THE FULL CIRCI

BOOK THREE

THE *Knowing*

Saga's Story

JEANNE SELANDER MILLER

Published by Seacoast Press, an imprint of MindStir Media, LLC
1931 Woodbury Ave. #182 | Portsmouth, New Hampshire 03801 | USA
1.800.767.0531 | www.seacoastpress.com

Printed in the United States of America
ISBN-13: 978-1-7356910-1-5

SEACOAST

PRESS

BY JEANNE SELANDER MILLER

The Knowing

The Seeker

The Seer

Privileged

The Healing Path Home

A Million Miles from Home

A Breath Away

For those who ask the hard questions
and are not satisfied with easy answers

"I used to think the top environmental problems were biodiversity loss, ecosystem collapse, and climate change. I thought that with thirty years of good science we could address those problems.
But I was wrong.
The top environmental problems are selfishness, greed, and apathy and to deal with those we need a spiritual and cultural transformation.
And scientists don't know how to do that."

Gus Speth

CHAPTER 1

2035

"Are you familiar with Rumi?" Annika asks.

"The Sufi poet?"

"Yes. In the words of Rumi, 'Sell your cleverness and buy bewilderment.' Perhaps it is your skepticism and bewilderment that keep you open to possibility. Perhaps there is still more to be revealed. Would you like to continue?" Annika asks.

"I think so," I say, settling back in the recliner before she covers my legs with a blanket.

"You are safe, and there is nothing to be afraid of…" Annika gently reminds me.

I close my eyes and find I am mesmerized by the sound of her deep and gentle voice, and even before she can say anything more, the colors behind my eyelids begin to shift in a way I am familiar with. Here I go again.

"I am much older now, no longer a child, it is cold here…" I shiver as I feel Annika tuck the blanket securely around my shoulders.

"Look down at your feet," Annika gently prompts me.

"I am wearing skis, wooden skis. My boots are made of an animal's fur. They are tall and cover most of my lower leg. The toes are turned up. I think they are made to accommodate the leather bindings on the wooden skis."

"What else do you see?" Annika guides me through this regression into my past, to a past life that heretofore I have had no knowledge of.

"I wear a woolen dress of cobalt blue that is embellished with stitching of red and yellow. My dress falls down below my knees and just hits the top of my boots. An embroidered belt of red, yellow, and blue threads cinches the waistline of my dress. Attached to my belt, I wear a leather sheath that holds a knife with a bone handle. I don't know why I need a knife, but the sheath is worn, and the knife handle looks well-worn, too. I wear a fur-lined hat and mittens, as well as a shawl of red and blue plaid across my shoulders." I pull the shawl close to keep out the chill.

"Are you alone?" Annika whispers unobtrusively.

"No, there are others here. Both men and women, and they are dressed much the same as I am. Something terrible has happened here. Everyone is upset. There are bodies of dead animals lying on the ice-covered tundra as far as I can see."

"What kind of animals?"

"They have white fur, just like the fur of my boots and mittens. They have antlers, and I think they might be caribou. The men are speaking to me in a language I understand. They call me Grandmother, and these dead animals are... oh dear God, they are our reindeer."

"Do you know where you are?" Annika whispers.

"I am above the Arctic Circle. I am a Sámi elder, and this is our herd. We are the Boazovázzi. We are the reindeer walkers."

Only once I recognize myself and who I am, do I fully embody this former version of myself.

"Grandmother," they say, first one and then another, as if begging me and pleading with me to help them come to terms with this horrific loss. They believe I know what to do. I am their spiritual leader. I am their *Noaidi*.

I bend down to release my skis from their bindings. Before I can even begin, one of the men is on his knees on the hard-packed snow doing this for me. I am the eldest of our *siida*, or group of families. It appears that both wisdom and respect are the consolation prizes bestowed upon the aged.

I will myself to keep silent as I walk among the carcasses of these beloved creatures, but I cannot keep myself from crying. I bend down and place my hand between their antlers to offer a blessing for the lives lost and to release their spirits into the spirit world. As I touch them, one by one, I thank them for their service and companionship on our shared earthly journey.

The others follow in silence, bowing to the animals as they place their mittened hands upon the head of each reindeer who has now passed over.

"We will meet tonight in the *lavvu*, in ceremony, to honor our beloved dead."

I hear the murmur of assent as I walk slowly back toward my skis. Still, even the soft-spoken whisperings carry in the stillness of this morning. My people want answers: Why has this happened and who is responsible?

One of the men bends to help me put my skis back on. Another asks, "Grandmother, what should we do with the remains?"

"They have not been dead long, and the night was cold. In the ways of our people, nothing is to be wasted. They will not have died in vain."

No further instructions are necessary.

"We must honor the circle of life and evaluate the role of mankind within this circle. We, too, are part of this circle. What happens to the reindeer will also happen to us if nothing changes."

I ski slowly back towards our village, as I hear Annika calling me. The next thing I know, I am back on her recliner and much too warm beneath the blanket that I now struggle to get out from under.

"Where were you?" Annika asks gently as I try to focus on where I am right now.

"I'm not sure, but I feel like I've just witnessed the apocalypse. There were hundreds of dead animals. Big beautiful reindeer, both male and female, old and young that appear to have starved to death. I was an elderly woman. They called me Grandmother. I was the sage and their spiritual leader. My people were looking to me for answers, and I did not have any. There was nothing I could say to take away their pain. I don't even know when this happened. I can't place it. I have no context for the location, the clothing, or the tragedy."

"I'm afraid I can't help you," Annika says, and I can hear the sadness in her voice. "Sometimes these gifts of *seeing* carry great sadness as well as great responsibility. In time, everything you need to know will be revealed."

"I need to spend some time with this. No doubt, there is a reason that my gift showed up like this today. I need to know more. If I am being called to act, then I must trust that everything will become clearer, just as it has in the past."

We sit in silence for a little while longer as I try to commit my visions to memory, lest I forget.

"I've been receiving bits and pieces of information from my past lives through dreams and full downloads in my knowings all my life. It is only since I had my first full regression that any of this has made any sense to me. What was it that Dev called them? Soul breakthroughs. I wonder how much really important information I have discarded or discounted because I didn't understand it?

"I believe that in my most recent life, I was Fiona Dolan, and I lived on a farm in middle America. The best I can figure I was born sometime in the late 1950s, but I don't know when I died or how.

"When I embodied Fiona, I was fully aware of my gifts as a Seer, a Seeker, and I experienced knowings, too. I even time-traveled back to my previous lives much as I do now. Perhaps I have always done that but simply lacked the awareness or the ability to remember until now.

"I don't know how many times I have been reincarnated, probably many more than I can remember. But I know I have experienced knowings where I fully embodied a young Jewish girl in ancient Egypt under Roman occupation, a child in Constantinople sometime around 550 CE, a child during the Spanish Inquisition, a young mother during the Armenia genocide, and now an old Sámi woman of an indeterminate time.

"I have so many questions, and it seems as if the more I know, the more questions I have."

"Tell me, what worries you?" Annika asks.

"I'm not certain they are worries really, although some of it causes me great concern."

"Okay, well, let's start with the questions."

"Well, I wonder if I have ever embodied a man," I say.

"I'm afraid I can't answer that for you."

"Somehow, I don't think so, as I don't understand men at all."

Annika laughs, "You're not alone."

"And I can't help but wonder where my soul has been during the interim, you know the period between lives. Do we linger somewhere in the cosmos, in heaven, or in the arms of Jesus and all of our loved ones that have gone before us until it is time for us to be recycled back to the Earth School? And if we linger before being reincarnated, do we have a choice about where we are going and who we are? If so, why do we choose one lifetime versus another? Are there specific things we are supposed to learn in each lifetime that are necessary for our evolutionary growth or the growth of our soul?"

"Certainly, every one of these questions is worthy of consideration and exploration. Do you want to write some of this down?" Annika asks as she hands me a leather-bound journal and a pen.

"Thanks," I say as I take them from her hand and settle back down on the sofa.

Annika stands and informs me, "I'm sorry to be so abrupt, but I need to get in the shower, I have plans tonight."

"I'm sorry, I'm so engrossed in my own stuff, I nearly forgot you might have a life that doesn't include me." We both laugh as I also stand up and head for the door.

"Mind if I keep these?" I hold up the journal and pen. "I'll bring them back to you next time."

"Keep them, my gift to you. Happy New Year, my friend," Annika says, as she hugs me.

I put my boots on and button up my coat.

"Until next time," I say as I close the door behind me.

Outside it is gently snowing; large, light, fluffy clusters of snow fall from the sky as I walk towards the Underground to catch my train. It's already dark, and the Christmas lights still twinkle in the trees lining the street. Fortunately, the snow and the clouds act as an insulator, and it's not too cold. I'm nowhere near as cold as I was in my past life. But was it really in the past or was it the future? I don't know why I think this, but I trust my intuition, and it's telling me that this time things were different.

There are very few people out tonight. Most people are probably home by the fire sleeping off what remains of last night's New Year's Eve celebration. Most people will be off for a few more days and do not need to return to work until after Trettondagen, or Epiphany, which is another national holiday.

Sometimes I wish I was like other people, just going about my business blissfully unaware.

CHAPTER 2

Rather than heading for home as I'd planned, I decide to hail a cab to my parents' home, Damgården. Although it has been dark since three p.m., it's still early. Tomorrow is my first official day in my new position as the Chief Executive Officer of Lundstrom Enterprises, and I am more than a little bit apprehensive. What in the world have I gotten myself into? I took this position at the request of my parents. The business has been in our family in one form or another since the mid-1600s, nearly four hundred years ago. I have a deep sense of foreboding and am in need of some information and a healthy dose of reassurance.

Mother may have dementia, but she also has moments of lucidity. She knows the cast of characters with whom I am expected to hold my own. If tonight isn't a good night for her, perhaps Father can help, and maybe Johan will be home, too.

The cab pulls up to the gate, and the cabbie asks, "Do you have a code or something?"

Rather than give him the code for the keypad, I say, "I'll just hop out here. There is an iris scan, or else you have to call the house for a passcode."

Too many people never change their codes or give them out willy-nilly to people they barely know, and then they wonder why there are so many burglaries. The news has been full of such stories. Or perhaps it is because there is such a disparity in incomes in this town, and desperate people will do desperate things. Either way, I'm not going to put my elderly parents, or my brother and his family at risk by being too trusting.

I run my credit card through the handheld meter and leave the cabbie a generous tip. "Thanks for bringing me all the way out here on this cold winter's night."

"You're welcome. Happy New Year."

I return the greeting and wait until he has departed before I have my iris scanned. It takes only a moment for the gate to open, and all the exterior lights go on. My father is standing at the front door before I even get to the front walkway.

"Saga, so nice of you to come by. We weren't expecting you, or did your mother just forget to tell me?"

"Happy New Year's, Father. No, I'm not expected, but I'm feeling a little nervous about my new position, and I thought maybe you and Mother might be able to offer me a little reassurance and alleviate some of my trepidation."

"Oh, my darling girl, you are always welcome here. You have always had difficulty with transitions," he chuckles softly. "I remember having to wait outside your kindergarten classroom for the whole first month, just in case you decided you didn't like it and wanted to come home."

With that said, we both start to laugh as he wraps his big strong arms around my shoulders and leads me into the house. "How's she doing today?"

"She's having a pretty good day."

"Edward, who's here?" Mother calls from the front room.

"Saga's come to join us this evening," Father answers as he helps me out of my coat, and I go into see Mother.

"Oh, darling, how nice of you to stop by."

I wrap my mother in my arms like she is a small child, and I am the parent.

"Come sit by the fire and warm up. Can we get you something to drink?" Mother asks.

"Maybe a cup of tea. Has Maryan already gone home?"

"She had the day off to be with her family. Have you eaten? Your father and I just finished, but there's plenty more in the kitchen."

"No thank you, I'm really not hungry."

"I'll make some tea," Father says, "You stay here and catch up with Mother."

Mother's face lights up with joy as we hold hands on the sofa before the fire and in the sparkling light of the Christmas tree.

"I'm feeling a little anxious about tomorrow," I confess.

"What about?" Mother asks, and I remind her that I am starting tomorrow in her newly vacated position as CEO of the family business, a multinational timber and mining corporation.

"Ah, yes, of course, I guess I'd just forgotten you were starting tomorrow. What is it that you are nervous about?"

"It's not something I can put my finger on. It's just a recurring sense of uneasiness. Perhaps my intuition is acting up. I guess I should have known that someday this responsibility would fall to me, I just didn't think it would happen so soon." I laugh a little nervously. "I guess I'm feeling a little ill-prepared."

Then Mother launches into the story of our family genealogy in a way that both clarifies and confuses. She tells me once again how the women in our family first acquired the land, which is now held in trust by Lundstrom Enterprises, our family's business.

"Please don't be afraid. There is something very right about this. The title, the land, and the position will all be yours, just as they have been mine. They have been passed from mother to daughter for the last sixteen generations, and God willing, they will continue to be for the next hundred generations to come."

As Mother's dementia progresses, she has started to repeat herself. She told me all of this just last week when she announced her retirement. It is heartbreaking. I choose not to remind her that I've heard this all before. Instead, I opt to make a little joke. "Of course, that would depend on me having a child and specifically a daughter," I laugh.

"There is plenty of time for that," Mother says reassuringly. "I didn't have you or Johan until I was well into my forties."

Mother continues to elaborate on a part of the story I am unfamiliar with. I have difficulty knowing whether I am just confused or if Mother is.

"My husband, the Baron Erik Lundstrom, was killed in battle in the service of the Crown during the Thirty Years' War. In compensation for his loyalty, bravery, and service, as his widow, I was bequeathed the timberlands in the north of Sweden by King Gustavus Adolphus."

"When was this Mother?" I ask, seeking clarification.

"In 1632, at the time, all the land of Sweden belonged to the king. He could do as he pleased with it, which included giving it to loyal members of the nobility."

It seems that in her confusion, Mother has cast herself in a leading role in this antiquated family drama. Part of me wants to ask my mother if she knows that today is New Year's Day in the year 2035. Instead, I ask, "If you were married to a baron, does this mean you are a baroness?"

"Yes, I was once the Baroness Kristina Lundstrom."

Tonight, since it is just the family, I wonder if Mother's guard is down, and so are the filters that she usually screens her comments through. I have heard modified versions of this story before. However, how our family rose to the ranks of nobility and acquired its wealth, is never openly discussed. And never before has Mother inserted herself into the role of the baroness.

Is she confused because of her dementia, or is it possible she knows exactly what she is talking about? Is it possible she was the Baroness Kristina Lundstrom in another life?

Just then, Father walks back in carrying the heirloom silver tea service, and two cups of black coffee for himself and Mother. "You're sure you wouldn't rather have coffee?" he asks as if he finds it hard to believe that anyone would opt to drink tea when coffee is available.

"I need to get a good night's sleep tonight, and the caffeine will keep me up." Father pours me a cup of herbal tea, which fills the room with the fragrance of cinnamon and cardamom.

"Can I make you a sandwich?" Father asks, and I shake my head no.

"Thanks just the same. Butterflies in my stomach tonight."

Mother takes the coffee cup Father hands her and takes a swallow before continuing with her story, "My husband was a better warrior

21

than he ever was a husband or a father…" Mother looks up at Father, and he looks perplexed. "Not you, my dear," she laughs as if this is just a silly little misunderstanding, "the Baron Erik Lundstrom. He was both reckless and wasteful. It was because of his shortcomings that I stipulated in my will that all land and assets were to be handed down from mother to daughter. It has been so in every generation since."

"What about the sons?" I ask.

"The mothers in our family have always taken care of their sons, but the title and the positional power and authority passes from mother to daughter."

Mother straightens her back and lifts her head before she adjusts the folds in her ankle-length, blue velvet skirt and interlaces her bejeweled arthritic fingers and places them in her lap. The light of the antique floor lamp creates a golden aura around my mother's silhouette and a luminous halo around her hair of platinum white. Sitting here in the elegance of this old manor house, she looks every bit the part, both noble, holy, and somewhat otherworldly.

I look to my father, and he holds my gaze for a moment then shrugs. Since Mother's diagnosis, we have all learned that it isn't always helpful or necessary to correct her episodic confusion. But is that what is going on here? Is Mother simply delusional because of her dementia? Or perhaps she is remembering things from another lifetime. Maybe I'm not the only one in this family who travels back in time.

There is so much that needs to be addressed in the present moment, but for now, I decide to stick with the subject at hand.

"Title?" I ask, seeking clarification.

"Yes," Father confirms. "Your mother is also a baroness, and someday, hopefully a long time from now, that title will pass to you."

I turn my head to look at my mother, "You never told me you are a baroness."

"Oh, for heaven's sake, why would I? It is simply an honorary designation. I never use it. It's just too pretentious and no longer important. What is important is how you manage the business and the assets that have been entrusted to your care. Your value and your legacy will not be found in any title you possess or the wealth that you may or may not accumulate but will be determined by how the decisions you make impact those who trust and depend on you."

Something has shifted, and now Mother seems to be fully grounded in present-day reality.

With that, the outside lights go on, as they are engaged whenever the front gate opens. Father stands and goes to look at the monitor to see who is here. "It's Johan. He's home early tonight."

"Where are Hanna and the girls?" I ask. It is the first time since I arrived that I realize how unusually quiet the house is.

"They left this morning to visit Hanna's mother in old town Malmö. She's none too pleased that Johan is going to the office tomorrow and cutting the holiday short."

"I guess that means she is none too pleased with me, either."

"She's going on holiday next week to the Maldives," Father says.

"Really? Don't Mia and Eve have to be in school on Monday?" I ask, already certain that my nieces need to return to school the Monday after Epiphany.

"The girls will not be going. Their nanny, Wilma, will be looking after them while Johan is working."

"No comment. If you can't say something nice, it's best to say nothing at all. Isn't that right, Mother?"

Mother looks in my direction and simply smiles. Again, she looks like she is a million miles away.

"Anyway, I'm glad Johan is here tonight. I need a little more information about the Sámi land dispute. It's the first thing on the agenda for Monday's board meeting and I'd like to understand the stated and unstated positions of the board on this issue before I meet with them next Monday night. I feel a little bit like I'm Daniel, and I'm being cast into the lion's den."

Father laughs, "Daniel and the lion's den. Now there's an old Sunday school reference I haven't heard used in a while."

"See, I was paying attention," I quip, feeling uncertain if the analogy I've just used is even close. But Father doesn't let it go.

"Well, let's see if the comparison holds together."

I groan. "I should know better than to quote or misquote the Bible around a man who knows something about everything."

"Just like Daniel, you have been appointed to a position of power and have been set to rule the kingdom, or at least Lundstrom Enterprises," he chuckles. "That part I get. But in the Biblical story, the ministers and governors are looking to discredit Daniel in the eyes of the king. They want to have him removed from power. So, who are the members of the Lundstrom board, the ministers and governors, or are they the lions?" Father asks.

"Hmm, I guess I *wasn't* paying close enough attention in Sunday school. Apparently, I missed the nuance of the old story. All I know is that I am feeling vulnerable, and I'd prefer not to be eaten alive if it can be avoided."

Father laughs, "Dearest Daughter, you forget how the old story ends. Daniel remains faithful to his God and to all he believes to be true. In the end, his faith saves him. The men who serve the king and the kingdom are those to be feared, not the lions. The lions are creatures of the natural world and honor the will of the Creator."

Father smiles as I contemplate the relevance of the analogy when my brother, Johan, opens the front door and walks in.

"Saga, to what do we owe this honor? I didn't know you were coming tonight." Johan reaches over to hug me, and I smell alcohol on his breath.

"Welcome home, son." Mother pats the cushion on the sofa bidding him to sit beside her. "Where have you been all day? I haven't seen Hanna or the girls all day."

I grimace as Mother has already forgotten that we have only just discussed their whereabouts.

"I kissed the girls good-bye after breakfast and then went by the office. Besides, the girls will be home Sunday night," he says as he takes a seat next to Mother. I can't help noticing he makes no mention of his loathsome wife, Hanna the Horrible. "I needed to look into a couple of things that have been bothering me."

"Really? Care to elaborate?" I ask.

"I ran into KP at the New Year's Eve party last night."

"KP?" I ask, seeking clarification.

"Klaus Pedersson Ek, the Third, otherwise known as KP for obvious reasons. He's Klaus Ek's son."

"Yes," Mother chimes in. "Klaus Ek is the chairmen of the Board of Directors. He was our former chief financial officer. He held the position for years, even before I took over."

I already know this as Johan and I dealt with him last week regarding the Löfgren lawsuit. "And…" I say, directing my attention back towards my brother. "How do you know KP? Does he also work for Lundstrom?"

"No, he's a trust fund baby and a member of the polo club. We play on the same team. Anyway, as he often does, he was bitching about his gold-digging stepmother Inga, who is five years his junior, and complaining about how she is spending all his father's money now that he's retired. In the past, he has expressed his concern and dismay that Inga will have it all spent before his father is cold in the grave. But last night when he was half in the bag, he said something about his father coming into money, big money, and that *we* will all be set. He included me in this *we* he was talking about. I pretended to know what he was referring too, but the truth is I had, and still have, no idea."

Father stands and fixes himself a drink, aquavit straight up. Then he looks in my direction as if to offer to make one for me. But I shake my head no. He knows that Johan has been out drinking tonight, so he refrains from offering him another.

Johan continues, "I went by the office today to see if I could figure out what was up but to no avail. So, I called KP and asked him to meet me for a drink at the club. Now he is back-peddling and acting like he never said anything about us coming into big money and that I don't know what I'm talking about. He even said that I was probably just intoxicated last night and dreamt the whole thing. You know, just wishful thinking. Something's up. I don't know what it is, but I don't like it one bit. Something is afoul."

"What do you make of this?" I ask my parents, given they are certainly more familiar with these people than I am.

"I've known Klaus for nearly sixty years," Mother says. "Isn't that right, dear?" She directs her question to my father, seeking confirmation. Father nods.

I, too, have known the man all my life, but I don't know him well. He usually attends Mother's annual party commemorating the Winter

Solstice. His name and face were seen all over social media a year or two ago when he went through a very contentious divorce and then married a beautiful woman who is younger than both of his children.

"Tell me what you know of him," I say.

"He's a card-carrying member of the Swedish Democrats, a neo-fascist, and an arrogant asshole, and these are just some of his most admirable characteristics—" Johan says, but Mother interrupts before he can say anything more.

"Johan," she admonishes, "Klaus Ek is a very smart man, and he has served Lundstrom Enterprises well for over forty years."

Father turns his gaze towards her, "Come on, Sigrid, I know it goes against your good nature to speak ill of anyone, but keeping your concerns about Ek to yourself will handicap Saga and Johan as they take the reins of the company. This is hardly idle gossip." In a manner I have rarely seen, Father presses Mother for full disclosure.

"Very well, Edward," Mother says with a sigh. "Perhaps you will find a little more compassion for Klaus if you have a better understanding of his childhood. Klaus was raised by his mother after his father was murdered by an immigrant on the streets of Stockholm when he was just a child. Overcome with grief and anger, his mother filled his head with a fear of outsiders and tales of danger. She struggled to make ends meet and was embittered by the early death of her husband. She filled her son with feelings of scarcity, all the while telling him that he must live up to his father's memory and make him proud by achieving both wealth and power."

"How do you know this, Mother?" I ask.

"After she was widowed, his mother took a position as our housekeeper. She worked for my mother while I was growing up. Klaus used to come by the house after school when he was just a boy. I'm afraid

I overheard many of his conversations with his mother when they thought I was reading or doing my homework. Hedda Klaus was a stern and oppressive woman. She was relentless with Klaus. He hasn't known a lot of love in his life. I suppose this was why my mother petitioned me to find a position for him at Lundstrom Enterprises after he graduated from university. And I suppose this is why I kept him on. It seemed like the right thing to do at the time." And then Mother turns her gaze into the golden flames that blaze and flicker in the fireplace as if they are possessed by an unseen spirit. Muttering softly, just under her breath, she says, "Although, over the years, he has given us pause to consider whether this was indeed a wise decision."

"Tell us what you mean, Mother," Johan prods gently, but Mother just closes her eyes, purses her lips together to keep herself from speaking, and subtly shakes her head no.

"Pappa?" I enquire, hoping our father will elaborate.

"Klaus Ek and some of the other members of the board hold views which conflict with the way your mother and I see our role and responsibilities to Lundstrom Enterprises. Correct me, Sigrid, if I'm speaking out of turn, but your mother has always embraced her position from a theological understanding of stewardship. Ultimately, she, and now you Saga, as CEO, are responsible to God for the utilization and management of the resources God has generously provided."

"Simply put," Mother states, "everything we have belongs to the Creator, and we will have to answer for our decisions."

"Whoa, that's a lot of responsibility, sister. Better you than me," Johan says as he gets up to fix himself another drink.

"Your mother's understanding is in complete alignment with your grandmother's and your great-grandmother's before her. This is the philosophical underpinning upon which Lundstrom Enterprises was founded centuries ago. All decisions on how the resources should be utilized should be run through this filter," Father adds. "In the times in which we live, people no longer speak of our responsibilities to our Creator or to one another. But that does not negate the obligation."

Visions of the stark beauty of the snow-covered land of my grand-mothers' triggers a memory from the knowing I experienced earlier today. There was a time when I was Sámi and a spiritual leader of the people. All this talk of generational stewardship leaves me wondering how far back our connection to this land goes.

Mother's voice brings me back.

"I'm afraid, my dear, that I am leaving you in a difficult position, but one that you are more than capable of handling." Mother leans forward to hold my hand. "As you will soon learn, unfortunately, some members of the board of directors do not share this understanding."

"Like our fearless leader, Chairman Ek," Johan grumbles as he downs his drink. "Want one?" he asks as he helps himself to another cocktail.

This time I agree. "Whiskey neat," I say to Johan. "Do you think God will forgive my ignorance and incompetence if I lack the intent to screw up?"

"Oh, ye of little faith," Father says, and he stands and walks behind the chair where I sit and places his hands on my shoulders and gives me a reassuring caress. "You need to trust your intuition. Your mother is right. You are more than capable of handling *this*."

Johan hands me my drink, and it looks like he has poured us both a double. I take a sip and feel the burn in the back of my throat as I swallow. "I wish I had some idea of what *this* even is. I don't even know what I should be looking for or what questions I should be asking and to whom." I take another sip and pause a moment when somewhere from the murky recesses of my mind, a question is called forth. "If Ek does not believe he is acting as a steward of the organization and its resources, then what motivates him? What does he hope to accomplish?"

Silence fills the room as we sit in the firelight and let the question simmer.

I set my unfinished drink on the table beside my chair. "I'm afraid at this time I have more questions than answers. Thank you for indulging my insecurities. You've given me plenty to think about for one night. It's getting late, and I should be heading for home. Good night Mother," I say as I stand and lean in to kiss her cheek. Father walks me out.

"I'm afraid our driver, Khadra, has already gone for the day. Would you like me to call you a cab?" Father asks.

"No, but thank you. The train station is only a few blocks, and the fresh air will do me good."

"Let me walk with you," Johan offers. "The night air will help clear my head as well." Johan puts on his coat while Father helps me into mine.

Now Mother is standing in the foyer as well. She reaches for my hand and pulls me close then whispers in my ear, "Call me tomorrow. I may have something that might help, but I'll need to find it."

I don't know what she is talking about, and perhaps she doesn't either.

Walking to the train with Johan, I ask him, "You were pretty hard on Klaus Ek. What was it that you called him? A neo-fascist asshole? Mother still seems to hold him in relatively high regard."

"Perhaps I see him in a different light. Things have changed since our mother was appointed CEO."

"That was nearly forty years ago. She was just a few years older than I am now. It's hard to believe. She took on all this responsibility and then went on to have two children when she was already in her forties. She was a force to be reckoned with and is a tough act to follow."

"I mean no disrespect to Mother, but there was a time when Sweden was held up as the best of what Democratic Socialism had to offer, but that was before the political climate of our country and the world began to change. Over the years, the population of Sweden has been bound together with both Norway and Finland to become an economic and political trading partner, much like the European Union of old. The Scandinavian countries withdrew from the European Union to strengthen their borders and control the immigration of people from the Middle East, particularly Muslims. This happened back in 2025, a little over ten years ago. Many people were surprised at the time because Sweden had long been heralded and admired by much of the free world as an exemplar of what the best of Democratic Socialism could offer. This changed when there was a power shift, and many of the Social Democrats, who had control of the Parliament for over a hundred years, were voted out and replaced as the Swedish Democrats grew in popularity after the elections in 2020. The Swedish Democrats were then and are still a right-wing, conservative ultra-nationalistic political power who campaigned on the slogan of *Keeping Sweden for the Real Swedes*."

"Thanks for the history lesson," I chide my brother, hoping to lighten his mood, but he is all wound up and will not let this go.

"Initially, the people didn't believe they stood a chance because everything they advocated flew in the face of the progressive policies of the time. But as the politicians gave voice to their long-held prejudice against outsiders, the people got behind them. The party was, and still is, backed by many, but particularly the less-educated men who were feeling displaced by both immigrants and women. Like many populist movements of the time in continental Europe and the United States, there was an emphasis on rolling back the hands of time to the *good old days*. The political rhetoric of the day was to send the immigrants home."

"And Klaus Ek is a leader in the Swedish Democrats. Is that right?"

"Indeed, he is. He's a card-carrying member of that neo-fascist regime. But he's savvy enough not to reveal his ethnic and racist prejudices directly. His far-right ideology is camouflaged under a nationalist veneer. He avoids public scrutiny because he has never run for public office, but behind the scenes, he wields a great deal of power."

"That's interesting," I say as we approach the entrance to the underground. "Thanks for walking with me. See you tomorrow, Johan."

"Just be careful, Saga," Johan calls as I descend the stairs to await my train.

Something about this doesn't sit well with me. I need to get a better handle on all of *this*. Most people won't be back to work until Monday, but I'm going to go in tomorrow. God knows I could use a few days' head start. I just hope it will be enough. The more I learn about the family business, the more I realize how much I need to learn.

CHAPTER 3

The Underground feels severe and so unforgiving. But unforgiving of what, maybe it is just devoid of humanity and warmth. The Tunnelbanna was once home to the world's longest art gallery that ran beneath the fourteen islands and the seventy-mile transport link. A wide variety of art graced these walls for over sixty years with different art installations at every stop, but that was years ago. Some of the work was considered offensive and pornographic by some. The truth is, in one exhibit, there were black and white drawings and paintings of women. It was feminist art, depicting women with splotches of red menstrual blood painted between their legs. It was the artist's intent to normalize a natural process that had long been considered shameful.

Perhaps she didn't understand the sensibilities of the audience. In an attempt to appease the outrage of their conservative constituency, the politicians of the day, in their infinite wisdom, decided to remove *all* the art and have the ceilings and the walls covered over in white—stark white.

Art is often the barometer of culture. I shudder as I remember an art history class I took at university. During Nazi Germany, the paintings of impressionists, post-impressionists, cubists, expressionists, and Dadaists were ridiculed and mocked as their work was classified by the Third Reich as degenerate art. The art reflected the period and actively advocated for change.

Now the walls of the Underground are tiled in white, and the concrete floor is cold. The leather soles of my boots offer little protection, and my feet are freezing. I shift my weight from one foot to the next, trying to warm my feet.

A sense of unease and vulnerability wraps itself around me like a damp blanket. What now? I take a deep breath to still myself before turning to look over my shoulder. I am all alone, absolutely alone.

A shiver runs down my spine as I look in the other direction. I see the light growing brighter with each passing moment. I feel the vibration beneath my feet, and then the whistle blows. My train is here.

I say a little prayer of thanksgiving. Does God really have time to listen to my prayers of gratitude about the timeliness of the subway train?

I need to get out of my head.

The car is nearly empty, and I am traveling to the other side of town. I pull the leather-bound journal I got this afternoon from Annika from the messenger bag I carry. It's time to make a written record of today's journey. No doubt there is a message for me here. There always is, even if I can't always decipher what the message is.

For the next twenty minutes, the train moves me closer to home as people enter and exit the subway car at each of the stops. I meticulously record everything I can remember from my travels back to another time when I was a Sámi elder, and a great number of beautiful snow-white reindeer perished. The question that nags at me, yet remains unanswered is why?

Why did this happen and when?

Although I have only a limited familiarity with the Sámi culture, I do know that the migratory route for the reindeer cuts through some of the land owned by our family business. Still, I'm fairly certain there must have been a chapter about the Sámi people in our history book back when I was in upper secondary school. But that was nearly twenty years ago, and those books were written from a nationalistic perspective giving only a brief nod to the history and culture of the native people of the Arctic Circle. The message was clear even then—*those people were not real Swedes.*

I think about Johan's rant as we walked to the train tonight. He is right. Much has changed since the conservative nationalists overtook the Parliament. I suppose there were always people who have held these beliefs, but there was a time when people would be ashamed to actually spew this kind of hatred aloud. Now you can't turn on the news without some political pundit going off on the immigrants and demanding all residents of our country speak Swedish. There is little understanding and even less respect given to anyone who doesn't look, think, speak, and even worship like the majority does. This includes the indigenous Sámi people. When did these people become the enemies of the state?

The train pulls up to my stop. I'm grateful I haven't far to walk tonight, just five minutes up the road and I'll be home.

Once inside, I flip on the gas fireplace. My apartment is small, like most city apartments, but it is also cozy and heats up quickly as I prepare my dinner. I fix myself a salad and plate of creamy dilled potatoes with a few pieces of pickled herring and a slice of dark bread and butter. I don't remember if I ate lunch today, and by now, I am hungry. Before sitting down, I turn on some music, "Clair de Lune" by Claude Debussy. I smile, remembering how Dev played this on the piano when we first met. But that was another lifetime ago. It was back when I was Fiona. I hum along as I let the music transport me. I open a bottle of wine, pour myself a glass, and take a sip. It's a Chateau Jean Bordeaux Blend. I take a deep breath and place my napkin on my lap. Dinner is simple and good, and I'm happy to be home.

However, I do not have the luxury of lingering very long. I still have work to do tonight. At the very least, I need to read through my correspondence.

So much has happened in the last few weeks. I've gone from working as a physical therapist at the Karolinska Institute to my new position as CEO in two weeks' time. It's still hard to believe. I always thought Johan was being groomed to take Mother's place. He is my older brother, after all. But Mother's dementia has progressed much more rapidly than any of us expected. It is so heartbreaking to lose someone you love a little bit every day. I don't know what any of us will do without her. The tears begin to run down my face, and I dry them with my napkin. There hasn't been much planning for my succession if there has been any at all. It was unrealistic to think that Mother might be able to continue indefinitely. I don't know if I am up to the challenge of stepping into her shoes. She has played her role flawlessly. It is hard to believe the board of directors did not voice any objections to my appointment, as clearly, I lack the experience, knowledge, and skills required for this position. Still, both Mother and Father insist that everyone will help me in every way and any way they can.

Perhaps they are right. But I can't help but wonder how the board, and the employees that have been passed over feel about such blatant nepotism.

I am beyond grateful that things went exceedingly well as we navigated the contentious lawsuit with Lars Löfgren. The board had my back, and they were supportive, every one of them. Still, something feels off. I remain skeptical. I have trust issues.

Mother, Father, and Johan have done their best to bring me up to speed, but as I read through the confidential correspondence meant for my eyes only, I can see that things have been overlooked and appear to have been slipping for a while. Mother has been trying to hold things together for longer than I have known. Given her cognitive decline, it is truly miraculous that things at Lundstrom Enterprises are not in worse shape than they appear to be.

I read through some of the correspondence from the board, all the while referring to the notes I took while Johan was bringing me up to speed in preparation for the Löfgren lawsuit. Everyone on the board is talented and has served the company or on the board for a long time, but do some of them pursue a personal agenda? I need to get a better handle on who these people are and what they may want before I make any more decisions.

Next, I read through the minutes of the past board meetings, and my discomfort increases. It is clear that I was not their first choice. Other qualified candidates were passed over, and I was only approved in deference to my mother and her years of service and leadership. It's more than a little unsettling to learn how tenuous my position actually is. Everyone has been so kind and gracious to my face, but it appears others are less than supportive behind closed doors.

There is so much to learn, and I will need to prioritize. I review the agenda for the upcoming board meeting that is scheduled for next week, and then take some time to read through some unlabeled attachments containing the relevant documents. It quickly becomes apparent that Lundstrom Enterprises is in the center of a public relations crisis. Johan warned me about this. It concerns the logging and mineral rights in the North and destruction of habitat used by wild reindeer and the nomadic Sámi people who herd them.

Annika's wise words come back to me, "Given time all will be revealed."

All my regressions have proven to be purposeful and have provided important lessons to be remembered. Only this morning, I learned I was once a Sámi elder and a spiritual leader among these people. It can hardly be a coincidence that I was guided to travel back to that lifetime only this morning.

It's been a very long day.

I check the time. It's almost ten o'clock, and it's too late to call Annika. Besides, she already told me she has a date tonight.

Instead of calling her, I pull out my journal and make a few notes for myself. Annika was my past life regression therapist, but now the nature of our relationship has changed since we have both concluded that she was my grandmother in another lifetime. Perhaps we have been in one another's lives across many lifetimes. Yet, given our past familial relationship, she believes it would be unethical for her to continue to be my therapist.

It all sounds so weird and difficult to wrap my head around when I try to put it into words. Now Annika is my confidant and my beloved friend, and I am grateful for that.

Closing my journal, I turn my attention back to the correspondence on my computer. Buried within my email, there is a slew of untitled, unopened documents of questionable importance. It is there that I find the minutes from a closed-door meeting entitled the Sámi Land Dispute.

Mother's position is clear. Promises were made, and she was adamant that they are to be honored. Her objections are all duly noted in the minutes. When the land in Västerbotten and Norrbotten Counties was given to our ancestors hundreds of years ago, an agreement was made that the lives of the semi-nomadic Sámi people would not be disturbed, as this land has been used by their people for thousands of years as they follow the migratory routes of their reindeer across the Arctic Circle.

Recently it was determined that this land appears to be heavily laden with both copper and gold. Now some members of the board are in favor of reneging on these long-held agreements. Our legal counsel is actively looking for a loophole, while the old meritocracy is giving voice to long-buried words of discretely hidden racism and privilege.

Johan's caustic words come back to me as I cringed when he referred to the chairman of the board Klaus Ek as a card-carrying member of the nationalistic, authoritarian, right-wing Swedish Democrats.

It is clear to me now as I read the minutes where the allegiance of several members of the board lies. Very little effort has been made to hide their ignorance or their prejudice against the Sámi people. Ek is even quoted as saying, 'It is our obligation to keep Sweden for the real Swedes.'

Who does he think the Sámi people are? They are not immigrants, but rather an aboriginal, nomadic people who have lived in and worked up near the Arctic Circle before the Germanic tribes settled in modern-day Scandinavia.

Perhaps he just wants to keep Sweden for those who look, think, worship, and live just like he does. A shudder runs down my spine as I recall the shameful rhetoric of Adolf Hitler during his reign over Nazi Germany and the horrific consequences of such propaganda and hatred. Words matter; they can harm, or they can heal.

I think I might be sick.

The board was split over Lundstrom Enterprises' obligations to honor the contract and their desire to pursue the extraction of mineral resources to increase profitability. These arguments were voiced and then tabled at the last board meeting in December, just before Mother retired.

As Johan explained it all to me, like it or not, we are not a publicly held company, and I do not answer to shareholders. As the newly appointed CEO, I have the ultimate decision-making power. However, the board sets the long-term goals and oversees the company, and according to the corporate bylaws, they have the power to fire the CEO and approve a replacement.

I don't want to go to battle with the board only one week into my new position.

Have I been appointed and approved as Mother's replacement only because they think they can manipulate me? Probably, this is the truth of the matter, and that doesn't feel good.

I need to find a way to honor Mother's legacy and all of the strong women who precede me.

Tomorrow, I will seek my brother's wise counsel.

I may have stepped out of the frying pan right into the fire.

Closing down the documents on my computer, I pour myself another glass of wine. I decide to sit a while before the fire because I am too agitated to sleep. The wine settles me, and the flames in the gas fireplace begin to lull me towards sleep. Part of me wants another glass of wine and to linger just a little longer in the firelight, but my higher self argues for a good night's sleep. Tomorrow is an important day; it is my first real day on the job.

Lately, my sleep has been anything but restful. I long for the deep, dreamless sleep that will leave me peacefully refreshed in the morning. Reluctantly, I take myself off to bed, and it isn't long before I am drifting off to sleep.

CHAPTER 4

I wake from a dream in the early morning hours with a start and in a cold sweat. I don't think I time-traveled, but I am overwhelmed with fear for thinly veiled within this dream was a cautionary tale. Biblical stories once learned as a child come racing back to me. Didn't God speak to the prophets and his people through their dreams? This is how it feels, like someone is sending me a message. Now if I can only figure out what it all means. My dream was fragmented with people from different places and different lifetimes, yet they were all together in the same dream. Dreams are often like that. It was peopled with those who would never be in the same room together, the insufferable priest Father Brendan from my life as Fiona Dolan in the 1970s, and the odious cardinal during the late Roman Empire from my lifetime as Sophia, and also Klaus Ek, the chairman of the board. This unlikely trio of disparate, angry individuals were scheming and plotting something evil, but before I could get a handle on it, they melded together as different versions of the same being, all with evil intent. But the intent to do what?

I'm totally creeped out. I turn on the lights as I try to get the visions and the corresponding feelings out of my head. It is only five a.m., but rather than going back to sleep and risk returning to this disturbing dream, I decide to get up and get an early start on the day.

I arrive at my new office—Mother's old office. It's just before seven. The building is quiet as many people are still on holiday, and most won't be back until after Epiphany, which isn't until next Monday.

This place runs like clockwork and is a model for efficiency. Still, I'm surprised to see my name on the door. I only accepted the position a little more than a week ago, and already the nameplate has been changed.

Part of me is pleased, yet it is a bit disconcerting. Was everyone so certain that I would be offered the position, that I would accept it, and be approved? The questions swirl nebulously through my consciousness. Do *they* know things I'm not privy to? And just who is this *they*?

I put the key code into the door and enter the outer office. As the door opens, the lights automatically switch on. This is expected, as most of the offices in the whole building go dark when they are not occupied. Environmentally responsible design is a point of pride around here at Lundstrom Enterprises. The thought no sooner takes shape in my mind than I notice the light streaming from beneath the door to my private office. Mother's office.

A tingle climbs from the base of my spine up to my neck.

The lights turn off automatically after fifteen minutes if no one is in the room. Someone has just been in there, or may still be in there, but why? My gut tells me to run, but my brain overrules my instinct as I reach for the handle to open the door. It is unlocked. To my great relief, no one is inside.

But someone has been here, and it is not the custodial staff, for drawers have been opened and left slightly askew. I place my hand on the computer, which sits on the credenza behind the desk. It is warm beneath my hand and purrs. I lift the cover, and it comes to life without needing to be rebooted.

Before taking off my coat, I lift the phone and call security.

In a matter of minutes, a woman in her mid-thirties dressed in the navy blue of a security officer is standing in my office. She looks disheveled and a little bleary-eyed after working the night shift.

"What seems to be the problem?" she asks.

"Someone appears to have been in my office. When I got here, the door was already open to my private office, the lights were on, the computer is running, and it looks like someone has been going through the desk drawers."

She appears confused.

Disregarding my concerns, she asks, "How did you get in? You didn't check in at the security desk in the lobby. If you had, I would have seen you." She states the obvious.

"I came up through the private entrance," I say, hoping to help alleviate some of her obvious confusion.

"May I see some identification," she says to me in a gruff and officious voice as she exercises her authority.

Clearly, she didn't get the memo about the change of leadership. I reach inside my handbag and retrieve my state documents and hand them to her.

She looks from my face to the photo on my ID and scrutinizes the documents but does not give them back. "Do you have your official Lundstrom ID?" she asks. She is all business and still has not put together who I am or why I'm here.

"No. Today is my first day."

"Then what are you doing in here? This is Sigrid Lundstrom's private office." She takes her handheld phone from her waistband and makes a phone call. "I have a woman here in the CEO's inner office. She says she gained access through the private entrance."

I can only hear this officer's side of the conversation.

"Saga Svensson," she tells the person on the phone as she reads my name off my papers.

Then clearly, she receives directives from whoever it is that she has called. "Yes, sir." Then she turns to me and asserts her authority, "Wait here. Chairman Ek is coming."

Her voice and her manner imply that I am in big trouble and should be afraid. I consider pointing out the fact that my name and title are now on the office door. I consider telling her that Sigrid Lundstrom is my mother, even though we don't share the same last name, but given her behavior, I decide to let it rest. She will know soon enough.

I can't help but wonder if this is the way she treats other people. Had my mother known this and condoned this kind of behavior? Certainly not. Instead, I choose to smile while she crosses her arms in front of her chest. The expression on her face remains gruff and unchanged, and we wait.

It isn't long before Klaus Ek comes bounding through the office door, "My dearest Saga, so nice to see you." He comes in close and hugs me as if I am a beloved child that needs to be restrained. He holds me close to his strong and muscular body. But it doesn't feel loving or welcoming as he holds me a little too long and a little too tightly. I am beginning to feel anxious and even a little claustrophobic when at last, he releases me. "I'm afraid you've caught us all a little off guard as we weren't expecting you until next week, after Epiphany."

"Ah Klaus, thank you for coming to my rescue. I was afraid this fine officer was going to have me handcuffed and call the authorities to have me charged with breaking and entering."

"Good heavens no," Klaus says with feigned dismay as he reaches over to wrap an arm over my shoulder. Then he turns to the woman in the security uniform and snarls at her like a vicious dog, "Good God, woman, have you lost your mind? This is Ms. Saga Svensson. She is Sigrid Lundstrom's daughter and the new CEO. She's the one who signs your check, so if you want to keep your job, I suggest you start apologizing and show her a little respect."

"I'm terribly sorry, ma'am. I guess I haven't been keepin' up with all the changes goin' on around here given the Christmas holidays and all."

"It was an honest mistake; no harm has been done. Just a little case of mistaken identity. What is your name?" I ask her.

"It's Gunilla, Gunilla Westberg."

"How long have you worked here, Gunilla?" I ask.

"It will be three years in February," she replies, and for the first time this morning, I see her smile. "Is there anything else I can do for you, ma'am?"

I turn and look over at Klaus Ek just as he thrusts his chin in the direction of the door. He is gesturing for her to leave. I had called her for a reason. Someone had been in my office. But there is something else going on here, so I decide to let it go. For now.

"Don't you have someplace you need to be, Ms. Westberg?" Klaus says with a sneer towards the security officer. His voice is harsher than it needs to be. She drops her gaze towards the floor as she hastens to make her way out of the room.

And then just as quickly as he turned on this young woman, he changes his tune and turns on the charm for me. "Come Saga, let us get a cup of coffee, and then I'll show you around the building."

"That's very kind of you, but probably isn't necessary as I've been in and out of this building many times visiting Mother. But a cup of coffee would be great. I'll be with you in just a minute."

I excuse myself as I take my coat and handbag into my inner office and close the door behind me. From somewhere deep within me, a question arises and asks to be answered—why is he so intent on getting me out of here? I hang my coat in the closet, then go to use the private washroom. I freshen up my lipstick, then leave the zipper of my cosmetic bag open on the sink with my lipstick setting precariously across the opening. Maybe I'm just paranoid, but I re-lock the desk drawers with the key Mother gave me and then slip the key into the pocket of my skirt before heading out for a coffee.

I decide to broach the subject with Klaus as we head back to his office for coffee. "The reason I called security was because it appears that someone had been in Mother's office."

He pauses before answering me. "Really? Well, I suppose it is your office now."

"Yes, I understand, but that's hardly the point."

Taking the keycard in his hand, he sticks it into the breast pocket of his shirt then clears his throat before asking, "What makes you think someone had been in there?"

"The light was on, the drawers were unlocked and left open, and the computer had been left on."

"I'm sure there is nothing to worry about. Probably just someone from the custodial staff. This isn't the first time, I'm sorry to say. Your mother was hell-bent on hiring immigrants, and I hate to say it, but I'm afraid that's what you get."

"What exactly are you referring to?" I ask. I want to hear him say it himself.

"Oh Saga, you know, carelessness, a shoddy work ethic, and sometimes petty theft. But your computer is encrypted and password-protected, and besides, your mother cleaned out all of her personal things when she retired. You don't need to worry your pretty little head about this."

Oh, my pretty little head. I want to scream at him. My pretty little head thinks you are a sexist bigot and a liar. But the voice in my head advises discretion. So instead, I say nothing.

We reach Ek's office in the other tower, where he gives his assistant a nod, and within minutes, she has prepared a tray of steaming hot coffee and cinnamon bread. How could she have gotten this together so quickly? Then it dawns on me that while I was in the washroom, Klaus was making phone calls. Clearly, he called this woman, but who else did he call?

"Thank you," I say as she sets the tray on the conference table. "I'm Saga. I don't think we've met before."

She stands there and doesn't say a word until Klaus stands up and says, "Forgive my manners. Saga Svensson, this is my personal assistant, Agnes Sandsgård." His smile barely covers his irritation as she nods in my direction before silently slipping from the room.

What is it with this guy and the way he treats women? He is cloyingly sweet to me and yet downright rude and dismissive of others. Does he just treat women this way, or maybe it doesn't have anything to do with gender? Maybe he is just as rude to both men and women if he thinks they are beneath him professionally or socially. Or maybe he treats everyone like this unless he wants or needs something from them.

My creep meter is going off.

What does he want from me, and what is he willing to do to get it?

He chats on and on about nothing of any particular relevance until I've had just about all I can stand of this time-wasting banter, which mostly revolves around himself, his family, and his accomplishments. Fortunately, I had set an alarm on my phone before leaving my office in case I needed to make an excuse to leave.

Klaus looks distressed as I stand to call an end to this little tête-à-tête. "Forgive me, but I have some things I must attend to."

"Oh, I had hoped to escort you around for a little meet and greet," he says with a smile.

"Now that sounds lovely." I tell a bald-faced lie as what he has just proposed sounds dreadful. This man treats me like a child, and if I'm not careful, I may tell him exactly what I think of him. "Let's schedule some time next week when everyone is back from the holidays." Two can play at this game, and I have no intention of letting this man manage my time and manipulate me into doing his bidding. "Thanks for the coffee," I call as I leave him sitting in front of the tray of sweets and close the door behind me.

I've been up since five, and it is now nine o'clock, and I haven't accomplished a damn thing, but I think at least I'm getting a lay of the land and starting to get a handle on the cast of characters or at the very least, that character.

Re-entering my office, Ulla, my mother's assistant, is seated at her desk. "Good morning, Saga. I hadn't expected you to be here until next week."

"So, I've been told." She looks a little confused, but I decide not to elaborate.

"Can I bring you a cup of coffee or get you some breakfast?" she asks.

"No, thank you. I've just had a cup with Klaus Ek."

"Oh," is all she says, but her face says so much more. I don't think she likes him any more than I do.

"Can you get me a copy of the agenda for the upcoming board meeting? I'd like to spend the morning preparing for it, so I don't look like the complete simpleton that Ek seems to believe I am."

"Yes, ma'am. You are your mother's daughter, and you are many things, but a simpleton is not one of them."

I laugh, and Ulla does too. "Maybe some night with a few glasses of wine, you will tell me what some of the other things are."

"Oh, I could tell you right now, but I don't want it all to go to your head."

"Thanks, Ulla."

"Don't worry. I've got your back. I promised your mother that she could count on me."

"Funny, I made her the same promise." I can barely get the words out as I'm getting choked up, and Ulla wipes her own tears away with the back of her hand.

"Now, don't get me started," she says as I open the door to my office.

It's not until I'm back inside that I remember how this morning started. I check all the desk drawers, and they are still locked. Good.

I walk into the washroom, and my cosmetic bag is still open on the vanity near the sink, but my lipstick is no longer resting on the top of the bag. Now it is inside, and not just on the top but on the bottom of the bag. Someone has been in my bathroom, and they took everything out of my cosmetic bag and repacked it. Were they looking for something, like what? Maybe the key to the desk.

Could it have been Ulla? I can hardly imagine that she would do that. Still, I would hate to embarrass her and myself by asking. She has been Mother's assistant for years, and Mother trusted her implicitly.

Or maybe Ulla just knocked it over, and it spilled.

My cowardice kicks in, and I decide to keep all of this to myself.

It's already mid-morning, and I'm finally getting to work. I find a copy of the agenda for the upcoming board meeting in my email.

I use the interoffice system to let Ulla know I have it, so she won't spend any more time trying to locate it for me.

The board meeting is scheduled for next Monday, January 8. Including the weekend, that is only five days from now. The first item on the agenda is the Sámi land dispute. I see that Klaus Ek, as the chairman of the board, isn't wasting any time trying to get this resolved. After all the weirdness this morning, I can't help but feel something devious and underhanded is afoot. But what is it?

Resonating deep within my chest, an unspoken voice I have never heard before comes up from the deepest wells of my being—*Beware of the powerful preying on the weak.*

I grasp the corners of my desk as my hands tremble. What the hell was that? The voice, although not audible, was no less real. It was deep and powerful and masculine. The sound still reverberates within my chest long after the words were spoken. The words were felt as much as they were heard. Was this the voice of God? Was it my soul speaking? Or is it the same thing? I don't know, but I do know that it is time to pay attention.

On shaky legs, I step into the outer office. I must look a fright as Ulla asks, "Saga, are you okay?"

"Yes, of course." I try to come up with a plausible explanation, "Maybe my blood sugar is a little low. I skipped breakfast this morning." I sit in the chair beside her desk as I don't trust myself to go much further.

"Can I get you something?" she asks as her voice reflects her concern. "Another cup of coffee, perhaps?"

"No, definitely not coffee. I'm already over-caffeinated."

Before I know it, Ulla is pulling a bottle of spring water and a box of knäckebröd from her desk drawer. "Here have a couple of these. I'll order you an early lunch."

"Thank you," I say as I take a long drink of the still-cool water. I wait a moment before taking a bite of the rye crisp. I take a deep breath and feel a little better, a little less shaky. "Ulla, would you call my brother and ask him to meet me in my office? Please see if he would like to join me for this early lunch." I stand still feeling a little wobbly as Ulla picks up the phone to call Johan and order our lunch.

I can see why my mother raved about this woman's efficiency. But it is more than that. She is good and kind, and she wants to see me succeed. I have a sense about these things, and this time it doesn't frighten me. No, this time, it makes me feel secure.

How much of all of this should I share with Johan? It feels as if I have no personal or professional boundaries when working in the family business. Even though I trust Johan implicitly, what would I tell him? That someone was in my office and moved my lipstick, or I have a sneaking suspicion that Ek is up to no good? Without any real evidence of wrongdoing, these kinds of allegations make me sound paranoid.

Beware of the powerful preying on the weak. The words come back to me. Am I the weak? Mother was pushed out by the board because of her progressive dementia, but why was I approved? Do they see me as a puppet? Do they think I can be easily manipulated to do their bidding? My intuition is acting up. I feel I am being called to do something, but what?

There is a knock on my door, and even before I can answer, Johan walks right in. "Hey, Ulla called and said you needed to see me." He looks me in the eye and asks, "Are you all right?" I nod and gesture towards the chair.

"You look a little peaked."

I disregard his comment and concern. "Have you looked at the agenda for Monday's board meeting? Klaus Ek has put the Sámi land dispute as the first item on the agenda. I'm not ready to make a decision about that, and I won't have Klaus try to railroad me into breaking that contract just to line his pockets. Can you clear your schedule for the next couple of days? I want to take a road trip to gather some information before any decisions are made."

"I can, or you could just table the discussion for another time," Johan suggests.

"I don't know, Johan. Something is up. I don't know what it is, but the feeling in my gut is telling me that this needs to be my top priority."

"Okay. No more explanation is needed. I don't trust Ek as far as I can throw him. If we attempt to break this contract, it will create a public relations nightmare, and that is one thing we do not need."

"I just need to see the land in dispute and get a better sense of what's at stake. I need to see it, stand on it, breathe the air, and meet the people. I need to get a feel for it. You know how I am."

"Yes, I'm afraid I do. Who am I to question your intuition? Okay, I'll call Hanna and have her pack me a bag."

"Must be nice to have a wife." I regret being snarky as soon as the words leave my mouth.

"Don't start with me," Johan smiles and laughs. I feel relieved he didn't take my comment as a judgment on *his* marriage. "Besides, I just remembered she has taken the girls and gone to visit her mother in Malmö."

"Guess you'll have to pack your own bag, just like a big boy," I smile at him.

"Yes, Boss," he says, shaking his head, and I realize I'm going to have to drop some of the sibling banter with Johan if either of us is going to be taken seriously.

"I'll have Ulla make the arrangements and have a car brought up from the garage. We can stop by and pick up my suitcase on the way out of town. It won't take me long to throw a few things together."

"It's going to be cold up there near the Arctic Circle. Pack your woolies and your Russian *ushanka*. There's nothing like a fur-lined cap with earflaps to fight the chill. Besides, I'm sure it will look fetching on you. You're sure you don't want to wait and make this trip in June?"

"That is probably what Klaus Ek is hoping for, but the board meeting is set for Monday. I'm sure Ek was counting on me to abdicate my responsibility and let him and his cronies make this decision. No, we're going today. If the Sámi can face the cold, then so can we. What kind of a Swede are you anyway?"

"One who's wishing for a tropical vacation and a mai tai. But, if we're going to go, then we'd better get going, because we'll be driving in the dark as it is, and the forecast calls for more snow."

Johan drives and drops me at my apartment, so I can pack a bag.

He waits in the car as he has to make a call to cancel some plans he had made before I asked him to accompany me to the North Country.

When I enter my building, Dagvin, the doorman greets me. "Ms. Saga, I haven't seen you in a while. I trust you had a good holiday." He smiles as I nod.

"I did, how are you? The family?" I ask.

"Everyone is well. Thank you for your generous gift. It helps more than you know." He smiles as he steps behind the desk and retrieves a long white flower box tied with a red ribbon. "These arrived about an hour ago. Would you like me to carry them up for you?"

"No, that won't be necessary. I can manage. Thank you." I rearrange my handbag and computer bag and place the long box in the crook of my arm.

"Looks like you have an admirer," he smiles as the elevator door closes behind me.

Using my thumbprint, I open the lock on my apartment door. The lights go on as I enter the foyer. I walk into the kitchen and settle my packages and handbag on the counter before I open the box of flowers. There are twelve long-stemmed red roses and a single white one. The card is signed simply—Anders.

Leaving the roses in their box, hang my coat on the back of the chair. I give myself a stern talking-to— don't read too much into this. Then the voice within my head protests—why not? A smile crosses my face as I open the cupboards and take out a crystal vase. The truth is I'm glad I'm not the only one who's smitten. Swedish men are not known for being overtly romantic, and I'm touched by his kindness. The roses are particularly beautiful in the gray, snow-laden months of winter. I breathe deeply as the fragrance fills the room. The holidays are behind us, and the roses brighten the room on this cold January day, I only wish I was going to be here to enjoy them.

It doesn't take me long to pack.

Then we stop by the house to collect Johan's things. Hanna may be out of town, but Maryan, Mother's good and faithful housekeeper, has packed Johan's bag. She comes out of the front door holding his overnight bag, so we are not delayed.

"I'm not really the little prince you think I am, but we have a very long drive ahead of us," Johan says in his own defense.

"I didn't say anything. Actually, I'm anxious to get on our way."

Within the hour, we are on the road heading to Västerbotten County and into the Lapland Province. The eight-hour drive north gives Johan and me plenty of time to talk.

"Tell me what you know about this land dispute. Everything I've read is from the carefully redacted version that Chairman Ek wishes me to see."

"Maybe a better place to start is to fill you in on what I know about the beady-eyed chairman. Are you familiar with Sun Tzu and *The Art of War*?"

"Sorry, it's not been on the top of my reading list. In fact, I've never heard of it."

"I hadn't expected you to. It was written in the early 1600s. Sun Tzu was a Chinese general and a military strategist. He said, *'If you know your enemy and know yourself, you need not fear the result of a hundred battles. If you know yourself and not your enemy, for every victory gained you will also suffer a defeat. If you know neither the enemy nor yourself, you will succumb in every battle.'*"

"Is Chairman Klaus Ek my enemy? Are we preparing for battle?"

"At best, he is a *noble* adversary. And yes, I anticipate a battle of wills and, at the very least, a struggle to see whether you will lead or will be led."

"This is more than a little unsettling. But okay, what do I need to know about my noble adversary?"

"Please keep in mind, he may or may not be noble. At this point, we are giving him the benefit of the doubt. Remember, Klaus Ek is a card-carrying member of the Swedish Democrats and member of the old guard. He sees nothing wrong with the acquisition of wealth and stripping the land of all the natural resources as long as there is something in it for him. He believes God favors those who help themselves, and he is going to help himself to anything and everything that is put before him. You've seen gluttons, those who have no self-regulation when it comes to eating?"

"Yes, it's one of the seven deadly sins."

"Klaus Ek is like that when it comes to the acquisition of wealth. He believes he wouldn't be in the position he is—wealthy, wise, and white—if he had not earned it. And simply because of his position, he is entitled to a higher quality of life and all the riches he can acquire. Any consideration of equity and fairness does not apply."

"Maybe we should rethink the *noble* adjective."

"You should hear him talk when he thinks everyone in the room agrees with him," Johan says as outside the snow starts to fall.

"Why would he think that?" I ask.

"Over the years, I have had lots of practice learning to keep my mouth shut and just listen. After all, I am married to Hanna." We both laugh.

"It's probably been a pretty good skill to cultivate in your current position as Director of Public Relations, too."

"I'm also fairly proficient at talking out of both sides of my mouth. But it has left me feeling morally weak and reprehensible as I shoot the shit with the arrogant and the affluent."

"Let's just get through this current crisis, and then we'll see if there is any remedy to strengthen your character. Look, Johan, you do know that I am only teasing you. You have already proven your worth to me, and I need to keep you in my inner circle if I am to keep the wolves at bay."

Johan drives on in silence. No doubt, he has a lot on his mind. I return to reading the brief our corporate attorney has prepared so I can familiarize myself with the issues and the cast of characters until the light leaves us. The computer dings as our itinerary arrives electronically, complete with our scheduled appointments, times, places, and the names of the people we are to meet. A thought passes quickly through my consciousness as I hope we are not being set up to see only what the chairman wants us to see. My mother trusted Ulla, and I trust Ulla. Klaus Ek may have influence over many people, but I don't think Ulla is one of them. This will be okay.

We arrive at the Grand Arctic Lodge, where Ulla has booked our rooms. The snowdrifts are deep, and the new soft powder has covered the grounds making everything look pristine and white. The lodge is painted a bright red with white trim. The snow-covered trees are trimmed in tiny white lights. I feel as if I've been whisked back in time as the whole place looks like something out of a fairy tale. It is so different from the art and architecture of contemporary Stockholm.

There is a roaring fire in the lobby as we check in. We opt for a drink by the fire before retiring to our rooms.

"Early start tomorrow," Johan says before we say good night.

"We'll meet Bierdna Heibmu in the dining room at seven thirty."

"Bierdna Heibmu? What kind of a name is that?" Johan asks.

"It means Bear Tribe. Traditionally the Sámi have not used surnames; instead they named their children for deceased ancestors. But for hundreds of years now, the Lutheran Church has applied pressure on the Sámi to use Christian names for their children. After years of forced assimilation, many of the Sámi are now returning to the indigenous names of their people as a means to preserve and defend their traditional culture, way of life, and ethnic identity. Bierdna is to be our guide tomorrow."

"How do you know all of this?" Johan asks bewilderedly.

"It was in the notes Ulla sent along today," I answer as a weird feeling starts to overtake me. How do I know all this? Some of this was in the notes Ulla sent me, but not all of it. This is just another one of those weird things I just know. I decide to keep it to myself. "I take it you haven't met him?"

He shakes his head. "I guess we'll meet him in the morning."

I head up to my room, for I'm tired, but a bit keyed up. The first thing I need to do is to send Anders Andersson an email to thank him for the lovely roses. The reminiscence of their sweet fragrance still lingers in my memory. I wonder how much of my true story I should share with him. I like this man, and I'd like to be able to be completely honest with him. Still, even I have to admit that any talk of time-travel and past life regressions might be a bit off-putting when two people barely know one another. I'm not very adept at the gamesmanship expected in an early romance, but I think I'll keep my idiosyncrasies private, at least for now.

He must still be working at his computer, for he responds almost immediately with an invitation to join him for dinner on Saturday night. Delighted with the invitation, I accept.

I run a hot bath and add some herbal bath salts I find in the bathroom. *Valerian and Hops* is printed on the label, with the tagline—*to quiet the mind*. I know valerian is good for insomnia. I don't usually have trouble sleeping, but quieting my mind, well, that is another matter entirely. I hope this helps.

After a long soak, I am warm and relaxed. I slip between the cool sheets and am encased beneath the eiderdown comforter. I turn the lights out and gaze out at the beautiful icicles hanging from the eaves. A rosy glow fills my darkened room as the twinkling white lights reflect off of the red wooden building. It isn't long before I drift off to sleep.

CHAPTER 5

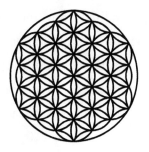

The alarm rings and I look at my phone. It takes me a moment to figure out if it is six p.m. or six a.m. All I know is that it's dark outside. Slowly, I begin to put it all together. I am in the Grand Arctic Lodge in the north of Sweden, somewhere near the Arctic Circle. It is early January, and the hours of darkness seem unending.

Oh, God, something's up.

I pull myself back to my current reality. I don't know how long I have been in the shower, but I do know that I cannot afford the luxury of lingering any longer this morning.

I need to keep my wits about me.

I need to be at my best today.

I dry my hair and put on my makeup before liberally applying moisturizer on the rest of my body as I attempt to protect my skin from the ravages of the cold, dry air. My skin welcomes the oil as I take my time massaging it in. Winter in the North Country can be brutal. The hotel room is still cool, so I dress quickly with a base layer of silk underwear beneath a cashmere turtleneck sweater, which will be warm but not too bulky. Next, I pull on a pair of fleece tights, then a pair of black merino wool palazzo pants, which fall to just above my ankles. Getting dressed can feel like such an ordeal when the winter weather is not just cold, but dangerously so. This should keep me warm today. Like most Scandinavian women, I dress simply.

I wrap a vintage shawl around my shoulders. It is handwoven with red and blue woolen threads, the colors of the Sámi people. This scarf once belonged to my grandmother, and it seems appropriate to wear it today. I do some quick calculations in my head. She was born in 1925, so if she were still alive, she would be 110 today. She led Lundstrom Enterprises before she passed the mantle to my mother, and now the responsibility to lead has been passed onto me. I come from a long line of smart and powerful women. I pray that I will be up to the challenge.

I pull my golden necklace from beneath the neck of my sweater and gently rub the Yggdrasil pendant between my fingertips—The Tree of Life. I say a little prayer for divine guidance and another of thanksgiving.

In all things, give thanks.

The Biblical words come back to me.

Now the golden tree with all its interconnected roots and branches rests on my chest against the black cashmere of my sweater. It feels like a sacred talisman providing wisdom and courage as well as a reminder of the love and protection of all those who have come before me.

I am almost ready. Lastly, I pull on my fur-lined winter boots then grab my hat and coat before heading down to the restaurant.

Johan and Bierdna Heibmu are already at the table when I arrive.

"I hope I haven't kept you waiting," I say as both men stand to greet me. I glance over to the corner of the dining room to the old

Mora clock with its painted floral face. It is seven a.m. and I am right on time.

"Not at all," Bierdna says. "I've only just arrived myself." Bierdna Heibmu is dressed in the *gakti* or the traditional clothing of his people. His wool jacket is cobalt blue, and the standup collar, shoulders, and cuffs are trimmed with red and gold embroidery where a pewter clasp both closes and embellishes the neckline. His jacket is belted at the waist and ruffles out around his hips where it is trimmed in a manner similar to his collar and cuffs. He is a little shorter than Johan, who is at least six foot three. Bierdna appears to be somewhere in his late fifties or possibly early sixties, although I've never been very good at guessing people's ages. His face is lined and weatherworn. He has a full white beard and sparkling blue eyes.

Johan makes the introductions.

"Thank you so much for making the long trip up from Stockholm. I am eager for you to meet my people and discuss our common interests and concerns. Today I dress in the *gakti* of our people so that you may come to have a better understanding of who we are and gain some appreciation of what is at risk of being lost." He extends his right hand to me. He exudes both personal strength and conviction, and yet he also has a gentle nature, which I had not expected.

I shake his hand, and he smiles broadly, showing his beautiful white teeth. "The pleasure is ours, Mr. Heibmu."

"Please call me Bierdna."

I nod, "Shall we have some breakfast?"

We take our seats at the table to continue this conversation and have something to eat. Johan has taken the liberty of ordering coffee for us, and thankfully, it is still piping hot.

After we order and while waiting for our breakfasts to arrive, Bierdna says, "I am truly delighted that you have come to the Sápmi lands to see the snow-capped mountains, wild rivers, pristine lakes and streams, the tundra, and the forests. Today you will meet our people and see for yourself how the Sámi people live."

I'm uncertain how to respond as these lands that he refers to as Sápmi have been in our family now for hundreds of years and are now owned by Lundstrom Enterprises. Although the Sámi do not have title to the land, they have used the land as it is right in the heart of the reindeer migratory path. The Sámi people have lived off this land for thousands of years, long before there were any national borders or even the concept of private land ownership, and certainly long before Lundstrom Enterprises was even thought of.

This is the essence of the conflict.

I take a long draw on my coffee.

Bierdna pauses in silence before he continues, "I had the pleasure of meeting your mother. It was years ago now. She was such a gracious and lovely lady. I had hoped we could get these land issues resolved before she retired."

I hesitate about how much I want to share about Mother's dementia. "Mother is getting on in years. I'm sure she would like nothing better than to see this resolved. I was unaware that you had been trying to reach Mother."

"Lately, the only person I have been in correspondence with is Klaus Ek. I'm sorry to be so direct, but the truth is that he and his minions have thwarted every attempt we have made to discuss the relevant issues and try to resolve this conflict."

Had Mother forgotten to tell me, or are my instincts right about Ek? Somehow, I believe it is the latter.

Johan pulls out his handheld computer to confirm the itinerary for the day. "How far are we from the winter grounds?" Johan asks just as the server brings our food.

"About thirty minutes, give or take," Bierdna responds. "We are expected in about an hour."

"We'd best eat up and get on our way, the forecast is calling for more snow," Johan says as he checks the time.

"Take as much time as you need. The land and my people will still be there when we arrive," Bierdna says with a chuckle that invites us to laugh along. Bierdna is a handsome man. The smile lines etched deeply around his pale blue eyes and his weathered face tell of a life lived outdoors. But his eyes sparkle when he laughs, and there is something in his smile that is welcoming and exudes kindness.

Still, we do not tarry long, and soon we have finished eating and are on our way.

Bierdna offers me a hand as I climb into the passenger seat of the elevated Land Rover while Johan climbs in the back. Bierdna drives. The vehicle has been equipped with large diameter snow tires and a snowplow to navigate the harsh and unpredictable Nordic climate. "In our homelands of Sápmi or the lands around the Arctic Circle that you call Sweden, Norway, Finland, and Russia, there are between 80,000 and 100,000 people who identify as Sámi. To try and help you understand our culture and our people requires gross generalizations that do not apply to all. Sámi are a diverse group of people who now work and live throughout Scandinavia. The more traditional among us fish, others are craftsmen and women, and only about ten percent of all Sámi are still Boazovázzi or reindeer walkers. In Sweden alone, there are more than 7,000 reindeer herders, and we herd over 200,000 reindeer down the mountain each fall from their grazing pastures.

Once the animals are down the mountain, they are separated by their owners into herding pens. Some of the reindeer go to slaughter, while others are kept for breeding, and a select few are neutered and trained to work either pulling sleds or for racing."

"How many reindeer does each herder own or claim?" Johan asks and I cringe.

Bierdna laughs, "Oh Johan, this question would be like asking you how much money you make or how much money is in your bank account. The herders measure their wealth and status in terms of the number of reindeer head."

Johan laughs, "Oh, dear, I'm so sorry. I meant no offense."

"Our livelihood is precarious at best. Our traditional migratory routes are being disrupted as more people are moving north to pursue work in the mines and climate change has led to later and later snowfalls here at the Arctic Circle. Some of the reindeer walkers stay too long in the summer pasture lands which has led to overgrazing."

I shudder as my thoughts return to the knowing where I once stood among the remains of these magnificent creatures. There were dead reindeer as far as I could see, and they had all perished by starvation.

Was that really just a couple of days ago? My entire understanding of time has changed since I've started to travel between my current life and other lifetimes. I am unable to place this knowing in any particular place or time. I know it took place somewhere in what Bierdna refers to as Sápmi or the homelands, but when did it take place? Has it already happened? Or perhaps it was a premonition. My head spins as I try to understand what, as of yet, is still incomprehensible.

Bierdna turns to me and asks, "Saga, are you okay? The color has drained from your face."

I close my eyes and nod my head. "Forgive me. I was just lost in my own thoughts for a moment," I say before returning to the concerns we are here to address. "Are the animals penned in the winter or allowed to run free? What do they eat up here with all this snow?"

Since the knowing, I've done some reading about this, and the stories are conflicting. I'd rather hear it from Bierdna. I trust he will tell me the truth.

"Ah, the reindeer are sturdy creatures and have survived up here longer than we have. God willing, with a bit of help from us, we will all survive this crisis of our own making. But back to your question as to what they eat, during the snow-covered months of winter, they use their sharp hooves to break through the ice in search of lichen. This year we have moved part of the herd into the forestlands for grazing. If their need for food exceeds the resources, then we will need to round them up and corral them. Providing supplemental feed domesticates the animals and severely cuts into any profit our people can hope to gain. Please understand that reindeer herding supports our way of life. Most of our nomadic people who walk with the reindeer earn only enough income for subsistence. There is not enough income generated to feed the animals *and* our families through the long cold months of winter.

"Climate changes and the warmer temperatures have led to ice melts exposing water. When the water evaporates, the air becomes wetter, inducing more rain. Last year we had an unprecedented rainfall which coated the ground, and then it froze. This makes it exceedingly difficult for the animals to break through the ice to find lichen to eat. Ten thousand reindeer across the region starved to death, and the entire herd was weakened. Subsequently, we had fewer calves born last spring."

I shudder as I try to grasp the implications of this loss. It sounds as if this has happened in Bierdna's lifetime. Clearly, I was not a witness to that tragedy.

"Now the government, in its infinite wisdom, has proposed a cull of 50,000 reindeer. Officials insist these killings are necessary to reduce overpopulation. The official position is that too many animals without enough access to food will weaken the herd and lead to widespread disease.

"However, since we are being forthright and honest with one another, let me tell you that we believe their motives are suspect. The killings are being proposed by Ek and his comrades in the government because they hope to profit handsomely on the energy and mining interests within the migratory path."

He doesn't need to say it. The traditional migratory routes pass directly through the land owned and mined by Lundstrom Enterprises. Ek's profit will be our profit, too.

This is the reason that we are here. He knows it, and Johan and I do, too.

It isn't long before we turn off of the plowed road and onto an unmarked road following the snowmobile tracks until we come to a one-lane wooden bridge over a frozen river. Before crossing, Bierdna puts the Land Rover in park, yet leaves the engine running. "Excuse me for a minute," he says, and he pulls on a fur-lined hat and leather mittens before opening the door to exit the truck.

Without further explanation, he bends his knee toward the bridge and a massive stone just on the other side. He lowers his head, resembling someone in prayer, and then leaves a coin on the wooden railing of the bridge.

"What the heck? Is he praying to the bridge?" says Johan as he tries to wrap his head around what is going on. "I thought these people were Lutheran."

"Just let it go. I'll explain later." I wish I had taken the time to bring Johan up to speed about the Sámi people and their beliefs.

"No problem. Better to keep my ignorance to myself than to open my mouth and remove all doubt," Johan says. "That's my mantra, and I'm sticking to it."

We watch in silence as Bierdna stands, dusts the snow from his trousers, and returns to the vehicle. "Just trying to keep those in the spirit world looking out for us. It could be a long, difficult winter without a little divine assistance," he says unapologetically.

We travel on for another few kilometers until the lights of the village can be seen in the distance.

"I don't know what I was expecting, perhaps an entire community of Sámi *lavvu* covered in reindeer skins," I say, expressing my own ignorance and lack of cultural understanding.

"The *lavvus* are similar to the teepees of indigenous people of North America, only less vertical and therefore more stable in the high winds of the Scandinavian tundra. In the winter, those *lavvus* in the valley along the riverbank are primarily ceremonial," Bierdna explains. "We have something planned for tomorrow night. We hope that you and Johan will honor us with your presence."

"Sanctioned by the Laestadian Lutheran Church?" Johan asks.

"Not exactly," Bierdna laughs. "There are those of us who still practice the old ways of our ancestors, given that the current government no longer burns us alive for doing so."

The silhouettes of teepees can be seen in the distance. We drive a little further into the rustic encampment. Many of the homes are dark and appear to have been all but abandoned. The houses are very small and poorly constructed. But there is little sign of life. There is a community center, a church, and a few shops, and they are all built of rough sawn wood and stained a dark brown with little or no external embellishment.

"Very few families choose to live here in these houses that were built for us by the government. Despite their best efforts to reconcile and play nice, after centuries of forced assimilation and attempts at annihilation, many of our Sámi families have gone back to more traditional, seasonal housing while we are here in the winter."

We drive around the bend where Bierdna gestures toward the river and the leeward side of the mountain where a collection of earthen mounds can be seen with smoke coming out of the chimneys and children ranging widely in age are playing together in the snow.

"Perhaps, they meant well," he chuckles. "But the governmental housing authority fails to understand that we are a nomadic culture and have little need for the little cookie-cutter, prefab houses they would like us to call home. Or perhaps it's just another attempt to try and change us and get us to live in a way that they can understand, control, and tax."

We drive on towards the settlement.

"Anyway, those houses they built for us are cold and drafty in these Arctic winds. They're poorly insulated and not designed for the permafrost, so they're falling apart and rotting as they're battered by the incessant storms of snow and wind. The government came in and gave us indoor plumbing, and that was all well and good until the pipes froze. These homes were not designed for our culture or our climate or built in sustainable ways.

"Most of our community has moved on from here, and we have designed our own homes below mounds of earth with super-insulated walls of sod with composting waterless toilets that dry out the human waste so it can be burned for heat. The building season is short up here, particularly for buildings which are off-road and off the grid, which is where most of the Sámi settlements are.

"There is a lack of cultural understanding. What works for people living in the South does not work well for the indigenous people of the North. For transient people, living in a fixed geographical area in permanent settlements is unnatural. What the well-intentioned fail to understand is that home is not necessarily the same as shelter; all of the natural world is our home. All of this land is our home." He extends his arm, making a large sweeping gesture.

As we drive into the settlement, both my phone and Johan's begin to buzz. We have been out in the hinterlands, and only now do we have service. "Ah, the blessing and the curse of modern technology," Johan says with a laugh. "We've been found."

"Do you need a moment to return messages?" Bierdna asks.

I look at my phone. There are three messages from Klaus Ek and one from Ulla. All have come in the last thirty minutes. This is just about as long as it has taken us to drive out here to this settlement.

"Did the chairman call you?" asks Johan.

I nod. "I think I'll call Ulla first and see if she knows what he wants."

"Good idea," Johan says. "Bierdna, I know our time here is short, but can you help me locate the men's room before we get started?"

"I'll only be a minute," I say to reassure our host that I have no intention of letting our plans be derailed. Still sitting in the front seat of the Land Rover, I place a call to Ulla while I still have service.

"Oh, Saga," she says, and I can hear the distress in her voice, "I hope I haven't made a huge faux pas."

"What's happened?"

"Mr. Ek called this morning looking for you. I told him that you and Johan left yesterday and were up in Norrbotten for a meeting with Bierdna Heibmu and a coalition of Sámi elders. He pressed me to share your itinerary with him, and I'm afraid I pleaded ignorance. I told him that Mr. Heibmu had made all of the arrangements, and all I knew was that you were expected home tomorrow evening. I hope everything is okay. He was most upset, angry, really. I can call him back and tell him where to find you if you want."

"It's fine, Ulla," I say as I wonder what this is all about. "I need to focus on a few things up here. I'm sure whatever Mr. Ek needs can wait until tomorrow or at least until I get back to my hotel room tonight. My phone service is spotty up here, so you may be unable to reach me for a few hours. I'll call you back when I get back to an area where my service picks up."

"Okay, but something is in the wind. I don't know what it is, but please be careful."

"Text me if you hear anything, texts often go through even when phone calls don't. And use the encrypted service, okay?"

"Sure."

"And if Klaus Ek calls again seeking more information, just tell him I'll call him back when I have service."

I have no intention of calling him until I can figure out what he wants from me. Ulla's right. Something is in the wind, and I don't like it either. I feel like I am being spied on. Something is going on here that he doesn't want me involved in.

It is still completely dark when Johan taps on the truck's window. "Are you ready to go?"

I open the door and smile, "All set. Where are we off to first?" I ask, directing my question to our host.

"I thought we'd go and see the reindeer in their enclosure and meet some of the reindeer walkers while you're still warm from the drive. Let me know if you get too cold because we can go inside and warm up at any time."

I have never seen a reindeer or a caribou except as a child at the zoo, and that was a long time ago. We stand at the fence line as my eyes begin to adjust to the darkness. Out of the shadows, shapes begin to emerge. I hadn't realized how big they are or how powerful.

Bierdna tells us a bit about the herd. "While they're not very tall, they are incredibly strong and can pull four to five times their own weight. The bull can weigh upwards of 500 pounds or 225 kilograms. Still, they are gentle and sweet." He reaches into a bag to retrieve an apple and feeds the female closest to the fence. Then he gently strokes her nose as she nudges his hand in appreciation. "They're not particularly aggressive except during the rutting season." He turns and hands me an apple as some of the other animals make their way to the fence line where we are standing. "This one is female. She will carry her antlers until after she has given birth. She may need them to help assure she gets enough to eat while nursing her young. The Creator is wise like that," Bierdna says and nods, affirming the truth of what he has just said.

I nod too. I want him to know that we are simpatico. So many people have forgotten our connection with the Creator and the natural world.

Bierdna returns his gaze to the magnificent creature at the fence. "We call her Vuorbbe. It means pure luck. She delivered two beautiful, strong calves last spring. Twinning is unusual in reindeer, yet it looks as if she is carrying twins again. Perhaps the luck isn't hers, but rather Droste's as she belongs to his herd."

The gentle reindeer leans over the split rail fence and nudges my arm to indicate that she is waiting for the apple I hold. I place the apple in the palm of my mittened hand as she retrieves it. I am reminded of my childhood when I would feed apples and carrots to my horse.

Bierdna notices, "You've done this before."

"I had a horse when I was a little girl."

"Do you still ride?" he asks.

"Not for years. Somehow the demands of my adult life have left little time for riding." I stand there for a moment more and pet her nose. She has a snow-white chest and face. There is something incredibly soulful about her eyes. They are the blue of a cloudless summer sky. She nudges my hand. I understand the request and continue to pet her. Then she looks me in the eye and holds my gaze. I sense she wants something more from me.

"It looks like you've made a friend," Johan says.

Bierdna smiles and interprets, "She trusts you and is asking you to help her and to help us."

A chill goes down my spine. It is as if Bierdna has read my mind. This is exactly the message I was receiving from the beautiful reindeer. She is worried about the future for her unborn progeny.

"She has such beautiful blue eyes. It is as if she can see right through me."

"Perhaps she can. The eyes of the reindeer change from gold in the summer to blue in the winter. The scientists tell us they see the world in glorious ultraviolet, which has a shorter wavelength than visible light and therefore is invisible to the human eye. It helps them find food and avoid predators. Perhaps it also allows her to look into your soul and see what is hidden there."

"Perhaps," I say under my breath.

Bierdna places a hand on my shoulder, indicating it is time for us to go. Before I leave, I take a moment to bow to this beautiful sentient being. In my heart, I make a promise to myself to remember her and the needs of the reindeer, and the people who walk with them. In response, she extends her right leg as she dips her head and lowers her gaze as if she is acknowledging what has been left unspoken between us.

CHAPTER 6

We walk away from the animals as three men in traditional Sámi dress drive up on snowmobiles. "Time to meet the elders, they have already gathered at the meeting house to discuss our concerns. We had planned to bring you in by a reindeer-drawn sleigh, but the weather is changing, and our time together is short."

"Perhaps next time," Johan says, and I am happy he seems to want to come back.

"Johan, you ride with Ado, Saga will ride with Gerda, and I will follow with Hugo."

Our drivers dress Johan and me in beautiful, hooded cloaks made of reindeer fur. Johan's is brown, and mine is white. The buttons are made of antler, and they tie the cloaks around our waists with embroidered belts. I feel like a character in *The Snow Queen*, the old fairy tale by Hans Christen Andersen.

I, too, am on a quest.

The snow has started to fall again, and the winds are picking up. But I feel warm in this luxurious coat. It is ten a.m., and it is just starting to get light. Up here, the sun still isn't expected to rise for a little more than an hour. Given the darkness and the snow, it is difficult to see. I hold on tight to my driver and hide my face behind his back, protecting myself from the driving snow. All of the snowmobiles have their headlights on, and I'm glad they know where they are going as I can't see much of anything in this whiteout.

We ride a long way through the blizzard, and I can't help but wonder if the Sámi people have also learned to see what is invisible to the rest of us. Gratefully, at last, we arrive at another community of Sámi people.

Bierdna takes my hand to help me off the snowmobile, and Johan follows as we enter one of the larger earthen dwellings. It takes my eyes a minute to adjust after coming in from the blinding snowstorm.

This must be some kind of a community center as there is a large roaring fire in the center of the room, and the smoke clears through a stucco chimney. A long wooden table has been set in front of the fireplace, and there are wooden benches around the perimeter that encircle the room, which are filled with people. The room is bathed in a golden glow and is lit by oil lamps hung as sconces on the exterior walls. The only natural light comes through the windows on either side of the door. Today, although dawn is breaking, there is little light coming through the windows due to the blizzard. The rest of the building is beneath the earth. The space is warm and cozy.

Bierdna calls out, "We're here."

Cheers go up from the twenty or thirty men and women. They all wear their *gáktis* or traditional dress. This traditional clothing has been worn by the Sámi for thousands of years and varies based on family of origin, personal interests, and even marital status. Today most of these people are dressed in cobalt blue woolen tunics or dresses with red and yellow hand embroidered trim. They stand to greet us as we are led to a semicircle of chairs facing the benches. One of the men comes to take our coats, and then Bierdna gestures indicating that we are all to sit down.

Clearly, these people have been awaiting our arrival. No sooner are we seated when a young woman begins to play a few notes on a small reed pipe, and the room goes silent as everyone turns their attention to the one young man who is still standing. He begins to *joik*. He sings a slow, deep, and beautiful song that resonates from the back of his throat. He sings acapella, without any accompaniment. His voice is ethereal, soul-stirring, and filled with emotion. Soon everyone joins in the ancient song. The words are all in Sámi, a language I neither speak nor understand, but there is something hauntingly familiar about the music, perhaps because it is eerily reminiscent of the sounds of the natural world, like the wind blowing through the forest. One moment the music is soft and gentle, then the timbre changes gradually increasing in both volume and power as others join in.

Oh, dear God, this all seems so familiar.

Once the song has been completed, an elderly woman slowly rises and walks in our direction. She is tall, and her long white hair is braided and falls like a thick rope down the middle of her back. It is the deep lines on her weatherworn face that tell of her age, but the sparkle in her pale blue eyes speak of her wisdom.

Bierdna stands, and Johan and I do the same. "Saga, may I introduce Grandmother Lejá. She is not my biological grandmother, but we are kin, just the same. Within our community, to be called Grandmother is a great honor. Grandmother Lejá is the *Noaidi* of our *siida*, or our community of families. She, too, is a seer and the eldest among us. We are honored to have her open our gathering today."

Despite my best attempt to conceal my intentions and remain neutral, I fear my eyes give it all away as I shoot Bierdna a look, for that one little word speaks volumes: *too*.

Apparently, Bierdna sees me for who and I am. If he sees me, no doubt this lovely elderly woman sees me and knows me, too. From the research I have done, I understand that this woman is not only a shaman or a healer, but she is also a *Noaidi*. She is a Seer.

Because of the deference given her, I believe this woman is a *mugga*, spiritually powerful, magical, efficacious, and therefore dangerous.

I utter a brief prayer for guidance, for I am in uncharted territory.

She smiles kindly as I extend my hand to her, but Grandmother Lejá opens her arms and wraps me in a warm embrace.

"Welcome home, child. We have waited so long for your return," Grandmother Lejá says softly in my ear so only I can hear. "I have heard how you charmed Vuorbbe. Perhaps she is your familiar. Only the strongest of the *Noaidi* and shamans have reindeer as their spirit allies."

How is it that she already knows of my encounter with Pure Luck, as this has only just happened, and we came here directly?

Before I can even begin to form a response to this kindly woman, the others come up to shake our hands as Bierdna introduces both Johan and me to the leaders from other communities who have traveled great distances across the tundra to meet with us today.

After the introductions have all been made, the room is filled with chatter as many of these people have not seen one another in a long time, and they have much to discuss, but Bierdna quiets the room with a call that is used for summoning the reindeer. Laughter erupts, and then everyone quiets down, "There is much to talk about today, but our time is short. Many of you have been up half the night and traveled a great distance through the blizzard. No doubt, you are hungry, but before we eat, Grandmother Lejá will offer a blessing over the food."

People begin to move, and out of the chaos, a circle is formed.

Grandmother Lejá speaks first in Sámi and then in Swedish for the benefit of their guests, Johan and me.

"The eyes of all wait upon you, O Lord,

and you give them their food in due season;

You open Your hand and satisfy the desire of every living thing.

Lord God, heavenly Father, bless us and these Your gifts

which we receive from your bountiful goodness. Amen."

I don't know what I'd expected, but the prayer is very similar to the Lutheran prayer said in homes all across Sweden.

"Please, everyone, fill a plate and eat," Grandmother Lejá requests as she indicates that Johan and I should be the first to go through the line.

There are plates filled with roasted reindeer meat, smoked trout and salted salmon, wild berries and barley, bowls of buttered potatoes, reindeer cheeses, and plenty of hot coffee.

We sit at a simple wooden table that has been adorned with pine branches and candles in burled wooden candle holders. The others return to their benches, balancing their wooden plates and cups on their laps like one would do at a picnic. The hospitality and courtesy are overwhelming, and the mood is jovial, for the most part. There are a couple of middle-aged men who seem less than pleased that we are being treated as honored guests, and they're grumbling about the lavish spread that has been put forth in our honor.

Bierdna excuses himself to deal with their rudeness.

It is hard to find fault with them for feeling that what little they have is being shared with people who have so much, and for all they know, on people who may be intent on their demise and destruction.

The conversation is light and convivial while we eat, no doubt the serious conversation will follow shortly.

When everyone has finished, young boys and girls scurry about clearing the dirty dishes and putting away all the remaining food while Grandmother Lejá stands again to pray. The room goes silent, and everyone bows their head:

"Oh, give thanks to the Lord,
For the Lord is good,
And your mercy endures forever.
We thank you for all your gifts,
May you live and reign forever and ever.
Amen."

It is then that Grandmother Lejá opens the meeting, "Our hearts are filled with gratitude that Saga Svensson and her brother Johan have traveled so far to meet with us, to learn about our ways, to share a meal and a celebration, and to help us find a way to survive in these uncertain times. We have been praying to the Almighty Creator that someone would come to help us, and now you are here, the answer to our prayers."

The very notion of being the answer to anyone's prayers is overwhelming and disconcerting.

When Grandmother Lejá has finished speaking, she lays a large bough from a juniper tree across the blazing fire. The smell and smoke fill the room, as the Sámi people ritualistically pull the smoke towards themselves, all the while murmuring prayers and blessing themselves. Only once Grandmother Lejá has taken her seat does someone else stand to address their concerns to both Johan and me.

An elderly man stands, and he leans against a wooden walking stick, his ceremonial clothing is clean and pressed but perhaps a little threadbare from years of wear. "Good afternoon, as Grandmother Lejá, has already said, we welcome you to Sápmi lands. My name is Mielat, and I have been asked to speak on behalf of our people. Forgive me if my Swedish is difficult to understand, as it is not my first language. We are a people who have relied on a rich oral tradition, stories of our people, and our history have been told for generations from grandparents to grandchildren around the fireplaces in the long cold months of winter. The stories are repeated again and again, lest they be forgotten. The strong and the powerful fear what they do not understand, and thus they have done their best to ensure that our stories, our language, and our culture do not survive. There are forces at work that are intent on our demise. They have taken our children and placed them in residential schools far from their families and the only life they have ever known. They have passed laws preventing us from speaking in our native tongue and practicing our religion while insisting that our ways are evil and our spiritual leaders, healers, shamans, and *noaidis* have been severely punished and even killed. Let there be little doubt that our people were coerced to join the state religion of the Lutheran Church.

"Please understand I mean no offense, for perhaps you are unaware of how our people have been treated. Trust me when I tell you that the Swedish people, the church, the monarchy, and the government have not always been on the honorable side of history. If you find us skeptical and reserved, please understand that we have reason to be. Too many times, we have taken people at their word only to be deceived, cheated, and lied to.

"Once this land belonged only to the Creator, long before the strong and the powerful claimed it as their own. They have done everything in their power, including declaring war to see who will profit off the land and control the lives of the people who live here.

"During troubling times decisions were made expeditiously, and deals were negotiated in exchange for freedom and protection.

"Allow me to remind you of the history of the North. Perhaps you have heard of the Thirty Years' War, which started in the mid-1600s as a religious battle between the Holy Roman Empire and the powerful forces embracing the Protestant Reformation.

"Cuius regio, eius religio—

the religion of the ruler,

dictates the religion of those ruled.

"Throughout this war, many battles were waged, and all the principalities in Europe were forming alliances for reasons that often had nothing to do with the practice of Christianity. For example, Catholic France helped finance the war being waged by the Protestant Swedes. They were more concerned with weakening the Catholic Hapsburgs of Austria than the saving of souls or even expanding the reach of the Roman Catholic Church.

"This was an era of almost endless warfare under the leadership of Gustavus Adolphus II, the King of Sweden, where battles were being fought on at least three different fronts. It is also a time when promises were made to the Sámi people of the North.

"The Sámis were promised the right to practice our faith in private and given exclusive sovereignty over our lands. Grazing rights on Crown land were secured, and in exchange, the Sámi shamans helped defeat the enemies of the Swedish Crown through our interventions with the spirit world.

"But when the threat of war was over and the victories secured, the promises made in the heat of battle were forgotten. Much of this land, the mountains, the forests, the lakes, and the rivers, which had been our ancestral homeland, was then sold off by the Crown to help cover the costs of this lengthy and extensive war or given away to the nobility and aristocracy in exchange for military service and valor in battle.

"My dear right honorable Lady Saga of the House of Lundstrom, it was your sixteenth great-grandmother Lady Kristina Lundstrom, the eldest child of noble birth who received the lands your family currently holds, as well as the title of baroness which your mother now bears. The land was given as a barony by Gustavus Adolphus II, the King of Sweden, after the Thirty Years' War ended in 1635 as remuneration for her husband's military service to the Crown and subsequent loss of his life on the battlefield.

"To the victors go the spoils.

"The king rewarded those who had been loyal to him in battle with a gift of land. Lady Kristina's husband died in the service of the king.

"This is how your family came to possess the land we have lived and worked on for thousands of years.

"It was then that the teachings of Martin Luther and the Lutheran Church became the state religion of Sweden. In the early 1700s the Sámi people were accused of practicing witchcraft. Our drums were confiscated, and our spiritual leaders were forced to renounce the teachings of our ancestors or be burned at the stake as heretics. This began a long period of forced assimilation and mandatory acceptance of the Lutheran faith.

"Many of our people are now practicing Lutherans and have left the old ways behind, some of us practice an integrated version of the old ways and the ways of the Lutheran faith, and some fully embrace the ways of our ancestors. We have a tolerance and an acceptance for different beliefs and practices—which is what we had been promised years ago by King Gustavus Adolphus.

"What were the Sámi given in exchange for the land, you might ask? We believe that no man owns the land, any more than one person can own another. We had no interest in owning the land, but we were promised we would always have the use of the land, the forests, the fields, and the water. Unfortunately, those promises have also been forgotten.

"The governments of Russia, Finland, Sweden, and Norway each attempt to tax us every time our people and our livestock cross one of the international borders. Our people live humble, healthy, and virtuous lives that are uncorrupted by commerce, materialism, and luxury. These taxes are crippling our way of life and our ability to be self-supporting and self-sufficient.

"The logging done by your company has already begun to encroach on the forests, disrupting the ecosystem and diminishing the lichen growing on the forest floor, which is the primary food source our reindeer rely on for survival during the long cold months of winter. The bullet trains that bring your timber to market run right through our grazing lands and put our animals at risk. And now gold, copper, and other minerals have been found right in the migratory path our reindeer have followed for millennia. We fear the environmental threat a mine poses to our people, our animals, the forests, the rivers, and the fresh water that we all depend on. We need your help to honor the promises made to our people so very long ago."

Mielat bows in my direction as he leans heavily on his old wooden walking stick and makes his way back towards his seat.

The Sámi people erupt in applause showing their affirmation.

Slowly the din quiets so I may be heard. "Thank you, sir," I say, feeling my thanks are completely inadequate. This kindly gentleman has taken it upon himself to understand and clearly convey the gravity of their situation, and still, he does not give in to anger or righteous indignation. Rather he is well-spoken and exudes both the grace and self-confidence that come from being in the right. Some of this story I have heard before, and some of it is new to me.

The room falls silent as the enormity of the issues fills the space.

Something nags at me, for there was something else that Mielat said, but what was it? Something about gold, copper, and other minerals. What other minerals? I wasn't told about any other minerals. I try to quiet the chatter in my head. These people need my full attention, and I need to listen. I'll come back to this later.

Then one person after another stands to speak, one at a time, until everyone who has something to add has a chance to do so. Many of these people are well-spoken in both Swedish and Sámi. Some whisper amongst themselves in Sámi, and those who are comfortable speaking Swedish translate for those who speak only in their native tongue.

Although their individual stories are varied in detail, the underlying concerns are nearly always the same. The way of life for these indigenous people of the Arctic Circle is being threatened by climate change, as the impact is amplified at the Pole. The temperatures here are rising twice as fast as the global average. Adding insult to injury has been the logging, and the high-speed train used to take the timber to market, and now the recent discovery of mineral and energy resources buried within the earth right in the ancient migratory path of the reindeer and in the heart of the winter grazing lands. The Sámi way of life and their very existence is at risk.

"We are concerned how the recent discovery of gold and other minerals on the land owned by Lundstrom Enterprises will impact the reindeer and the reindeer walkers. The mine, the excavation, and the trucking of ore are already disrupting the migratory pathway. We fear the loss of habitat for our reindeer and the negative environmental impact the mine is having on our ancestral homeland and our way of life," a younger man in his twenties reiterates the concerns already put forth by others.

He is the second person who has referred to other minerals, and he speaks as if the mine is already in existence. Could this just be an error in translation? All the reports I've read indicated the presence of gold and copper. I've heard nothing about any decision to mine. Has this young man misspoken, or am I just ill-informed?

Before he returns to his seat, I ask for clarification. "I was told gold and copper were discovered up near the Gulf of Bothnia, but I'm not aware that any mining has taken place."

A look of shock and confusion comes over his face, and it spreads like a contagion throughout the room. In an instant, this quiet and polite gathering is abuzz as people turn to those seated on either side of them, whispering to one another in Sámi.

Johan leans over to me and whispers, "What just happened? And what the hell is this all about?"

Bierdna stands and addresses the members of his community, "Let us remember that Saga and Johan are our guests, and we will treat them as such while maintaining a sense of decorum." The room grows quiet, but you can cut the tension with a knife.

Then Bierdna turns to me, "Saga, both you and Johan seem to be both upright and honest people. I draw this conclusion by the fact that you and your brother have traveled north to Sápmiland to meet with us. So, I must ask, do you mean to tell us that you do not know about the mine which has been built and is operational on land owned by Lundstrom Enterprises near the Gulf of Bothnia and the Finnish border?"

My stomach heaves as I turn to look at my brother. He looks as bewildered as I feel. Now it is my turn to feel a sense of shock and dismay.

"Do you mean to tell me that the mine has already been dug and is operational?" I ask, hoping I've misunderstood, and this is all just a bad dream.

"Bierdna nods, "Yes, it opened a few weeks ago."

"This is the first I am learning about this." I turn to my brother as I have to ask, "Johan, do you know anything about this?"

"No," he says. His face is gray. He turns his hands upward in a gesture indicating he has no more information on this than I do.

The room erupts in a din of angry rumbling as the elders speak amongst themselves in their native tongue. I don't speak their language, but I know what they are saying. They have been lied to before. Now, I, too, am pleading ignorance. Almost to a person, the council of elders have crossed their arms defiantly over their chests.

Grandmother Lejá stands and approaches me, placing her hand lovingly upon my shoulder, "Well, it looks like you have a fox in your hen house. A fox by the name of Klaus Ek."

So many questions race through my mind, I wish I weren't sitting here on display as I try to process this news.

"Please understand I have heard you, and your concerns are also my concerns. I intend to make this my highest priority." My words sound and feel so inadequate. These people are angry and in need of reassurance, and all I am capable of offering is a promise to investigate further.

This is wrong in so many ways.

Still, the questions come: What is Ek up to? Has he really prepared to mine gold on company land without my knowledge, or, for that matter, without my mother's approval, as clearly this mine was dug while she was still the CEO? Or the written consent and direction of the other members of the board?

I have read and reread the minutes from every board meeting for the last few years, and there is not so much as a footnote about a mine being dug on our land. Who is he working with, and what does he intend to do with the gold he extracts? Where did he get the funds to build this? I met with the chief financial officer over the winter holidays, and there is nothing budgeted for an expenditure of this magnitude.

My insides feel like they are on fire, and I don't trust myself to speak. I may not have the details or the answers to the questions that seek to overwhelm me, but I do know that this is an organizational crisis, potentially a major environmental faux pas that puts the Sámi people, their livelihood and their reindeer at risk. These are stoic Scandinavians who are slow to anger, but they have been manipulated and deceived. They are enraged, and so am I.

"I don't know what is going on, but you can be assured I have every intention of finding out," I say the words aloud, and the young woman acting as my interpreter delivers them in Sámi. The elders nod their heads as if my words give them some modicum of comfort. Finally, someone has heard them, but now what?

"Bierdna," I address our host, "I had been told that gold had been found on the land, but until this moment, I was completely unaware that a mine had already been dug. I understand your concerns, as promises made long ago have been broken. Before the sun sets on this day, I need someone to take us out to the mine so I can see the scope of this operation."

"I appreciate your sense of urgency, but given the blizzard, it is too far to travel today. It will be dark long before we arrive. Let me take you and Johan back to the hotel, and we can leave for the mine first thing in the morning," Bierdna suggests.

Johan looks over at me, and I nod in agreement with the wisdom of this. "You exercise good judgment, Bierdna, and I can use the time to investigate and make a few phone calls. I can assure you that I don't like having the wool pulled over my eyes or being deceived any more than you good people do."

The Sámi people approach both Johan and me, forming a line to shake our hands and thank us for hearing their concerns. Lastly, the eloquent, elderly speaker Mielat approaches. He takes my hands in his. The joints of his fingers are knobby and gnarled with arthritis, but his grasp is gentle as he brings my hands to his lips and kisses them. "Thank you, my dear." Tears well up in his eyes and threaten to overflow and run down his lined cheeks just as they are running down my own.

And then out of nowhere, the young people arrive carrying the beautiful reindeer cloaks, and we are redressed for our snowmobile ride back to Bierdna's Land Rover, which is still parked back near the reindeer enclosure.

Before we leave, Grandmother Lejá rises again to address the group. She comes to stand beside me and places her hand on my shoulder, and the room goes silent, "It looks like this trip has already proven to be worthwhile. You have learned many things and understand many things." Then she folds her hands and offers another simple prayer:

"May Biegkegaellies,
the God of the winter winds and snow,
protect you and guide you safely on your way.
Mother Earth thanks you for your care and concern
and on behalf of all our people,
we thank you for coming here to help."

One of the young men who assists Grandmother Lejá lifts a long burning stick from the fire and lights a braid of vanilla sweetgrass and walks around both Johan and me as the smoke from the burning plants encircles us.

"Sweetgrass will bring you blessings and protection," the young man explains as we prepare to leave.

The blizzard rages on as we travel across the icy Arctic tundra while the roaring sound of the snowmobiles prohibits any conversation. My thoughts turn to Grandmother Lejá as visions of her praying hands come to mind. There is something familiar about her, and her gnarled and arthritic hands folded reverently in prayer. I hold onto the driver of this mechanized sled while allowing my mind's eye to focus on her hands, recreating the image from memory. On the back of her right hand, there is a birthmark in the shape of a mitten. It has faded with the passing of years and is a light brown, like the color of coffee with cream. I have seen these hands before, on other women who have helped me through other challenges in other lifetimes. This spirit is kind and gentle but unwavering in fortitude. I take comfort in the feelings of love and protection that come over me.

The storm rages on until, at last, we arrive back at Bierdna's Land Rover.

The reindeer pen has been totally obscured by the storm. I'm disappointed as I had hoped to reconnect with the mother reindeer they call Pure Luck. It is almost as if the pen and the animals contained within it have completely disappeared into the snowstorm. No sound carries above the wailing din of the Arctic wind. The white winter coats of the reindeer offer them complete camouflage and concealment in the snow.

Ah, the wisdom of mother nature prevails. Now, if only we don't go and destroy all that we have been so generously given.

Just as we are removing the beautiful reindeer pelts we wore while traversing the tundra on the snowmobiles, a long, low, blowing sound blasts from the direction of the pen.

"Sounds like Vuorbbe. Pure Luck is asking you to remember your promise," Bierdna says as a matter of fact.

But I don't need him to interpret for me. I, too, have understood her call.

CHAPTER 7

We travel back towards our hotel in silence as Bierdna drives slowly through the near whiteout. The temperature has dropped. The snow is dry and light, so it blows and drifts across our path. As we cross back over the frozen Torne River, again Bierdna slowly brings his truck to a stop and exits again chanting loudly, he asks the river for permission before we venture across the bridge. Johan shoots me a sidelong glance, as I suspect he knows even less about the ancient Sámi beliefs than I do. I know they believe the spirit of the Creator lives in everything in the natural world, including the Torne River, as well as in all the beings in the spirit world.

I believe this too.

These people may worship at the Lutheran Church on Sunday mornings, but many still hold onto the pagan beliefs of their ancestors and communicate with the spirits of the natural world and the spirits just beyond the veil.

We ride along in silence as Bierdna devotes his full concentration to getting us through the blizzard and back to the hotel. When at last we arrive, I breathe a sigh of relief and thank God for our deliverance from the storm.

The blizzard rages on as he puts the vehicle into park near the entrance to the lodge. Bierdna asks, "Would you like to have dinner in the hotel this evening?"

"It has been a long day, one full of surprises and certainly not all of them pleasant. Besides all that, I'm not the least bit hungry after that wonderful lunch," I say. "I have work I must do before we head out to see the mine tomorrow. There are phone calls to return, and I need to let my assistant know we will be staying another day." I'm yammering on like an overgrown child. I've always tended to talk too much when I get nervous and afraid. He doesn't need to know any of this. What is wrong with me? Taking a breath, I regain a bit of self-control and say, "Thank you, but perhaps it will be best if we just meet in the morning."

"Very well, then I will wish you a lovely evening and will return in the morning to take you out to see the newly constructed mine. The sunrise is about eleven tomorrow morning, why don't I meet you in the dining room at eight thirty so we can have some breakfast before we head out. It's at least an hour's drive out to the mine. It's likely to be another long day, and there will be nothing to eat anywhere near the mine," Bierdna says as Johan, and I get out of the car.

"Thank you for today, as Grandmother Lejá has so aptly stated, 'this has been a successful day as we have learned much that we did not know before.'"

Johan nods, "Thank you, Bierdna. We will get to the bottom of this. See you tomorrow."

We close the vehicle doors and walk toward the entrance and the lobby. The outside fairy lights twinkle and sparkle on the snow-laden evergreens which line the walkway. Johan takes my elbow as the sidewalk is slippery. "If I go down, I'm taking you with me," I say as I hold on tight to my brother.

"Do you mean that literally or metaphorically," he laughs.

"Both, I'm counting on you to get me through this… all of this," I say as I give his arm a squeeze.

Once inside the hotel lobby, we take off our outerwear before the snow covering our clothing begins to melt. There is a roaring fire in the large fieldstone fireplace. "Care to grab a drink and talk about this before you call Klaus Ek and ream that man a new asshole?"

"Are you speaking as the Director of Public Relations or as my brother, an heir to the family fortune?"

"Both, we need to strategize on how we intend to handle this illicit debacle. I think we need to get a handle on what is going on before we tip our hand, and he learns that we are on to him."

"Okay, but I was all for reaming him a new asshole."

"I'm not opposed to that, however, let's figure out a few things first."

I smile at my brother. "My clothes are damp, and I need to change into something a little more casual and a lot more comfortable. In fact, I could really use a short nap. Do you mind?"

"I'll be in the bar," Johan says as he leaves me at the elevator.

"If I'm not down in an hour, call my room."

"Okay. But, don't call anyone or take any calls until we've had a chance to strategize. Now I am speaking as the Public Relations Director," Johan says.

The elevator door opens, and I step in. "Don't get too far ahead of me," I say as the door begins to close. I regret my comment and wish I could retrieve it as I see my dearly beloved brother cringe at the mention of his drinking.

It's only three thirty by the time I reach my room. It seems so much later as the sun has been down for hours already. I hang my wet clothes near the heating vent and climb under the duvet. It has been a stressful day, and it feels so good to leave it all behind, if only temporarily. I begin to drift between worlds before I even turn off the bedside lamp.

It feels like dreaming, or maybe watching an old movie where everything is in black and white and shades of gray. An alarm has rung. I leave the wet laundry in the basket out back by the clothesline and rush to find my mother. She holds my little brother in her arms, and I take my little sister by the hand. Today, I am a child, thin and scrawny. My bare feet are covered with fine gray dust. I am an observer.

Nothing grows here. The ground is dusty. We need rain. The sky is gray and overcast, and it threatens to rain again. A crowd of people, mostly women in old cotton house dresses and other little children under the age of ten, wait in the dust behind the split rail fence. But what are we waiting for? The women whisper amongst themselves. They are worried, and their thin ashen faces are heavily lined and careworn. Life is difficult here, and these are young mothers, but they look much older than their years. The air is filled with coal dust, and I begin to cough. I am having difficulty breathing.

Men, covered with soot, emerge one by one from beneath the surface of the earth. The first man out carries a small cage. The only color in this world of gray haze is the bright yellow feathers of a little canary that lies dead on the bottom of his cage.

Then I wake up. My heart is pounding, and I'm sweating. I feel I have had a premonition. Something bad is going to happen, something really bad.

It seems as if every time I fall asleep, I am being sent messages from the great beyond. Why is this happening so frequently now? And then like a cosmic download, I have the answer to my question. Time is of the essence. Critical things are happening, and I need to know what I am up against.

I look around my now-dark room for my phone. I want to call Annika. I need her guidance. I need her perspective. I need her to help me understand what is being asked of me. Finding my phone beneath my pillow, I see that I have many missed calls, one from Anders, one is from Ulla, one from Mother, and four from Ek all in the last hour.

I had promised Johan we would strategize on how best to handle Ek before we tip our hand.

I want to talk to Annika. Perhaps she can help me sort this out. How quickly she has become the person I turn to. She is my most trusted advisor, my confidant, and my confessor. But before I call her, I take a moment to listen to my voicemail.

Anders called to chat. The warmth in his voice wraps around me like a soft blanket, and in spite of everything else, I smile at the prospect of seeing him again. How nice it would be to be spending the evening with Anders rather than trying to find my way out of this quagmire.

The next call is from Ulla. She is heading home early as another snowstorm threatens to bury the city and make the roads impassable. She leaves me her cell phone number in case I need to speak with her at home tonight. She ends her call with a plea for caution, "Please, Saga be careful."

Mother's call is next. She sounds agitated and anxious. She whispers into the phone as if telling me a secret that she doesn't want anyone else to hear. She sounds distressed and more than a little confused.

I listen to the recording again. "We are on firm legal ground, and everything has been addressed and recorded in the deeds, the will, and the trust." Then her voice becomes emphatic, "You must secure the documents before they disappear."

I'm not certain what she is talking about. What documents? And is this confusion due to her dementia or just my lack of understanding? Why is she whispering? Is there someone at the house that she doesn't want to hear what she is saying to me, or is she just being paranoid? Or am I the one who is suffering from paranoia?

Although there are four missed calls from Klaus Ek, there are only two messages. In the first message, he is overly solicitous about my whereabouts. "Hi Saga, it's Klaus. My dear, I've stopped by your office twice in the last few days and left numerous calls requesting you return my call. And yet, I still have heard nothing back from you. I am starting to get worried. I have surmised that you are with your brother, but perhaps not as he is perpetually unavailable. Even dear Ulla is evasive with regards to your whereabouts. I even took the liberty of stopping by to see your mother. I thought perhaps you might be there. But alas, no. Given the frightful storm which is raging outside, I am praying that you are safe and warm and out of harm's way. Perhaps it is just the storm that has interrupted the phone service. In any regard, if you would be so kind as to call me back at your earliest convenience."

Apparently, he doesn't know that I spoke with Ulla. Why is he so evasive and cagey? Ulla told him yesterday that Johan and I were up here meeting with Bierdna and a delegation of Sámi elders. Perhaps he suspects that I am on to him. The cloying sweetness and insincerity of his concern that radiates from his voice cause me to shudder. I feel like he is baiting a trap and trying to lure me in, but for what?

I play the next message. This time he merely says, "Shit." He let his true feelings out before he had the chance to hang up.

I'm troubled that he would go to see Mother. Was this the reason behind her call? Perhaps she is not paranoid at all. Maybe in spite of her cognitive decline, her ability to discern evil and malicious intent has just become that much more acutely honed.

As much as I would love to know what transpired this afternoon in our absence, I resist the urge to call Ulla at home. I check the time; I don't even have time to call Annika. It's already been over an hour, and Johan is waiting. I dress quickly to go downstairs.

I can hear the piano as I step from the elevator. Johan is playing. I recognize the new song he was working on over the holidays. I turn the corner into the lounge as he finishes. There are a few people listening who begin to clap.

A pretty woman who looks to be in her late twenties says, "That was beautiful. It sounds almost Indian or perhaps Middle Eastern. What's the name of it? It sounds vaguely familiar."

My brother looks up and smiles at her, "It's an old one by a Canadian composer named Dev Singh. It's called *Ode to Fiona*."

My heart nearly stops in my chest as I lower myself onto an upholstered chair near the fireplace. Oh, dear God, it is now so obviously clear to me that my brother Johan was once my beloved in another life. He left me to attend to the needs of his mother and his family, only to return as my brother in this life. Does he know this? I don't think Johan is gifted with the same awareness this time through. Still, when issues from one lifetime are left unresolved, perhaps karma is evoked, and we are given another chance to make things right. Dev walked away from me and away from love when he left Fiona, and now, he appears to be destined to live a life of misery with Hanna, a woman he can never please.

It seems like it would be kind of creepy that someone who was my lover in another life is my brother in this life. Perhaps love is just love, and it takes different shapes and forms in different lifetimes. There is nothing remotely sexual or intimate about my relationship with Johan. I don't understand it, and perhaps I have no need to. I trust the Creator knows what he or she is doing.

The more I seek answers to the questions that plague me and my consciousness, the more I see, and sadly the less I understand. I shudder as I wonder which mistakes I have made, or will make, in this life will need to be paid for in the next. I fear the decisions that currently belong to me. The consequences seem so overwhelming, and the answers elude me.

"Saga," Johan calls my name as a worried look crosses his face as I stand with my back against the wall. He closes the cover over the piano keys and comes to stand beside me. He reaches for my elbow and leans in and whispers as if we are the ones involved in a major conspiracy, "What's up? You look like you've seen a ghost."

I just shake my head. There are so many things I want to discuss with my brother, but believe me, this is not one of them. Instead, I say, "I'm sorry about what I said earlier." Johan looks confused.

"That comment I made about your drinking."

"Oh, that. I know I tend to drink as an escape from the drama and heartache of my marriage, but it's not necessary now, it's not necessary here."

"I meant no offense, and I'm sorry for being insensitive. It's just that I love you, and I depend on you. You're wise and understand so many things I only have a superficial grasp of."

"Forget it, Saga, your apology is accepted. There is so much at stake right now, and it behooves us to be clearheaded."

A sense of relief washes over me. The last thing I need right now is to be at odds with my brother.

"I've been thinking. We need to go slow here. Well, maybe not slow, but we need to exercise caution and restraint. If Ek gets wind that we're poking around in his nefarious business, it could all blow up in our faces."

"So, let me get this right, you're saying I shouldn't express my outrage and take legal action against the chairman of the board because he has proceeded to dig a gold mine on company land without obtaining any of the necessary permissions or authorizations and because it appears that he is profiteering on the extraction of precious minerals, to say nothing of his intent to violate long-held agreements with the indigenous people who live here. Is this where you would like me to go slow and exercise caution and restraint?"

Johan takes a long pull on his drink, and then a smile creeps across his face while he sits quietly holding my gaze before asking, "Are you done?"

"Yes," I mutter under my breath.

"The operative words in that long litany you just delivered are— *it appears.*"

"Yes, it appears."

"If you come at him with guns a blazin' he could make a very strong argument that he fully intended to bring you up to speed about this at Monday's board meeting, that you only officially were instated into your position on Wednesday and then immediately left town before he had any chance to discuss this with you."

"But—"

"I'm not finished. He could say it was discussed with Mother, whether it was or not, and that she gave her approval, and given her dementia and subsequent cognitive decline has simply forgotten."

"Oh, for the love of God, you don't believe that any more than I do."

"I didn't say I did. All I am saying is that we have to have some solid proof before we begin making any accusations."

I take a hearty swallow of my drink. The vodka tastes mildly bitter with a hint of citrus. Giving a loud audible sigh, I say, "Goddamn it, I hate it when you're right."

Johan smiles. "I think we'll have a clearer picture tomorrow after we visit the mine."

"I think we need to follow the money, as they say. I have a lot of unanswered questions."

"Such as?" he asks.

"How is this whole thing being funded, for one? And then the question of who is profiting? If Ek is not running this through the company, then who are his partners? Does this qualify as embezzlement if he is building a gold mine on company land and siphoning off the resources? Is this criminal? Yes, there are way too many unanswered questions."

"I'll send a note to an analyst I know in the finance department. She'll be discreet. She doesn't trust Ek anymore than I do. In fact, she's had her eye on Ek for a while. There are too many inconsistencies and things that don't add up. Those are the kind of things accountants look for, and Ebba is a good accountant. I can ask her to investigate any large expenditures or inconsistencies that Ek has signed off on in the last six months. The money to build that mine is coming from somewhere, and I can assure you it isn't coming from Ek's personal account. Let's just keep this between ourselves until we have a more complete understanding of what's going on."

The pretty blonde server hovers nearby. I nod to my brother, "Do you think you can trust her?"

"Her name is Ebba Lennart, and she's as honest as the day is long. We can trust her."

Taking another deep breath, I ask, "Did you get a call from Mother?"

"No. Why?"

"I don't know. I guess I'm just a little concerned. She left me a cryptic message about being on firm legal ground and that the deeds and documents are all in order."

"I don't know what she is referring to."

"Neither do I. But she was whispering like she didn't want anyone else to hear what she was telling me. She begged me to hurry before they all disappeared."

"I know it is difficult to accept, but maybe she's just confused and feeling a little paranoid."

"That was my initial thought, but my next voicemail message was from Ek."

"Oh…"

"Actually, my next four messages were from Ek. He said that when I didn't return his earlier phone calls that he went to the house to see Mother under the guise of being concerned about my whereabouts given the blizzard."

"You think Mother was whispering because she didn't want Ek to hear?"

"I don't know, but the thought crossed my mind, and there was something rushed and almost fearful in her voice." Before I've even finished speaking, Johan has taken out his cell phone and is standing beside the table.

"Excuse me. I'll be right back," he says as he exits the dining room with his phone in his hand.

The young blonde server approaches the table. "May I bring you another drink?" she asks as she hands me a menu.

My glass is nearly empty, so I order another vodka on the rocks and peruse the menu while I wait for my brother. It's been a couple of hours since Mother called, but Johan was quick to pick up on my concern. He doesn't trust Ek. Mother has always been so strong, and now she's become so vulnerable. I'm sure that Father is home by now if the storm is as bad as they predicted. Self-chatter fills my head as I wonder if Mother is safe, but safe from whom, or are the demons she battles all in her head?

The pretty young woman brings me my cocktail with a small plate of pickled herring. I take a sip of my drink and help myself. It has been a long time since lunch, and I'm starting to feel hungry again. So much has happened in the last two days. It's hard to believe it was only yesterday that I started in my new position. I wander around in my head as I recreate the images of walking into my office early yesterday morning to find that someone had already been there and had gone through my desk. Is there a connection between the perplexing message I'd just received from my mother and the fact that someone had been going through her computer and her files?

A sense of foreboding wraps itself around me. I take another sip of my drink in an attempt to quiet my fears and feelings of impending danger. I wipe my mouth on the white linen napkin and stand, leaving it on my chair. I need to talk to Johan.

Just as I prepare to leave the dining room, Johan appears in the doorway. Taking my seat again, I wait for him to join me.

"Is everything okay?" I ask.

He also takes a seat then motions to our server that his glass is empty, and he'd like another before he answers my question. "I spoke with Father. Mother has already gone to bed. He said she seemed particularly agitated this evening. He was in his study on a conference call this afternoon, but Maryan confirmed that Ek had been by the house. She didn't know how long he stayed because she had run an errand for Mother. Father found Mother in her study hiding beneath a blanket. She was beside herself carrying on about some document insisting it had been with the cache of others and fearing it may have gone missing from the locked safe in her study. Father didn't know whether this was just delirium, or what it was that had set her off and why she was so concerned about the documents. Mother was so distraught that against his better judgment, he gave her a sleeping pill to help settle her."

"Something is up, and I don't like it, not one little bit. I didn't tell you about what I encountered when I arrived at the office the day before yesterday."

"No, as a matter of fact, you didn't. Now would be a good time," he says as I wait for the server to leave his drink before continuing.

"Are you ready to order," she asks. I shake my head.

"Can you give us a few minutes?" I ask as she turns away with a pout. Perhaps she is hoping to turn the table. She lingers at the server's station just within earshot. Perhaps Mother isn't the only one feeling paranoid.

Leaning in and whispering to my brother, I tell him, "It was my first day, and I wanted to settle in, you know, in my own way and in my own time without a lot of fanfare. I arrived at the office early, and using Mother's passcode, I entered through her private entrance, avoiding the security officer in the front lobby. To my surprise, I found that someone had been in her office, I guess technically it is now my office, and the desk drawers were open, and so was the credenza. The computer was all lit up like a Christmas tree as if someone had just stepped away from it."

"No shit. What'd you do?"

"I called security, and a sleepy night shift guard responded. Poor thing, she had no idea who I was and started reading me the riot act as if I was the intruder. Then she called Klaus Ek, who appeared like the knight in shining armor. He chastised her ruthlessly for not knowing who I was, and then he whisked me away to his office for some coffee and chitchat."

"Do you think someone was just making themselves comfortable in your office, just trying it on for size. You know, no harm, no foul?"

"Do you?"

"No," he says as he shakes his head.

"I thought I might just be feeling overly suspicious and insecure, so before I left for a bit of a coffee klatch with Klaus, I set up a little trap."

"What kind of a trap?"

"I wanted to see if I could figure out who had been snooping around Mother's private office and why, so I left my makeup bag open on the bathroom sink with my lipstick setting precariously on top. When I came back, the lipstick was in the bottom of my makeup bag."

"Really? Well, that was rather clever and conniving of you. Who do you think is wearing your lip shade?"

"I'm going with Ek or one of his minions. I wonder how he looks in Autumn Rose?"

"Perhaps he or they are looking for Mother's treasure trove of documents. Perhaps she is not as paranoid as others make her out to be. Maybe it's not mental illness or cognitive decline. Perhaps she is just as shrewd as she has always been."

"She has always been as clever as a fox. Always two to three steps ahead of everyone else."

"Do you think Ek was looking for Mother's mysterious documents?" Johan asks.

"I don't know, but Mother's reaction to Ek's unexpected visit is rather telling, don't you think?"

Again, the server approaches the table, this time she doesn't ask if we are ready to order but instead starts reeling off the list of tonight's specials. This time she is no longer smiling. Both Johan and I order the special—fried herring with mashed potatoes and lingonberries. Something seems a little off. The server types into her cell phone the whole time we are ordering. How difficult is it to remember two specials? Or maybe she was busy communicating with someone else?

After she leaves the table, I ask, "Do you think Ek stays here at the Grand Arctic Lodge when he is up here supervising the construction of *his* mine?"

"Well, that's an interesting thought. This is the nicest inn or perhaps the only inn in this region."

"Are you sensing a change in our server's temperament or attitude?" I ask.

"I didn't notice. Most women start out friendly then turn rather frosty, at least towards me, or maybe that's just my wife," he says with a sigh.

"I'm sorry, Johan. More than likely, she's only messaging with a friend and has no interest in this nest of intrigue we find ourselves in. I'm not certain who is more paranoid, me or Mother."

"Does it qualify as paranoia if the threat or danger is real? Perhaps neither of you are paranoid. Perhaps you are both just being wise and astute. I do wish I knew just what those old documents revealed and why after all this time, they are suddenly so important that Klaus Ek is searching for them and Mother is so intent on hiding them."

"Maybe," I answer with a shrug for fear my brother has greater confidence in me and my abilities than may be warranted.

We both fall silent when the server again returns to top off our still nearly full water glasses. Once she leaves, Johan continues, "Anyway, I've been thinking we should keep our concerns to ourselves. I don't think we should tip our hand and make any formal accusation implicating Ek for impropriety, acting without authority, for use of company assets for personal gain, and dare we include embezzlement. No, we are just entering the fact-gathering stage. Fortunately, at this time, people are still willing to talk to us freely. I fear when Ek gets wind of this, these same people may clam up if they fear Ek and his need for revenge and retribution."

"Really? I'm not certain. I'm feeling afraid."

"Afraid of what?" Johan asks, gently encouraging me to put words to my fears.

"I don't know exactly, but I have a sense of imminent danger. But who is in danger, and what is at stake? I can't say."

We table this discussion when our dinners arrive, beautifully plated, and piping hot. Again, our server lingers within earshot. Is she eavesdropping? I change the conversation to Johan's girls. "Did you get a chance to talk with your girls when you called Father?"

"No, he said, "they'd already gone to bed. I was happy to hear they'd been out playing in the snow before the winds kicked up and the temperature dropped."

"With Hanna?" I ask, not quite able to visualize my sister-in-law playing in the snow or able to keep the surprise out of my voice.

"No, they were with their nanny. Wilma took them to play outside. Hanna is already on her way to the Maldives to get a little sun. She says this pregnancy is really wearing her out, and she needs some rest after the holidays."

"The Maldives? I thought they were nearly underwater due to climate change."

"That was one of the reasons Hanna gave me for going this winter. She's afraid they will completely disappear in the near future."

"I'm glad to hear she is becoming a climate change activist." I almost can't help myself; the only thing that woman cares about is herself.

Johan rolls his eyes. "Anyway, she'll be back in a week. Hopefully, a little rest and sunshine will improve her disposition. It can't be easy having a baby in your forties."

"I wouldn't know, but Mother seemed to manage."

"We both know that Mother was and is exceptional. To expect Hanna to handle what Mother has with the same grace and ease is, well… what can I say, it's unrealistic, to say the least."

We both continue to eat in silence. Before we have even finished eating our dinner, this pesky server is at our elbows, asking, "Would either of you like dessert?"

Johan answers for both of us, "No, thank you." Then he turns to me, "I didn't get a nap like you did, and I can hardly keep my eyes open. Do you mind if I say goodnight now?"

"Not at all, go ahead upstairs and get some sleep. I'll meet you down here in the morning."

"Eight thirty?"

"Okay. Sweet dreams."

And with that, my brother leaves me in the dining room. Unlike him, I am still wide awake. Perhaps a cup of chamomile tea will help me sleep. I look around the dining room, trying to locate our server but she has her back to me. Unable to get her attention, I go to meet her at the coffee station. She is talking on her phone.

"He just left the dining room… No, she's still here."

I don't know who she is talking to, but suddenly I have no desire for a cup of tea. If someone is in my room, I want to know who it is.

I stand by the elevator and can see from the indicator light above the elevator that it is on the third floor. This is the same floor where both Johan's room and my room are located. I take a deep breath before pushing the call light for the elevator. Perhaps the elevator is just taking my brother to his room, but perhaps not. Not willing to wait, I decide to take the stairs, climbing the stairs two at a time I pass two men in the stairwell. Both men drop their heads as I pass. Neither of them looks up or speaks to me. I hurry past them quite certain I don't want to confront two men in this heavily shadowed stairwell.

Opening the door from the stairwell onto the third floor, I see nothing amiss. Using my hotel keycard, I enter my room. Things appear just as I left them an hour ago. I flop down onto the bed, and the old adage plays on in my head—*but things are not always as they appear.*

CHAPTER 8

Again, Bierdna and Johan are already sitting in the dining room waiting for me when I arrive. Unlike yesterday, this morning they appear anxious to get on the road. They both stand as I approach the table, and Johan hands me a coffee in a paper takeaway cup with an insulated sleeve. He has already prepared it just the way I like it.

I look at my watch. It's only eight fifteen. I'm fifteen minutes early. "I'm sorry, did I misunderstand. I thought we were having breakfast before we went out the mine."

"No, you didn't misunderstand. It's just that our plans have changed. It's at least an hour's drive out to the mine, and as you might expect, the security in the area is pretty tight. The weather looks clear today, but we did have quite a storm last night. We should be able to make pretty good time if the snowplows have been out. Otherwise, I might have to do a bit of the plowing myself," Bierdna says, shifting his weight from one foot to the other. He is anxious to get on the road.

"Oh, I hadn't considered that," I say, chastising myself for my ignorance.

"The roads we can deal with, and that is truly the least of our concerns, but there is a security crossing on the road, and one of the members of my *siida* or community has taken a job there as a security officer. He is working today, but only until ten o'clock. I spoke with him last night, and he will let us pass."

I reach across the buffet table and make myself a smörgås—an open-faced sandwich with a piece of cheese and a slice of tomato. I open a paper napkin and fold it around my breakfast. "I'm ready. Let's go."

It's still dark when we leave the hotel, but the sky is clear, and the stars sparkle like diamonds. It's colder today without the cloud cover, and it will still be dark most of the way out to the mine. Sunrise is not until after eleven this morning, so if all goes well, we should be there under the protective cover of darkness. We drive on through the stillness of the night, respecting the quiet and one another. Fortunately, the plows have been out, and the roads have been cleared. At about nine thirty, we approach the fork in the road that leads to the mine.

"Just keep your heads down and don't say a word," Bierdna cautions. "Let me handle this."

I feel like a spy trying to leave East Berlin through Checkpoint Charlie during the Cold War. I push the thought from my head. Maybe I've just seen too many movies.

There are two large signs with bold red lettering posted on either side of the narrow, snow-covered road that read:

INGET INTRÅNG BORTOM DENNA PUNKT
PRIVAT EGENDOM
ÖVERTRÄDARE ÅTALAS

OR

NO TRESPASSING BEYOND THIS POINT
PRIVATE PROPERTY
VIOLATORS WILL BE PROSECUTED

I bite my tongue, and my blood boils as I remind myself that Bierdna has asked us to say nothing.

There is a red and white railroad crossing bar in place across the road. There is a chain link fence, nearly 3 meters high, topped with rolls and rolls of razor wire on either side of the gate as far as I can see that prevents us from going any further. A light goes on in the guardhouse, and a man dressed in a uniform similar to that worn by those in Swedish Security Service approaches the car with a large Alsatian shepherd. I do not see a weapon, but I assume he has one concealed beneath his navy blue coat. Bierdna lowers the window, and the officer asks to see our credentials. His voice is strong and gruff. Clearly, he means business. I can't help but wonder if there has been a mistake. Where is Bierdna's friend? I'm starting to sweat, and my heart races.

Bierdna hands him an envelope, and the man looks inside before he activates the wooden crossbar causing it to lift and allowing us to enter.

Bierdna raises his window and slowly drives through the gate and enters the compound.

I take a deep, calming breath, and then I remind myself I have just gone through all of this rigamarole to gain access to land which has been owned by my family and our family business for hundreds of years. Now I am angry.

"What was in the envelope?" Johan asks.

"Money," Bierdna smiles. "You know the old Russian proverb, *'When money talks, truth keeps silent.'*"

"Not anymore," I murmur beneath my breath.

We drive another ten minutes down the road, and I am fuming with anger as dawn breaks, and the first glint of daylight begins to peek over the mountains. I don't know what I was expecting, but it certainly wasn't this. The mine is a big open pit where a circular road has been carved deep into the earth that leads towards the center of the mine. I'm not good at estimating the size of it, but it looks to be larger than ten football fields long by ten football fields wide.

Bierdna estimates, "It probably covers about a hundred hectares."

Johan concurs as he pulls his phone from his pocket and begins to take some pictures. "You know, a picture's worth a thousand words."

"Indeed," I say, completely stunned at the size and scope of the operation. "No wonder these people are upset. This is a hideous scar on the landscape of their homelands, to say nothing of the danger and disruption for their animals."

We sit and watch in silence, this is no small operation, and it certainly hasn't been only planned recently. There are half a dozen big dump trucks already in use for hauling something out of the mine. A crane can be seen loading the trucks at the bottom of the mine.

There's no way this is copper or gold they're mining. I don't know how I know it, but I do. Sometimes I just know what I know. But if not copper or gold, then what is it?

The level of daylight increases, and we can see that there is already dust of some sort covering the newly fallen snow making everything look dirty and dingy. A thin layer of dust covers the windshield before we've even exited the car. We stay inside Bierdna's Land Rover and watch for a while. I'm not ready to make our presence known.

"Do you want to get out and talk to anyone?" Bierdna asks.

"No, not yet. Let's follow the next pickup truck. I want to see where they are going." Bierdna puts his car into gear. "Let's hang back a little bit and don't follow too close behind. I don't want the driver to take us on a wild goose chase."

There is only one road into and out of the mine. The truck emits plumes of dark exhaust into the now clear blue morning sky as it burns its diesel fuel making it easy to follow at a distance. After traveling less than twenty minutes, we stop at the crest of the hill as the truck we were following descends into some type of a transfer station. From within Bierdna's vehicle, we can see over a hundred different-colored, metal shipping containers. About half are sealed and appear ready for transport, and the others are still open and ready to be filled. A flatbed truck is being loaded with containers. The dump truck we followed here backs up onto an earthen ramp and dumps its load directly into an open-topped shipping container which rests on a flatbed truck. Just what is this—ore of some kind? Is that what you call this gray material being dug out of the earth?

We sit and watch for a while, when again Johan takes out his phone and takes some more pictures. "I can see the label on the side, but I can't read it. Perhaps we can get the photo enhanced so we can see just what this is and where it's going."

"Some of the Sámi work here, too. I've already made some inquiries, and we will know before long. They are coming to the ceremony tonight. Grandmother Lejá has extended the invitations, and there are some invitations that are never refused."

A sense of foreboding threatens to overwhelm me. "I think we should get going."

"Okay, but before we leave, I'd like to know where these trucks are going," Johan says. "Ek clearly has a buyer for this. Whatever this is, it belongs to us and to Lundstrom Enterprises. Before we start making any accusations, we need to be certain we know what we are talking about and who we are dealing with."

Against my better judgment, again I consent to follow the flatbed truck carrying one of the large containers across the tundra. There is only one road in and out of this mining compound, so we have to exit the same way we entered. Fortunately for us, the guard is busy granting entry to a luxury SUV, a large black Volvo. I turn around to look at it as we pass. Just as I suspected, our company logo is visible on the back panel of the vehicle, but who is inside?

We haven't gone too far down the road before Bierdna begins to suspect we are being followed. "I think we need to lose whoever is following us. Their Volvo is no match for my Land Rover. If they choose to follow us, they may find themselves stuck in the snow. I can always drop the plow and clear our way. I know where those containers are headed. It's going by ship as they've just taken the road towards the port of Piteå."

Johan gives his consent to Bierdna's proposal. "Let's lose them."

Bierdna looks at me, and I give him a nod. To my surprise, he slows down to let the Volvo catch up, then unexpectedly, and without using his indicator light, he takes a quick right turn onto a slippery snow-covered road then leaves the road entirely, barreling through chest-high snowdrifts and then onto the tundra. Johan laughs in the front seat, and once I catch my breath, I turn around to see what is so funny. The black SUV is in the ditch, and the deep, drifted snow covers the doors and is up to the windows.

Once it is certain that they are no longer capable of following us, Bierdna drops the plow and clears a path to get the Land Rover back on the road

As much as I'd like to know who is driving the Volvo, I decide to let it go. No doubt someone will need to file a vehicle damage report, so I'll figure it out when we're back in Stockholm. Bierdna drives right past the stranded vehicle, clearly having no intention of stopping while both he and Johan laugh like naughty children.

"I think that should do it for this morning," Johan says.

"Let's head back to the hotel. I'd suggest you both get something to eat and take a little rest this afternoon as we'll be awake all night during the ceremony."

In spite of my best intentions, the stress of the morning has exhausted me, and I fall asleep in the car as Bierdna drives us back to the Grand Arctic Lodge.

It's early afternoon by the time we get back. "How about if I pick you up in the lobby at three thirty," Bierdna suggests. "We can have dinner at the community center before the ceremony and meet with some of our people who are working at the mine."

The three of us go our separate ways to rest, and agree to regroup before the indigenous ceremony. After the events of the last few days, I can't even imagine staying up all night in a teepee in the midst of a blizzard. If someone ever told me I would agree to this, I would have said they were mad, but then again, perhaps I am.

"Do you want to get some lunch," Johan asks.

"It's been a stress-filled morning, and my appetite is a bit off. Besides, I'm afraid I need sleep more than I need food. I might grab something from the mini-bar in the room." Johan and I make our way to the elevator, as the door closes, I ask, "Do you think you could send me copies of the photos you took today?"

"No problem. Is there anything in particular you want to look at?"

"No…" Something's up, and I feel it in my gut. "I just think there might be some wisdom in having a second set of photos and another pair of eyes to review them. Send them to my personal, encrypted account, will you?" Better safe than sorry.

I hear my phone ding as we step off the elevator, and I see the photos are already here in my hot little hands. "Thank you. See you in a couple of hours."

I take a moment to plug my phone into my laptop computer so I can get a closer look at the photos. I fill the electric kettle to make myself some tea. I slip out of my winter clothes and get into bed with my laptop and a cup of tea and start to shuffle through the images that Johan has sent.

A list of questions runs on in my mind. To break with this circuitous thinking, I write them down.

What are *they* mining?

Who are *they*?

Where is this being shipped?

Who is covering the expenditures?

Who is buying the contents? Who is profiting?

If this is all above board, then why don't I know anything about it?

I compare the photos Johan has taken of the mine with photos of both copper and gold mines that I find on the internet.

I don't know what I was expecting, but they don't look like they contain any copper or gold. It all just looks like dirt to me. Somehow, I had expected copper to be either a copper color or a verdigris green patina that copper takes on when it is exposed to moisture, and I thought gold would look like, well… gold as if it had been found in a vein of gold. But the images on the internet look similar to the ore being dug from the open pit on the property owned by my family and our business. It all just looks like dirt to me. I could scream or have a good cry as I have no idea what is being mined.

I enlarge one of the pictures and zoom in on the guy running the crane and another of the guy driving the dump truck. There are clouds of dust everywhere. It coats the machinery and the workers' faces and clothing, and no one is wearing any kind of respiratory protection or safety glasses. One of the workers appears to have tied a cotton bandana around his face, but his eyes appear irritated.

Even photos of miners from fifty years ago show pictures of people wearing respiratory protection and full hazmat suits when they are in the mine or transporting the ore, whether copper or gold. Clearly, there are health and safety regulations that are being ignored, but what else?

Next, I zoom in on the label affixed to the blue container to see if this offers me a clue about what is being mined and where it is going. The first two images of the label are too blurry to read, but the third and final one reads: RU KGD. It takes me only a moment on the internet to determine that this container is being shipped to the Port of Kaliningrad in Russia. The next set of letters indicate from there it is to be shipped to Rosatom in Almaty, Kazakhstan.

Whoa. Oh no. I take a deep breath as I try to comprehend just what this might be.

Kazakhstan is located on the Caspian Sea and shares a border with Russia. Whatever this is, I have little doubt it will be moved by rail across Russia to its destination in Almaty, Kazakhstan. I search the internet, and there is a little information available about Rosatom. It is the Russian State Atomic Energy Corporation and is headquartered in Moscow.

It was established in 2007 by Vladimir Putin, who was the Russian president at the time. It comprises hundreds of enterprises and is now one of the world leaders in the nuclear energy industry, supports scientific research within the organization, and has authority over the Russian nuclear weapons complex.

Just reading this causes my blood to run cold. A shiver runs up my spine.

Rosatom currently has one-third of the global supply of uranium.

I close the cover of my computer. What in the name of heaven have I gotten myself involved in?

Every question answered leads to more questions, but the essential question that remains unanswered is: What the hell is Klaus Ek up to?

I still don't know for certain what is being mined. I can guess, but I pray I'm wrong. The implications are both illegal, amoral, and dangerous.

I pull the blankets up around my shoulders and lie back against the pillows and close my eyes. The voice within my head speaks—*Don't ignore the obvious.*

I still have an hour before I need to be back downstairs, and I am bone-weary and afraid. I am in so far over my head, and I don't know what to do. My tears begin to soak the pillowcase as I lie there and try to figure out what course of action I should take. Fear and an overwhelming sense of vulnerability threaten to overtake me. I have options, but each seems fraught with peril. I think back on all the science I have learned. I cannot predict the outcome of any possible course of action because I don't have enough information. There are too many variables.

I pray for divine intervention, or at the very least, some guidance as I ask my spirit guides, angels, saints, and anyone and everyone who might be listening, for help.

Just as I'm starting to drift off to sleep, the phone rings. As I reach over to the bedside table to find my phone, I wonder if this might be the answer to my prayer, or if I am just a madwoman? "Hello."

"You sound sleepy. Did I wake you?"

"Oh, hi Anders. I had just laid down for a nap. How are you?"

"All is well in my world. I thought perhaps I should make a reservation for dinner tomorrow night, so I called to see if you had any thoughts about where you'd like to go."

"What day is it today?"

He laughs. "It's Friday."

"Things have gotten so crazy up here. I'm sorry, but I'm afraid I won't be back tomorrow."

"Oh, well..."

I hear the disappointment in his voice. "I'm sorry, Anders. So much has come to light in the last couple of days, and I'm in over my head." Despite my best intentions not to cry, my voice catches in my throat, leaving me at a loss for words and overcome with emotion.

"Saga, it's okay. We'll get together another time when you're less busy."

"Okay," I say as I am overwhelmed with regret as the line goes dead, and Anders is gone.

Overcome with grief and fear, my heart cries out, *Help me, please help me.* I plead with the Almighty while asking all the angels and saints to intervene on my behalf. I do not know what else to do. My sobs give way to a whimper, my pillow is wet, and sleep threatens, as somewhere in that space between sleep and wake, the words take form—*Ask, and it shall be given to you.*

I'm sound asleep and far away in dreamland when the alarm on my phone buzzes to wake me. I hit snooze and then lay there for a moment trying to determine if I was dreaming, or did I time-travel? The clouds lift on my dreamlike state, and I am crushed by the reality of my current predicament. This was not just a far-fetched dream. I'm a little surprised I didn't time-travel, given that I specifically called on my spirit guides to help me. Maybe they are busy, hopefully busy concocting a foolproof plan for this foolish woman to execute.

Again, the voice within my head speaks—*Stop demeaning yourself. This is not helpful.*

I pull the covers back and turn on the light. I give myself a good talking-to. "Let's get going. Tonight is an important night, and I should feel honored to have been asked to participate in the sacred Sámi ceremony. There is much at stake for me, my family, for the business, for these indigenous people, for the country, and for the planet. Now is not the time for self-doubt. Be present."

I wash up and re-apply my makeup before putting on a long woolen skirt. The rough weave scratches my bare legs, so I pull on a pair of fleece-lined tights beneath my skirt then step into my fur-lined boots that have been drying on a boot rack. The boots are warm and dry and lined with sheepskin, so they feel as luxurious as new moccasins. I add a woolen pullover on top of my base layer. I need to get out of here before I roast.

I gather up my purse and my phone when I realize my computer is not sitting on the desk connected to its power cord. I pull back the blanket, did I fall asleep with it in or on the bed? But it's not here. My hotel room is tidy as well as small, so it doesn't take me long to realize that it's not here. It has been taken. Someone was in my room and took my laptop while I was asleep. There is something very creepy about this. Who was in here? How did they get in? And why have they taken my computer?

I'm not just being paranoid. That server last night, she was watching us and monitoring our every move, but for whom?

Again, I am the last one ready to go, both Johan and Bierdna are waiting for me in the lobby when I get there.

"Are you okay?" Johan asks.

A look of concern passes over both of their faces.

"I think we should go. I'll tell you about it when we get in the Land Rover." They both nod simultaneously as if this has been choreographed, then Bierdna leads the way, and Johan and I follow behind.

It is a clear night, and the snow is fresh and light. The moon is just rising and is nearly full. The golden orb fills the night sky as it comes up over the horizon. I notice that Bierdna has had his car cleaned, and all of the dust from the mine has been washed away.

"I see you've had the car washed," I say.

"Yes, I don't often do that during the winter. A little ice, snow, and road salt are one thing, but I don't know what might be in that mine dust that was airborne and ended up all over my vehicle. There's an auto wash not far from here, the only problem with the winter wash is that sometimes the locks freeze afterward. I have some deicer with me if we need it."

"Anyway, what was bothering you earlier?" my brother asks me.

"Well, someone was in my room this afternoon while I was napping, and they took my laptop."

"What?" Johan says in a voice loud enough to wake the dead. "What was on it? What do you think they were after?"

"Whatever it is they are looking for, I highly doubt they'll find it or even get in. Everything but my personal email has been run through the latest encryption software. The tech department had it all set up for me; it's supposed to be super secure."

"Who do you think the techs report to?" Johan says as he shakes his head.

"Oh, you mean Ek? There's not a formal reporting relationship to him."

"He was the chief financial officer. A little extra money flashed about can buy a lot of friends."

"Oh God, I hadn't thought of that. I guess I'm still rather naïve."

Bierdna raises his finger to his lips, indicating we should not say anything else. I know what he is thinking, the car may be bugged, and this conversation may not be private after all.

Without missing a beat, Johan begins to fabricate a story about how he once left his computer at the bar and yammers on for whoever might be listening all the while he searches the vehicle for any kind of surveillance device.

This time is precious, and there is so much we need to discuss; my anxiety is mounting with each passing mile. It is all I can do to stop myself from asking Bierdna to pull over so we can get out of the vehicle and I can talk freely with these two men. But we have somewhere we need to be, so instead, I begin to make notes detailing my concerns. I share them with Johan, who passes them onto Bierdna once they've been read. Bierdna's reading glasses sit on the tip of his nose as he glances over the note before returning his eyes to the snow-covered road. Unlike Johan and me, Bierdna has a poker face and gives nothing away. We keep this up until we finally pull into the Sámi compound.

"Let's go check in and see if we can find a cup of coffee," Bierdna suggests.

My stomach is already acting up, and another cup of coffee is the last thing I want. I need to mind my manners and remember that I am a guest here. My frustration is not with these people; my frustration is with my own people.

"Of course," I respond as Johan and I follow him out of the car and toward the community center.

Instead of walking towards the main entrance, we go around the back and find the *kåta*. Smoke pours out of the center of the hill, and a small wooden door with a window opens to welcome us in. There is a fire in the center of the room and a hole in the earthen ceiling allowing the smoke to find an escape. Large cushions act as backrests around the circular walls, and others are available for sitting. There are reindeer pelts scattered on the floor and around the roaring fire, and just as Bierdna has promised, an old blue and white enamelware coffee pot hangs over the fire.

I start to talk, and again Bierdna puts his finger to his lips. One of the women approaches and leads me behind a wooden screen where traditional Sámi dress is hanging on a hook on the wall. She gestures toward the clothing, and "Please," is all she says. She wants me to dress for the ceremony. I change quickly then emerge from behind the screen where the same woman picks through my clothing. Only now does it dawn on me that she wants to be certain that I have not been bugged, with or without my consent. When I return to the fire-place, I see that Johan and Bierdna have changed into traditional Sámi dress as well.

"We can't be too careful. There is too much at stake." Once the room has cleared, I bring Johan and Bierdna up to speed about what

I learned before my computer was stolen. I tell them how I enlarged the images on the shipping containers. Perhaps whoever took my laptop believes that without the photographs, it may just be our word against theirs."

Without the need for any more explanation, Johan removes his phone and sends a duplicate set of the photographs taken this morning to Bierdna and another set to me using my encrypted email. Ulla set it up for my use before we began this grand adventure. Then we shift our conversation and talk about the possible implications of illegally exporting uranium to Russia and the very real threat some people believe that Russia is to Scandinavia. With every national election, politicians talk about keeping Sweden militarily strong to prevent the Russians from trying to make another land grab, others claim our strength is in maintaining neutrality, and still others propose the wisdom of joining the NATO alliance. How much of this is fear-mongering, I don't know. But if new gold, copper, or uranium mines have been located on our land, there may be an even greater risk of foreign invasion.

It doesn't take long before Johan has decided to send another set of today's photos to Maryan, our parents' housekeeper, with specific instructions not to open or delete.

The tension is so thick you could cut it with a knife, and I nearly jump out of my skin when I hear someone knock on the wooden door of the *kåta*. Both Johan and Bierdna laugh out loud. "Hey, it's just a natural reflex to jump when startled," I laugh. But part of me wonders what my body knows, maybe we have every reason in the world to be afraid. But afraid of whom? And why?

Bierdna calls out, "Come in." And two men clothed in traditional dress enter and stand in the doorway waiting to be introduced.

"Welcome," he addresses the men. "These are our guests, Saga and her brother, Johan, from Lundstrom Enterprises, this is Márten and Silvu, both members of our *siida*, and both are currently employed at the mine."

I notice that Bierdna does not use our last names or theirs. As if reading my mind, Bierdna explains, "Given names will be enough tonight, as this is a longstanding custom among our people."

I stand and Johan follows as we both extend our hands to the Sámi men. It is difficult to guess how old these men are, as even in the glow of the firelight, they look wan and gray. Most of the Sámi people usually appear robust and strong from all the time spent living and working outside, but not these two.

"Please, come warm yourselves by the fire," Bierdna invites us all to sit down.

The men sit quietly as if waiting for me to speak. I have questions, and now is the time to try and get some answers.

"Thank you so much for agreeing to meet with us. Bierdna drove my brother, Johan, and me out to see the mine today. And I have some questions I hope you can help me with."

Both men nod in agreement but still do not speak.

I proceed, "Can you tell me when this mine was dug and how long you have been working there?"

The men exchange glances and then Márten, the older of the two men, speaks, "I'm afraid that is a difficult question to answer. I can tell you this—it was not here last year when winter gave way to the spring season, and we left for the summer grazing lands. This we refer to as *gidá* as it happens in April and May. When we returned to the winter grounds in early winter or *tjaktjadálvve*, it was early in November, and the excavation equipment was here. The pit had already been dug."

"That was two months ago," I say as I want to get a handle on the timeline and scope of the deception. "This was done on Mother's watch," I whisper my comments to Johan. "I'm sorry for interrupting. You were saying…"

"The migratory path had been disrupted by the mine, the roads, the trucks, and the dust. Most of the Boazovázzi and their herds had to be rerouted, and we were late getting back. The herd suffered losses, and those who survived have been weakened."

"How do you account for the losses?"

"The reindeer travel over 1500 miles and up to 150 miles per day to reach the winter lands. They leave the summer lands fattened up to ensure survival throughout the winter. When we were rerouted because of the open-pit mine, we traveled across rocky soil where there was little for the herd to eat. Fat stores meant for their winter survival were expended on the journey. Predators such as wolves separated the weak from the herd. Then once we arrived here, we found that the water is no longer clean and fit to drink, and the air is gray with dust from the mine," Márten says.

"That is one way to look at this. But others believe these people who mine the land have not honored the *sieidi* or the spirit of the sacred land. They have desecrated the land which is essential to our common survival. If nothing changes, we will go the same way as the reindeer," Silvu says, and Bierdna nods his head in agreement.

"How long have you been working at the mine?" Johan asks.

"It was only in late-November when we learned they were taking on miners for the winter, no experience necessary." Márten answers as he exchanges a look with Silvu encouraging him to contribute to this exposé.

"There were others who had agreed to meet with you, but they are now too ill to leave their homes."

"I'm so sorry to hear this. What ails them?" I ask. Perhaps this is none of my business, but, then again, maybe it is.

"It might be some kind of miner's flu. Seems like those working in the mine are a lot sicker than those who work the gate or in the office, like Márten and I."

I ask the questions I have been trained to ask when taking a medical history as a physiotherapist, "How many of your people are ill?" Silvu and Márten talk amongst themselves in their native Sámi tongue before switching back to Swedish to answer, "Ten to twelve or so."

"What kinds of symptoms do they have?"

"Coughing, shortness of breath, fever, fatigue, weakness," Silvu offers.

"But it's a weird flu, if that's what it is. Some of the guys are bleeding from their noses, and some have dysentery, too."

"Dysentery?" I ask.

"I don't mean to be inappropriate and indelicate and all, but they're shitting blood."

"Good God," Johan says, "that doesn't sound like any flu I've ever had."

"My training as a physiotherapist only touched briefly on infectious diseases, but I have worked with people in pulmonary rehab, and this sounds more like an exposure to a respiratory toxin than a virus. It sounds like they need to be in the hospital."

"Grandmother Lejá, is already preparing to send some of the women out with homemade split-pea soup and special teas to feed and care for the ill. We take care of our own. Tonight, we will pray for them and ask the spirits to return them to health."

A chill runs down my spine, for I recall how Fiona and her large Irish family embraced this same philosophy, as if we didn't have an obligation to care for one another whether they belonged to our tribe or to another.

"I just don't want the caregivers to get sick, too." I know they think I'm talking about exposure to a contagion, like an influenza virus, but my real fear is cross-contamination from uranium dust and any subsequent radiation sickness. If that's indeed what this is.

Bierdna nods to me, and I see that he understands—he'll take care of it. I don't want to alarm these men and the rest of this community with my concerns and with a diagnosis that has not yet been confirmed, but neither am I willing to risk the health and safety of anyone else.

"It's nearly time for the ceremony. Perhaps we should have some of Grandmother Lejá's healing soup. It may be a long night." Bierdna stands, and the rest of us do the same.

"I think that's a very good idea," I say. "But I just have one more question before we head back to the community center."

"Yes, ma'am," Silvu says, and I shudder to think how much undo respect this older man shows me. I feel so unworthy.

"Can you tell me who you report to or who your supervisor is?"

"Kapten Norberg is the onsite supervisor we report to on a daily basis, but it is Kommendor Ek who gives the orders."

"Kommendor Ek? Do you mean Klaus Ek?" I ask, seeking confirmation to what I already know. Again, I shudder as he bestows military titles on people who have not earned the honor.

"Yes, ma'am. He's been up here three or four times, and if I can speak candidly, he is one scary dude."

"What makes him so?"

"It's hard to put into words, but he emits a muddy brown aura of darkness and evil that can leach the light from the room. He puts everyone on edge with his faux militaristic garb and persona. He is in control, and everything and everyone else is expendable."

"What do you mean, faux military garb?"

"Maybe it's because he insists on being called Kommendor or perhaps it's that every time he is here, he wears this long blue coat with gold epaulets on the shoulders and an insignia of some sort on his sleeve. And he wears those knee-high, black, shit-kicking boots with his pant legs tucked inside. He gives the impression of being from another place and time and that he's here in some official military capacity. I think he's a poser, a dangerous poser."

Márten gives Silvu a swift nudge with his elbow as if to tell him to shut up.

"What?" Silvu turns and addresses his comment to Márten, which is met with a glower. Clearly, now Márten wants Silvu to stop talking.

"It's all right. Can't you see it? She's bathed in golden light. We can trust her."

"I want to thank you for being so forthcoming. I can assure you that you can trust me. I will get to the bottom of this."

"Let's not keep Grandmother Lejá waiting. First, we eat, and then we will ask the spirit world for guidance," Bierdna says as he lifts a reindeer pelt covering a doorway. Johan leads, and the rest of us follow through a passage leading to the community center.

The community room is dark as the lights are low, and most of the light emanates from the central fireplace. The room is quiet as everyone is already eating. Silently Grandmother Lejá gestures toward the buffet, indicating that we, too, should get some soup and eat.

A sense of guilt overcomes me, and I chastise myself for being late. It is a sign of great disrespect to arrive late for dinner when others have been busy all day preparing the food.

Once we have been served, Grandmother Lejá is escorted out to the *lavvu* to prepare for the ceremony.

The soup is hot, thick, and meaty, more like a stew than a soup, and quite unlike anything I would prepare for myself or order out. But on this cold night, it is both nourishing and warming. I say a silent prayer of gratitude. The bread is still warm from the oven, and the butter softens and melts on it as it sits beside my bowl of warm stew. I hurry to finish as others take their dishes up to be washed and then depart for the *lavvu*.

CHAPTER 9

It is already eight o'clock when we leave the community center, and the sky is dark. The sun has long since disappeared beyond the crest of the Scandes Mountain range to the west. Even the gray light of day is limited here near the Arctic Circle during January. It is still snowing, and the wind is creating drifts of new powder outside the door, but while we were meeting with the mine employees, some of the younger folks must have cleared a pathway through the snow from the meeting house to the large *lavvu* a short walk away. A chill runs through me as I cannot imagine spending the evening in a teepee up here near the Arctic Circle. I am thankful for the reindeer cloak I now wear. When we enter the *lavvu*, I am surprised by how warm it is. The fire is roaring in the center of the teepee, and reindeer pelts have been placed on the ground all around the perimeter. Only one wooden armchair has been placed opposite the doorway. I am shown to my place, clearly a seat of honor next to the chair, which is reserved for Grandmother Lejá, as she is both the Shaman and the *Noaidi*. Johan is seated on the ground beside me, and our interpreter, Elssa, sits behind us.

Others enter the *lavvu* in silence. Everyone kneels on the reindeer pelts around the fire. Even the children are included in the ceremony as they sit behind their parents or have been laid down to sleep and are covered with blankets and pelts to keep them warm. No one speaks as the fire keeper brings in more wood to keep the fire blazing. The ceremony will begin soon. Johan and I sit up on our knees as this seems to be customary.

Once everyone is situated, Grandmother Lejá enters. Slowly, she walks around the fire drumming on a reindeer hide that has been stretched over an oval-shaped wooden frame. She holds the drum in her left hand by the strips of reindeer hide on the backside of the drum, which secures the skin to the frame while drumming slowly with a padded drum hammer or a *vuorbi*. The face of the drumhead has been enhanced with a variety of symbols, including those of a reindeer, people, the sun, mountains, and a structure with a cross on top that looks like it might be a church.

I nod, and Johan looks over to me with a questioning look. Again, I nod to reassure him that despite the frightening information we have just learned, we still need to do this. A sense of calm comes over me, as I honor my intuition and I feel reassured that I am making the right decision. Grandmother Lejá circles the fire again before coming to sit beside me. She turns her gaze toward me and gives me a knowing smile as she lowers her eyes and nods to both Johan and me.

"Saga and Johan, we welcome you as our invited guests. Perhaps those in the spirit world can help you come to terms with this daunting responsibility which now rests in your capable hands," Grandmother Lejá says reassuringly. "There is nothing to be afraid of, my dear ones." Others around the circle murmur softly and nod their heads, affirming Grandmother's sentiments.

I can't help but wonder what Grandmother Lejá sees when she looks at me, but she is a wise woman, and her words and her presence are comforting.

Grandmother Lejá passes the drum to the left, and this woman takes up the drumming while she raises her arms and begins to *joik* and chant in Sámi, the native tongue of her people. There is something eerie about the *joiking* that resembles a magic spell. Soon others kneeling around the fire begin to chant as well.

"Grandmother Lejá is offering thanks to the spirit world. She is the mediator between the spirit world and this world of the body," Elssa whispers first in my ear and then to Johan. "Grandmother is praying for you, Saga. She is invoking assistance from benevolent spirits that you may travel as a free soul and traverse the divide separating the spiritual netherworld from the world of the body."

The drumming and the chanting continue gaining in both volume and tempo until Grandmother Lejá turns to offer me a two-handled earthenware vessel.

"Drink the tea," Elssa says, and I do.

Grandmother Lejá begins to drum again, and then I begin to slip away hearing the drumming and the *joiking* in the distance…

I start to drift, and as much as I want to remain kneeling as the others do, I cannot. I recline onto the fire-warmed earth, and someone covers me with a heavy reindeer pelt, which feels like the weighted blanket Annika uses in her office. I close my eyes, for I cannot do otherwise. I hear the drumming, familiar and yet far away, and then the voices join in, *joiking* in ethereal melodies that are carried in the sound of the wind while the blizzard rages with discontent and the leather walls of the *lavvu* quake and rattle. I feel the earth tremble beneath me and the heat of the fire in the center of the *lavvu*. I am warm now and have no need of the reindeer pelt that covers me. Underneath the reindeer cloak, I am dressed in traditional Sámi dress. I rub the rough woolen weave of my skirt between my thumb and forefinger. I sit back on my haunches with my legs folded beneath my body. On my feet, I wear fur moccasins with turned-up toes. I reach a gnarled hand up to touch my long, white braid that has fallen over my shoulder. I straighten my back and try to come to terms with where I am, and who I am.

My head is spinning as someone hands me the drum. It is only when I begin to drum that the unfamiliar words of the *joik* begin to take shape in my head and my mouth, and soon I am leading the singing, and the others are singing with me in Sámi. I stand to walk around the fire only to realize I am no longer Saga, but I am one of the elders. I am the *Noaidi*. I am the Shaman and the Seer, and it is my responsibility to hear the prayers of the people gathered around this fire and intervene with the spirit world on their behalf.

Again, I have traveled back in time. I have traveled back to *another* time when the lives and the lifestyle of our ancient indigenous ancestors were at risk. Again, we are in the *lavvu*. The *joiking* continues, and someone rhythmically beats upon the drum as we sit around the fire circle and pray. We have a guest, an outsider who sits on a beautiful brocade chair while all others sit on the ground around the sacred fire. She wears the attire of a noble woman, both a beaded cap worn close to her head and an apron of silk damask in shades of pale blue and trimmed in gold. Both have been outlawed by the king for women in the burgher class and other women of lesser birth. Wearing these beautiful embellishments are the prerogatives of the nobility.

I don't know how I know this, but I do.

It is sometime just after the Thirty Years' War, somewhere in the mid-1600s. Over eight million people have died due to the violence of war, famine, and plague. Some still believe this was a religious war between the Catholics and the Protestants, but in truth, it is no different from any other war. It was fueled by greed. Greed for power, land, and wealth. To the victors go the spoils, and now the Swedish Crown is parceling off the land we have lived on long before the Germanic people moved north to the Arctic Circle, and giving it to the nobility who remained loyal and defended the Crown.

I have heard this story before, from the deep recesses of my memory; I can almost hear my mother's voice as she recounts how we ended up as the beneficiaries of someone else's misfortune.

I straddle the memory as I attempt to be fully present in this lifetime. The drum is passed around the circle and others take a turn as it makes its way back to me. Again, someone hands me the drum, and I continue the drumming while *joiking* until the visions become clear to me. I am the *Noaidi*, and it is my responsibility to save this land for our people. A voice I do not recognize as my own calls upon the spirit world for protection and guidance. And then I know, sacrifices will be required to preserve our families, our animals, our way of life, and the good earth that provides for us. This is the way it works.

The nebulous haze lifts, and the path to our survival opens before me. This noble woman is someone I must trust to do right by our people. Our land, the land upon which we have lived and worked since the end of the ice age, must be signed over to this woman. There is something very familiar about her, something in her countenance and the dignity with which she carries herself that makes me certain I know her. And then it all becomes clear—she is a prior incarnation of my own beloved mother.

Something nags in my memory. Like a dream that has dissipated upon waking, I know there are memories just beyond my grasp that are lost from another lifetime. I try to focus, for whatever it was that has just slipped away now seems of utmost importance. Still, I cannot grasp it. Panic threatens to overcome me. Is this what it is like to be my mother? Is this what is is like to have dementia? I push the thought from my head. Without words, I acknowledge her forthcoming struggle. I nod to the baroness, and in return, she gives words to this elusive understanding.

"These lands where you live and work have been bequeathed to me by our King Gustavus Adolphus as recompense for my husband the Baron Erik Lundstrom's years of service to the Crown and for the ultimate military sacrifice, the loss of his life in battle."

One of the young men grumbles audibly in Sámi, "We, too, were made promises. Promises made and promises broken, trust erodes." For the next few minutes, there is an underlying murmur of agreement while the drumming which had quieted to a slow, steady beat becomes louder and faster, acknowledging the betrayal.

The moment hangs there, and I am mindful I am holding my breath while waiting to see how this will unfold. The tension is thick, and my people are seething.

Waiting for the voices to quiet, the drum steadies and slows as one of the elders in our community prepares to speak, "We acknowledge that as a nomadic people we do not hold title to this or any land, nor do we recognize your king as our king. We, too, are sick and tired of the war, the violence, disease, and poverty that has ravaged this land and our free and sovereign people.

"We do not wish to do battle with you or the king's minions. We wish to live in peace. Therefore, we will submit to the will of your king with the understanding that you and your descendants will hold these lands in safekeeping for the Sámi people with your solemn promise to respect the land and the people who live here, respecting the earth, the trees, and the water. But this is not forever, for if at anytime should you disrespect Mother Earth, then you will be asked to return the land to us, or we will harness the strength and power of all creation to set things to rights. No one owns the earth, but jointly we can agree to use it and be good stewards of the earth."

The baroness nods her head, giving her assent. But the elder is not finished, "Clearly, your king is not bound by his word. However, our memory is long, and your promises will not be so easily cast aside or put asunder. This covenant will be recorded, then signed, and sealed for posterity."

Again, the baroness nods, and then two of our people carry in a plain pine table that is set before her with two hand-inscribed parchments, a small wooden box containing a quill and an old inkwell to sign the agreed-upon treaty.

Only once the baroness has signed the documents are they sealed with the red sealing wax and the stamp of our people. Embossed in the molten wax is the impression of the Yggdrasil, the tree of life. It is the same ancient logo that has been used by the Lundstrom family since we became merchants and involved in the timber trade almost four hundred years ago. My head spins as time feels so fluid. Was that then, or is this now? To which reality do I belong?

I reach for my necklace that rests between my breasts. There it is, still around my neck. I close my eyes, and the power of the Yggdrasil medallion burns my fingertips. Perhaps it is not either/or but both.

The drumbeat continues calling me back while the ethereal voices sing and *joik* across the generations as I return to my current life, no longer the Noaidi, but simply Saga, a guest here among these kind and generous people of the North.

I now believe I know what my mother was so intent on hiding for safekeeping.

CHAPTER 10

In the early morning hours, long before the sun is scheduled to make its appearance, Bierdna drives Johan and me back to the Grand Arctic Lodge. We travel on in near silence as the snow softly falls to the earth, and it drifts across the windswept road. Bierdna appears lost in his thoughts, and Johan is uncharacteristically silent. I want to talk this over with my brother, but I'm hesitant to do so with Bierdna in the car. Perhaps he'll think I've lost my mind. Perhaps Johan will too. There are risks to being a Seer when others seem so firmly planted in their own perceptions of the here and now.

Just before we take the turn towards the inn, Bierdna suggests, "These ceremonies and staying up all night can lead to exhaustion, if you are not careful. I suggest you both go directly to bed and I will bring Grandmother Lejá in for a late dinner. She needs her rest, too, and no doubt you both will need some time to process all you've just experienced. We can talk about your experiences and strategize about what to do next when we return. I'll book the special dining room for dinner so we can have some privacy. Dinner at eight?" Bierdna proposes.

Johan nods and commits for both of us. I can barely keep my eyes open, let alone put together a coherent thought. No one needs to insist I go directly to bed as I am already beyond exhausted.

The smell of coffee, bacon, and cinnamon wafts in from the dining room where some of the other guests are just sitting down to breakfast. I'm hungry, but my need for sleep greatly overwhelms my need for food.

As we step off the elevator and head down the hall to our respective rooms, Johan says, "Set an alarm so we can meet before the others arrive. I'll meet you downstairs at seven tonight." I check my watch. It's already six-thirty in the morning, leaving time to shower that should give me nearly twelve hours to sleep, and that should be enough.

"Okay," I say as I unlock the door to my room. Once inside, I throw the deadbolt, then strip off my clothes. They still smell of smoke and incense from the ceremony. For a moment, I consider taking a shower, but I'm too tired, just too damn tired. I settle my naked body beneath the eiderdown, and the mattress gives just enough to support and cushion the weight of my body. I roll over and inhale deeply. My long hair crosses over my shoulders. My last conscious thought brings an awareness of the fragrance of burning pine and resin that lingers in my hair.

The flames glow golden as they lick and burn the split log in the fireplace. The room is warm. Annika's words resonate from past regressions, and I look for my feet to give me some context as to who I am and where I am. Is this what is meant by lucid dreaming? Something is amiss. I cannot see my feet or any other part of my body. I feel as if I am a disembodied spirit hovering in my parents' home.

I am definitely in their manor house at Damgården. This is the house I grew up in, the house that has been in my family for years, but things are different. I struggle to make sense of how they are different and why it matters, but I know that it does. I am in my mother's study. The desk and the carpets and the fireplace are all the same, but the painting over the mantle is of a young girl. It is a portrait of my mother. This is my grandmother's study.

Just as I am about to put this all together and place myself in another time, a blond-haired boy of twelve or thirteen enters the room with an elderly gentleman that I recognize from old photographs as my grandfather. Grandfather carries a book.

"Settle yourself here by the fire, young man." The boy does as he is told and sits on the fine brocade chair. My grandfather hands him the book. "You might want to read this while you wait for your mother. She shouldn't be too long."

"Thank you, sir," the young man says politely, giving deference to his mother's employer.

My grandfather closes the door behind him as he leaves the boy alone in the study.

He waits in the chair with the unopened book in his lap. The sound of the older man's footfall on the hardwood floor recedes, assuring the boy that he has gone. He leaves the book on the chair and moves to the wall opposite the fireplace. He slides his fingertips beneath the lower right edge of the gilded frame, which surrounds the portrait of a long-dead ancestor, Baroness somebody. I'm sure I've been told who she is but have long since forgotten her name, and now this is of little importance. The frame moves like he is opening a book, and a wall safe is revealed behind the massive oil painting. The boy kneels on an upholstered chair, placing his ear next to the dial.

Spirits hear what mere mortals cannot; I know this somehow. I hear the tumbler click and watch as he takes note of the number and slowly counts to five as he advances the dial. He has done this before. He has the first number of the combination, but he hasn't figured out the second, at least not yet.

With patience, he listens and tries each number individually, listening carefully for the tumbler to fall. Given enough time and opportunity, he will crack the safe.

Before he has a chance to finish, his mother thunders down the hall calling out his name, "Klaus, let's go." Before he can set the room to rights, the door to the study bursts open. A big woman still wearing her dirty apron stands in the doorway with her hands on her hips.

Klaus shakes his head almost imperceptibly as he closes the frame over the safe and returns the chair to its usual place. "Not yet," he whispers.

"You'll get it," she says as she ruffles the hair of her adolescent son.

The door closes behind them as my gaze is drawn to the book left unread on the chair, *The Ego is the Enemy*—a collection of short stories.

CHAPTER 11

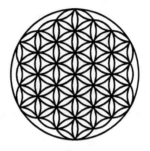

My phone rings and I am relieved to find I have returned to my own body. Caught somewhere between my dream and this reality, my mind wanders a moment longer as I try to put this all together. Searching for the light switch and the whereabouts of my phone, I seek to quiet the incessant buzzing. I can't help but wonder if perhaps it would have done young Klaus Ek some good to have read the book or spent a little more time with my grandparents. Or perhaps the influence of his family and the circumstances of his life had already impacted his character and set the path for his life.

"Hello?" I answer, uncertain who I might find on the other end as the number is unrecognizable.

"Sleeping again?" the low, slow, deep voice asks.

"Anders?"

"Yes, am I disturbing your afternoon nap?" he asks playfully.

I am so relieved to hear from him for so many reasons. "Oh, I'm so glad you called. I was afraid I offended you when I didn't get back for our date."

"You don't know me very well if you think I could be so easily discouraged," he laughs.

And with that, I break into tears. I try to stop myself, but the floodgates have opened. I'm sobbing and having difficulty catching my breath.

"Do you want to talk about what's wrong? Help me understand why you are crying. I'm a pretty good listener." His dulcet voice is low and soothing, and it doesn't take long before I have regained my composure.

"I'm sorry to be so emotional. I don't know what came over me, except perhaps your kindness." I wait for him to say something, but he lets the silence build between us as I try to decide what I want to tell him.

"I had a bad dream," I start and realize I don't really want to go *there* with him, at least not yet and definitely not over the phone. I decide to stick with the objective and the verifiable. "Someone broke into my room and stole my computer."

"When did this happen?"

"Yesterday, while I was sleeping. Someone must have a key to my room. I don't know what they were looking for, but I'm afraid." I take a deep breath before I'm able to continue, "In less than a week on the job, I find myself embroiled in an ethical and legal quagmire. I really could benefit from some legal advice to help me understand the risks and clarify my options."

"Well, I just so happen to be a lawyer. I'd be happy to help if I can." His voice is calm and reassuring.

"I don't know. I don't want to get you messed up in this."

"I can't help you if I don't know what you're talking about."

"You'd have to promise to hold everything in strictest confidence."

"Well, I suppose if you send me a couple of kronor, then you will be my client, and everything you say will be covered by attorney-client privilege. Would that make you feel better, and a little less vulnerable?"

I take another deep breath and wipe away my tears with the back of my hand. I wonder if this is a good idea, and if I consent, will this agreement protect him? Will it protect me? "I don't know what to do, but I feel like I'm out of options."

"Trust me, Saga."

"Okay, do you use *Swish*?" I ask as I'm sure he does, as everyone under the age of eighty has an account and the app on their phone.

"Yes, I use it. But you must understand there may come a time when I don't want you to be *just* my client?" he says with a teasing air hoping to lighten the mood.

"Well, I suppose if that should happen, I could fire you." I laugh with a modicum of relief as I open the app and send the money. Almost instantaneously, I hear the ding through the phone, indicating he has received the money.

"Okay, Ms. Svensson, your retainer has been received. Now let's find out what has you in such a state."

The playful banter rapidly gives way to the sobering reality of what I am up against. It doesn't take long for me to fill Anders in on my concerns that Ek may be mining uranium on our land. I tell him about following the trucks to the shipping area and how the cargo containers are being shipped across the Baltic Sea to Kaliningrad, Russia. "And if this isn't bad enough, I fear this may be weapons-grade uranium."

"How do you know that?"

"I don't, but I have a sixth sense about it. Perhaps because some of the containers are labeled to be sent to Kazakhstan." I hear Anders exhale loudly as I try to reel it all back in and stick with what I do know. "At the very least, Ek is having it sent to a Russian entity which may be selling it to foreign powers."

"There are legal implications for this. What he is doing is in clear violation of international law, specifically the Nuclear Non-Proliferation Treaty," he says, reflecting on the grim reality of what I have just told him.

"The legal concerns are secondary at best. The moral and ethical issues being raised by his behavior are of far greater concern. But my primary concern is for the safety and security of the planet should weapons-grade uranium get into the hands of people with nefarious motives."

"You have good reason to be concerned. Let me help you make a plan to stop this, and to protect you and your family. Let me make some inquiries. I'll be discreet."

"At this point, I need to have a clear understanding of the law and the names and contact information of the people who are charged with protecting the public from this kind of malfeasance. We need to do the right thing. And quickly."

"I'll call you with the names. When do you expect to be back in Stockholm?"

"Probably on Sunday night."

"That's tomorrow."

"My internal clock is all messed up. After being up all night, I truly don't know if I'm coming or going. All I know is that I have a board meeting on Monday night."

"Let me see if I can set something up for Monday morning with either the International Atomic Energy Agency or Euratom. You will need legal representation to protect you and your family. Let me go with you when you blow the whistle on Ek. I may be in over my head, but I know people who know people. I'll find the best legal minds in the country to represent you if need be. In the meantime, say nothing to anyone."

"Call me when you know something."

"Will do."

"And Anders…" the silence grows as he waits for me to continue. "Thank you."

"Ah, the things we do for love," he says as the line goes dead.

I pray to God that I have not just made a huge mistake in trusting this man I barely know, when another thought pushes my fear away, or is Anders Andersson the answer to my prayer. Was he the help that I was asking for? Is he heaven sent, an angel among us?

I don't even know what I don't know.

CHAPTER 12

I lay there for as long as I can, until I cannot afford to rest a moment longer. I'm running a few minutes late as I desperately needed to shower, wash, and dry my hair before meeting the others for dinner.

Entering the bar, Johan is actively engaged in a conversation with an older man. Although the man has his back to me, I can see he is dressed in some kind of a military uniform, dress blues of crisply pressed wool gabardine with gold epaulets embellishing his shoulders, and highly polished knee-high black leather boots. Am I having some weird kind of déjà vu? Whatever is going on? My brother looks as if he is literally being backed into a corner. This tall, imposing man encroaches on his personal space. Johan, who is usually so even-tempered, glowers at this man as his lip curls in response to something that is happening. Never quite able to resist adding my two cents, I step forward to intervene as someone grabs my elbow. I yank my arm free and turn to confront whoever feels entitled to touch my person without permission. To my great relief, I see it is Bierdna. He presses his index finger to his lips to silence me.

What the devil is going on?

Bierdna places his hand on the small of my back as he escorts me to a private dining room, where a beautiful smorgasbord has been laid out for us on the bar. Grandmother Lejá appears to be asleep on an overstuffed chaise near the fireplace.

Once the dining room door has been closed behind us, I ask, "What the hell is going on? Who is that with Johan?"

"Did you not recognize him?"

"No, I didn't see his face. He had his back to me," I say as I try to put the scene back together. "It's Ek, isn't it?"

Bierdna nods, "Kommendor Klaus Ek in all his power and splendor."

"Oh my God, what's he doing here?" I ask aloud, expecting no response. "Do you think I should go out and confront him? Is Johan in danger?"

"Please just stay here. I can't imagine that Ek will do anything to Johan, at least not now and certainly not here. There are too many witnesses. It is standing room only in the bar tonight, and every table in the dining room is booked. Besides, we don't know why Ek is here or what he knows. We must trust that Johan will know what to do."

"Sometimes the most difficult thing is to do nothing." I ease myself down onto an upholstered chair just inside the room. Bierdna pulls a chair up beside me and places a hand on my shoulder as I drop my head towards my knees and fold in on myself and begin to pray to whoever might be listening.

I don't know how long I am sitting there when at last, the door to the private dining room opens, and Johan walks in. His face is as white as a sheet. He closes the door behind him and then leans his back against it as if he is barring the door from any and all unwelcome intruders.

Bierdna stands and goes to Johan while it takes every bit of self-control I can muster to contain the questions I would otherwise release like artillery fire against my dear sweet brother. I breathe a sigh of relief and bite my tongue as my need to know is only superseded by my compassion, for Johan is clearly distraught. Johan already looks like he has barely escaped an enemy ambush. He slowly lowers himself onto the overstuffed armchair beside mine. Bierdna joins us in an intimate gathering of three.

We wait in silence until, at last, Johan speaks, "Jesus Christ, I feel like I've just had a tangle with the devil incarnate."

"What's Ek doing here?" I ask as my heart races, and my hands begin to sweat.

"He didn't say. He acted as if he was as surprised to run into me as I was to run into him."

"He's a manipulative poser. He absolutely knew where to find us. Ulla told him we were here meeting with Bierdna and a consortium of elders."

"Well, he's a pretty good actor then. He immediately went on the offensive about my not returning his phone calls and being unable to locate you. He wanted to know what I was doing up here. Since he didn't mention you, I told him I was doing some reconnaissance, trying to get a handle on the Sámi issue before Monday's board meeting.

"Before I could get another word in edgewise, he charged at me like a crazy man saying, 'The rules of the game have changed. Your mother can no longer protect you. I know what you are up to.' When I asked him what he was talking about, he started pummeling me with a litany of things I was guilty of, implying grounds for dismissal. He went off running the gamut with accusations of disclosing company secrets, illegal activity, disrupting trade, harassing workers, insubordination, and poor job performance.

"He was so angry, and right up in my face. I tried to hold my tongue. But I could smell the alcohol on his stale breath as his spittle began to spray my face. I'm afraid I lost it. I put my hands on his chest and pushed him away. Probably with greater force than I intended. To my own surprise, in a low controlled growl, I informed him that I did not report to him. By then, a crowd had started to gather when two of his comrades-in-arms pulled him away from me. I don't know if that was for his protection or mine."

"Well, isn't this interesting," I say.

"That might be one way to look at it, but only if it didn't happen to you," Johan says incredulously. He is visibly shaken.

"I didn't mean it like that. To paraphrase good ole William Shakespeare, *methinks the gentleman doth protest too much.* I have a pretty good idea of what he is up to, and he has reason to be afraid."

Just then, the same server from last night walks through the door with a tray holding four glasses with a round of vodka on the rocks in each with a lemon twist. She has drinks that no one has ordered. All conversation stops while she is in our presence. She's a pretty girl somewhere in her early twenties with white-blonde hair and ice blue eyes that dart nervously about the room. There is something off about her.

Grandmother Lejá gets to her feet. Tonight, she leans heavily on her burled cane as she walks over to join us. No doubt, her body is tired from staying up all night in the ceremony. She refuses the drink when offered, explaining, "Alcohol muddles the senses and messes with my gift." Then she turns and addresses the server in Sámi. The server looks confused, so Grandmother Lejá translates her request into Swedish. "How is it that you betray your own people and sell your soul for a small offering of gold? Remember who you are and what you are worth." Without acknowledging Grandmother's comment, the young woman's face glows red, and her hand begins to shake, causing the vodka to spill from their nearly full glasses. She sets the tray on the table before she turns and flees the room. Once the door closes behind her Grandmother adds, "She's a spy for Kommander Ek."

"I thought you were asleep, Grandmother," Bierdna says as he pulls out a chair for the elderly woman.

"I was in and out," she smiles. "I learned long ago not to disregard my intuition or the messages sent to me through my dreams. She is one of ours. I have seen her before, and I know what she is up to."

We help ourselves to some food from the buffet when there is another knock on the door, and every one of us falls silent as Bierdna goes to the door. Two Sámi men are standing in the doorway. The shorter of the two breaks into a broad smile, "I'm not certain who you were expecting, but I can assure you we don't bite."

Bierdna returns his smile and steps to one side, "By all means, please join us." The men embrace both Grandmother Lejá and Bierdna.

"Lenne, it has been too long, far too long," Grandmother Lejá says to the shorter man. And then to his companion, she says, "Aako, welcome. I would know you anywhere for you are the spitting image of your father."

"What about me?" the man she's called Lenne asks as he extends both sides of his skirt and gives a little twirl.

Grandmother Lejá laughs, "Oh Lenne, perhaps a little less so."

The man called Lenne is dressed in traditional women's clothing but has facial hair and masculine features. There was a time when people were free to love whomever they chose, and gender expression was open and fluid. But that was years ago. To do so in this day and age is bold and courageous.

Then Bierdna introduces Johan and me to Aako and Lenne. "Aako and Lenne have traveled a great distance to meet with us. They are the *Noaidi* from other Sámi communities across the Arctic north. And our dear Lenne is of two spirits."

I take note, not wishing to embarrass myself or make Lenne uncomfortable for this must be the agreed-upon language used by the Sámi for homosexual and transsexual people, *to be of two spirits.*

Lenne smiles broadly as he takes my hand and kisses it. The gesture and his smile are so familiar that I am certain that I know him, but from where and when I cannot say.

"Do I know you?" I ask.

Again, he smiles broadly, and then he curtseys. "You don't remember?"

I shake my head no, "I'm sorry."

He just smiles and lets it go. "I believe we have other things that need to be attended to. Time is of the essence."

"Now, at last, it is time to rehash, recap, and strategize." Bierdna takes control of the gathering, and I am grateful for his leadership.

We take our plates and gather at the round table closer to the fireplace, as we take our seats Bierdna stokes the fire before adding another log. It isn't long before the log is engulfed in flames, and the light of the fire fills the room. Johan distributes the glasses of vodka, all of the *Noaidi* refuse. Resisting my desire for a good strong drink, I decide to do the same.

"Don't worry. It won't go to waste," Johan informs us as he takes two drinks off the tray.

"I hate to be suspicious," Bierdna says. "But given everything that has happened today, let me get us a round at the bar." He gathers up the glasses on the tray and places the tray of untouched drinks back on a table near the door.

"You don't think they've put something into our drinks, do you?" I ask.

"There are many things that are beyond my imagination. Tonight, I choose to err on the side of caution."

Our guests look confused. Bierdna leaves to go to get the drinks while Johan describes what happened just before their arrival and his encounter with Klaus Ek.

When Bierdna returns, he has an unopened bottle of vodka, an ice bucket, and half a dozen empty glasses. I guess he brought the extra glasses in case someone changed their mind.

"You Saga, are the Seer, our *Noaidi*. Tell us what you see. Tell us what you know," Grandmother Lejá says.

I am humbled. I am the CEO and have only recently stumbled onto my gifts of seeing and knowing. I feel so ill-equipped to guide these people, to guide my family's business into the future, to protect us all against evil and malfeasance, but someone must. We are at a tipping point, where if nothing is done, everything could be lost. I think back to earlier times to a young climate change activist, Greta Thunberg; she was a prophet, really. If no one else will speak, then maybe I must. I wander around in the silence, uncertain how much to share.

I take a deep breath and then begin, "Last evening, I was present at a ceremony where an agreement was reached, and documents and contracts were signed outlining the terms of land use and stewardship of the Sápmiland." Grandmother Lejá smiles as the men nod their heads, and I can't help but wonder who else among us might also have been present back then and have firsthand knowledge of this sacred agreement. "Two copies were signed; one was given to the Sámi people, and another was given to one of the women of my family. Is it possible the one given to your people is still in existence?" I direct my question to the delegation of Sámi elders.

"I cannot say for certain. But we do not have it, and I'm afraid all evidence of any land treaty was probably put to the flame back in the 1800s during the evangelical Christianization. Our people suffered and were forced into total subjugation, our *Noaidi* and shamans were murdered, our drums were confiscated, our culture, spirituality, and entire way of life were attacked by the state and the state church."

I start to tremble as if I have a personal recollection of this time and the reign of terror. Is this just an empathic response, or was I there? Right now, it doesn't matter; right now, I need to stay focused on the magnitude of the problem at hand.

We finish eating and everyone fall silent as another young server scurries about clearing the dirty dishes. Only once he has left the room does anyone speak. "Let us start with the timeline and see what is possible. I must attend the board meeting at seven on Monday evening. The Sámi land dispute is the first thing on the agenda. I have consulted with an attorney and laid the issues out as best I can."

Bierdna's eyes grow wide as he presses his index finger to his lips then pulls on his ear.

I nod towards him. I understand. He fears Ek may have had the room bugged, and others may be listening in as we strategize. "We all know what the issues are, so I won't elaborate here." The others nod in agreement. They, too, understand Bierdna's concerns.

I decide to keep silent about the mine and our suspicions that Ek and his henchmen are selling weapons-grade uranium—if this is revealed, the reindeer will not be the only species at risk for extinction. Any talk of this kind will put us all at risk, long before those containers cross the sea towards Russia. The chatter runs on in my head as I try to decide what to say to this brave group of whistleblowers. I close my eyes and take another deep breath before continuing.

"A meeting has been set for Monday morning, but before that, I need to search the company archives and consult with Mother. She may be able to locate the document signed long ago which secured this land for the Boazovázzi and reindeer herding. I want *our* legal experts to weigh in and to know if we have any legal standing to protect this land. To accomplish this, I'm afraid we will need to leave first thing in the morning." The others murmur their assent.

I retreat momentarily into my own thoughts. I feel as if I am playing chess, trying to anticipate my opponent's next move while setting up my pieces to be in an advantageous position two or three moves from now if I am to have any hope of securing the desired outcome. I must think strategically.

If Ek is listening in, I want him to assume I am consulting with our in-house lawyers. This may create a distraction, for he may attempt to manipulate those who report to him. I make a mental note to have Johan schedule and attend a meeting with them on Monday morning to discuss the land dispute. I don't want to tip our hand that we are seeking outside counsel.

Bringing my awareness back to the room, I notice everyone has gone silent. Hands are folded, and heads are bowed in prayer, even Johan sits in silence. I wait in shared silence as they finish praying and begin to lift their heads. I make eye contact with them individually; one by one, I pause and hold each of them in my gaze a moment longer, offering a sacred promise to do my best while holding each of them in my heart.

Grandmother Lejá breaks the silence, "Godspeed, dear Saga. We will be praying for you and await your return." The others smile and nod.

"The hour is late." Grandmother stands, leaning heavily on her burled cane, indicating it is time to go. She opens her arms to offer me her warm embrace. As we hold one another, the others stand and place a hand upon my shoulders as I feel the strength and power of this community. Then the men exchange handshakes with Johan thanking him for coming as we walk them out to the lobby.

The lobby has emptied out, and even the bar is quiet. "Nightcap?" Johan asks.

"Not tonight, I think a good night's sleep is in order."

"Okay, I guess we'll have plenty of time to talk tomorrow on the drive home. It's been an interesting week."

"It feels like a week, but it has only been four days."

"True enough. What time would you like to leave tomorrow?"

"We have at least an eight-hour drive ahead of us, and that's if the roads are clear."

"The forecast calls for snow. Breakfast at seven and then on the road before eight?" Johan suggests.

"That settles any ambivalence I was having about that nightcap. See you in the morning," I say as I head for the elevator.

"Saga," Johan says as I turn back towards him. "I know you're the one with the full-blown intuition, but try not to worry and get some sleep. These are good people, and we're on the right side of this issue."

"I agree, these are good people, but the Sámi are not the people who worry me," I say with a smile and Johan nods his head in agreement. "See you in the morning."

CHAPTER 13

To my great relief, I fall asleep quickly and sleep the sleep of the unencumbered. Sometime in the early morning hours, I am visited in a dream by Lenne, the *Noaidi* from another Sámi tribe who met with us earlier in the evening.

"Once upon a time, a long time ago, you befriended me, and I have not forgotten your kindness. I was then as I am now, a man of two spirits. Then I was called homo and fag. But you called me Barry, and you were Fiona.

"Barry," I say his name, and now I cannot believe I did not see him for who he was then and who he is now." In my dream, I reach out to embrace my long-lost friend. "You left us so tragically and so young."

"An autoimmune disease, a plague upon my people, and an entire generation."

He enfolds me in his arms. And then as if he can read my mind and my confusion, Lenne says, "I was in danger of failing, and you were patient and kind and a friend to me. Now you are here among my people, and we are all in danger. We are being called to fulfill our destiny.

"Grandmother Lejá has sent me to deliver a message to you. She wants you to know that you are more powerful than you know. We are here to help you access your power as a Seer, a Seeker, and to finally and fully embrace your role and be One Who Knows. You have prepared many lifetimes for this. Remember, Saga, you are a *Noaidi*. If you need help, all you need to do is ask. We will be there for you."

And with this, Lenne slips away like an apparition back into the world of dreams.

I wake and am filled with wonder as I lie encased in the warmth of the eiderdown while the fairy lights twinkle in the dark on the new-fallen snow. How is it that I could not see Lenne for who he is, and now I can see so clearly? I could easily become overwhelmed by the task that rests upon my shoulders, but there is something comforting and reassuring, knowing that others love me and will stand with me in this world and the next. I wonder who else might be out there to help me if all I need to do is ask?

Perhaps there is only a fine line between being psychic and psychotic. I ponder the differences, and I'm left to wonder, at any given point in time, just what side of that line I find myself on?

Closing my eyes and just as I begin to drift off back to sleep, my phone rings. It's only four-thirty. Who could possibly be calling now? "Hello?"

"Saga, sorry to be calling so early. I couldn't sleep. I've been up watching the weather. There's a big storm coming this way, and unless we want to get snowed in, I think we should leave right away."

"Oh, okay," I say, just coming back to the present and grasping the reality of what Johan is saying. "I can be ready in ten minutes."

"I'll meet you downstairs. I'll see if we can get some coffee and perhaps something for breakfast that we can take along with us."

"See you in a few," I say as I hear Johan click off, and the phone goes silent.

Johan has already cleared the snow from the car as it appears it has been snowing softly throughout the night, giving everything a fine dusting of light powder. He helps me put my luggage into the back of the vehicle. He has already warmed up the car and hands me a large travel mug of hot coffee and a bag of cardamom buns as I climb into the passenger seat of this oversized SUV. At a time when I seek to find my place in the world, it is so nice that my brother has looked for ways to make my life a little easier and attended to my comfort. Johan is so considerate. He has considered me and my needs, and his kindness has not gone unnoticed. "Thank you for seeing to all of this."

"It is the very least I can do. We have important things to attend to today."

Johan waves to a man standing just inside the lobby as we drive away, and in return, the man raises a gloved hand and salutes him. This strikes me as odd. He is dressed in black outerwear and a black watch cap rather than the red coat worn by the doormen and most of the employees of the Grand Arctic Lodge. "Who was that guy?" I ask.

"His name is Oskar," Johan replies as if this name should mean something to me. "When your laptop went missing two days ago, I took the liberty of hiring Oskar to sweep the car for any surveillance devices that may have been planted here for nefarious purposes by your old friend Klaus. Once it was cleared, he spent the night in the vehicle to be certain no one came and reinstalled another listening device."

"Seriously? What do you mean another? Did he find something?"

"Indeed, he did, something for listening in real-time as well as a GPS tracking device so they, whoever *they* are, would know exactly where we are at any point in time. I also took the liberty of having your apartment, and the manor house at Damgården swept."

"Johan…" I have so many questions, but I don't know where to start. "You think we are in danger, don't you?"

"Saga, there is a lot of money involved, international laws have been broken, weapons-grade uranium is being sold to countries who harbor terrorists and are intent on world domination and destruction of our way of life and possibly the extinction of the planet. We are getting ready to expose all of this. Do I think we are in danger? Absolutely. We are in danger."

I sit in silence as we head out into the darkness.

"Is there really a big storm coming, or did we slip away in the dead of night to avoid detection?"

"There is always the possibility of snow. We're up near the Arctic Circle for God's sake," Johan says with a sly smile.

Johan is steps ahead of me on this. "I'm just glad you are working with us, rather than against us."

"Well, you may not feel that way when you get home."

"Why?"

"Oskar has a security officer stationed outside your apartment and another at Damgården."

"Is there anything else you think I should know?"

"I'm sorry if you think I have gone over your head making these arrangements without discussing them with you first, but we have not had a moment to ourselves, and I did not know who might be listening in or who could be trusted. These last few days have helped me see this in an entirely different light. There is more than the future of Lundstrom Enterprises, and the fate of the reindeer and the Sámi people at stake. As if that wasn't enough. But after the encounter I had with Ek last night, he is one angry and scary dude, I believe he is capable of anything. You need protection, and so does Mother, at least until we get through this."

"Okay," I whisper softly. I know he is right. "Thank you for looking out for us. We haven't had any time or space to talk, and I need to tell you a few things, too."

I tell my brother about my conversation with Anders, and he laughs when he learns that I sent him a couple of krona via *Swish* to bind him to attorney-client privilege.

"I guess you are taking precautions, too."

"I'd like to say I thought of it, but it was Anders's idea."

"Either way, I like it."

"Anders is setting up a meeting tomorrow morning with some legal experts to look into the violations of international laws regarding the sale and shipment of uranium. The meeting is set for nine tomorrow morning in Anders's office unless I hear something different today."

"I heard you mention this last night, but I thought you were meeting with the in-house legal team."

"Good, that was my intention. I was fearful that Ek may have put the private dining room under surveillance. Still, I want you to schedule a meeting with our lawyers to discuss the signed agreement that was made with the Sámi when Baroness Kristina Lundstrom first acquired the land and the deed restrictions which were agreed upon at the time. In the meantime, I will meet with the team of legal experts Anders is putting together to discuss the international violations, who we need to inform, how to bring this to light and stop Ek before it is too late, all the while protecting us in our role as the whistleblowers."

"Anders knows people who deal with this kind of thing?" Johan asks.

"He has been an *advokat* and an active member of the Swedish Bar Association for over ten years and even received the European Law Institute's Young Lawyers Award for a paper he wrote on Civil Liability in Blockchain Technology."

"Sounds fascinating," Johan says as he yawns widely. "Is this the kind of thing you two discuss on your dates?"

"No, it came up at Sigge Markus' New Year's Eve party. Sigge was associate counsel for Ulf Lang and was at the Löfgren settlement hearing."

"I know Sigge. He's on our polo team."

"Well, it was the first time I'd met him. Apparently, he had just been telling Anders about this woman who'd given Ulf Lang a good waxing earlier in the day, and then I walked into the party. He'd already had a few by the time I got there, so he began telling me all about my illustrious date. I guess he wanted me to know that Anders was smart and could hold his own."

"Sounds charming," my brother laughs.

"I have to agree, in the retelling, the encounter does sound pompous and boastful. Perhaps Sigge is all that, I don't know, but Anders is humble, and I like that about him. He offered to help and told me he knows people who know people. I trust him."

"I've known Anders for a long time. I agree, he's cut from a different cloth than some of the assholes I usually hang around with."

"Maybe it is time for you to choose some new friends."

"Maybe, but my asshole friends accept me for the asshole I am. You know, birds of a feather—"

"Flock together." I finish the old adage for him.

"Still, maybe it's time to fly the coop, make a new start, and leave behind childish ways and all those other overplayed lines."

This time I quote my yoga teacher. "It might be something to think about. Letting go of that which no longer serves you."

"You're not talking about my wife, are you?" he says with a laugh.

"I won't dream of trying to advise you on your marriage, particularly now that you have another baby on the way. Speaking of your family, what are you doing to protect your girls? Aren't they expected back this afternoon from their visit with Hanna's mother?"

"They are staying in Malmö for a few more days, at least until I get home and can assure their safety. They're still little, so it won't be the end of the world if they miss a day or two of school. Hanna left yesterday for the Maldives, and I don't expect her to be back for a week or so."

"What reason did you give her mother?"

"I made up some cock 'n bull story about a frozen pipe in our wing of the Manor House and how the water had been turned off until we could get it repaired. Minna loves the girls and is delighted they will be staying a while longer."

"You seem to be pretty proficient at manufacturing the truth," I say.

"Side benefit of hanging out with assholes. Just borrowed the tale from one of the guys who needed a reason to send his wife and family away while his mistress was visiting."

"Ugh," I say with a tone of disgust. "I reiterate, you need some new friends."

"Point taken," Johan concedes.

We drive along in silence for a while until Johan suggests, "Why don't you try to get some rest. There's likely to be a couple of long days ahead of us. Perhaps you could drive a bit once you've had a nap, and then I'll take a turn and catch up on my sleep."

By now, the car is plenty warm with the heat blowing full force, so I take off my coat and press it up against the window to cushion my head. As I begin to drift off to sleep, something is nagging at me. "What was the name of that book you were telling me about?" I ask my brother.

"What book?"

"During the drive up here, you asked me if I'd read a book written by some ancient Asian emperor?" I ask groggily through the threat of impending sleep.

"Do you mean Sun Tzu? He wasn't the emperor. Sun Tzu was a Chinese general and military strategist."

"Yes, that's the one. You quoted something he said in the book. Could you repeat it?"

"I think you mean, *'If you know your enemy and know yourself you need not fear the result of a hundred battles. If you know yourself and not your enemy, for every victory gained you will also suffer a defeat. If you know neither the enemy nor yourself, you will succumb in every battle.'*"

"Yes, that's what I was trying to remember. I feel I am gaining clarity on myself, my motivations, and my purpose in this battle we find ourselves embroiled in, but still, it seems as if a piece to this puzzle is still missing. There is something about Chairman Ek that eludes me. I don't know what it is, but it feels important. It's as if I'm being nudged, or rather shoved, to draw back the curtain to see Klaus Ek and to know who he really is."

"The trouble is once you see it, you cannot unsee it."

"Or to use the Biblical reference, *what was hidden, will be revealed.*" My coat has slipped down the frost-covered window. I retrieve it from between the seat and the door and reposition it as my makeshift pillow. Leaning against the window and securing it with my head and shoulder, I close my eyes for a much-needed nap. My head knocks gently against the window, and I'm barely conscious of the crunching sound of the metal-studded snow tires rolling over the snow-covered pavement as the heater blows warm air in my direction until I am enveloped in its embrace. It doesn't take long before I'm drifting back towards sleep.

I am a teenage girl in a farmhouse in middle America. I'm dressed in blue jeans and a flannel shirt. It is the 1970s. I know who I am. I am Fiona, and there is an older man in a Roman collar lecturing me about morality and my sinful ways.

He insists I reconsider my testimony. "You are nothing but a whore, and a whore cannot be raped."

Unable to defend my virtue, the unspoken words get stuck in my throat.

The scene shifts, and again I am Fiona. I am at a funeral. I think it is my grandmother's funeral. I approach the altar with my hands folded and my head bowed when this same priest denies me the sacrament of Holy Communion. Again, the priest is Father Brendan. I burn with fury and public shame.

The scene shifts to an earlier era; perhaps it is the time of the early Christian church. Now I am a small child, barefoot and dirty. I hide within the recess of a cave and silently watching in the shadows as a pompous man dressed in the red liturgical garb of a cardinal, demands that a scribe to alter some sacred text that he is translating. If he refuses, he will be charged with heresy and be sentenced to death.

The scribe sees me hiding in the alcove and calls for me to run. He calls me by my name, "Run, Sofia. Run." The scribe is my father.

My father calls my name with great urgency, "Sofia," and then as I go around the corner, and just before I'm out of earshot, I hear his heartbreaking plea for my escape. "Run, Fee." And so, I do. I run through the dark, dank tunnels into the courtyard where a platform has been erected and the funeral pyre prepared. This time this evil being is not intent on hurting me. This time he will hurt someone I love. This kind of assault inflicts an unbearable, soul-wrenching pain from which one may never recover.

The Cardinal, dressed in red vestments, does not resemble Father Brendan, but he is the same. I see clearly now. He is an earlier incarnation of the same dark spirit.

I cry but make no sound as once again, the scene begins to change and shift. The wind blows hot and dry, and the desert sand stings my face and eyes. I am thirsty. I am no longer a child but a woman. I am clothed in a headscarf and the long black dress of a widow. I am an Armenian woman in the time of the genocide and diaspora. I have lost my parents, my siblings, my husband, and my children to the brutality of the Young Turks and the Ottoman troops.

I am a stranger in a strange land, grieving the loss of my loved ones. I find no comfort here from the other women of the harem. I am an unwelcome outsider.

A dark-haired woman accompanies me as we leave the women's tent for another. She pretends to be my friend, but she is untrustworthy. She does the bidding of the powerful. I don't know how I know this, except that I do. I have lived this life and suffered these losses and indignities.

I stand before a big and powerful man robed in the finery of a Bedouin sheik. He does not care about my losses or my grief; I am being held as a sex slave. I am to be part of his concubine.

I do not love this man. His touch disgusts me, and I find him despicable. Lost and alone, I am powerless and degraded again and again. The Sheik uses my body until my novelty wears off. I cannot pretend what I do not feel. I do not please him. My value is diminished, and I am expendable.

The scene shifts, and I am brought back to the women's tent where I am beaten by the women of the harem. They hold me down as my face is tattooed with the symbols of my captors. Once so marked, I am cast out, no longer suitable for marriage to any man as I am marked as an Armenian sex slave in a Muslim country. I am discarded and left on the streets to beg and die alone.

This man and his dark-haired accomplice bear the face of pure evil. Across many lifetimes, he has been intent on my destruction. I fear I will encounter him again and again in other lifetimes until I stand up to him and stand in my own power.

The scene shifts again, and it is the present time. This time he bears the face of Klaus Ek. He is dressed in full faux military garb. He tells me I am weak and merely a figurehead, as were all the women in my family who have come before me. He threatens to have me removed from my position and expose me as a psychotic fraud in need of imprisonment in a psychiatric hospital. I start to protest, but my tongue is tied, and I cannot find the words to defend myself. I know who he is. I have seen him for who he is.

I wake with a start. My heart is racing, and I am sweating. It takes me a moment to realize I am back in the car with Johan.

Johan reaches over and puts a hand on my shoulder. "I think you were having a bad dream."

It's already dark, and the lights of some urban area glow in the distance.

"How long have I been asleep?" I ask, trying to keep the panic from my voice.

"Awhile, I guess you needed the sleep."

"What time is it?"

"Just about four o'clock. We're thirty minutes from home. It's been slow going as we ran into a bit of snow north of here. I guess they were right about the storm they'd predicted after all."

"Why didn't you wake me? I thought you wanted me to help with the driving."

"I'll sleep tonight. Besides, I took a little nap when I stopped to get the car recharged. I got myself something to eat and a cup of coffee. You must be starving."

"Come to think of it, I could use something to eat."

"I saved you half of a meatball sandwich in the bag, and the coffee in the thermos should still be hot."

"Thank you," I say as I look in the bag. "As hungry as I am, I don't think I can stomach a cold meatball sandwich, but the coffee sounds good."

Johan looks at the grease-stained bag and turns up his nose, "I see what you mean. It wasn't too bad a couple of hours ago."

"I think we should stop at the Damgården and see Mother and Father before you take me home. I want to see if we can locate a copy of the Sámi land contract."

"The deed that was signed by the Sámi elders and Baroness Kristina Lundstrom back when we acquired the land from King Gustavus Adolphus in the 1600s? You, my dear Saga, are forever an optimist."

"I'm hoping Mother has it in the archives or the safe. How are you at reading and translating Old Swedish?"

"Probably not that great, although I can't say I've ever tried. If this document even still exists, I'm putting my money on Father to be able to read it. He is the resident scholar in our family."

"You're right. If any one of us can read it, Father would be the one. Maybe I should call Mother and see if we can wrangle an invitation for dinner."

"I'm already expected, and you know Maryan. There's always more than enough to eat. She still thinks she's back in Somalia cooking for the whole village."

I laugh as I call Mother to let her know we are on the way.

CHAPTER 14

When we arrive at the manor house of Damgården, the motion of the car triggers the floodlights, and the whole place lights up like a Christmas tree. A large man dressed in black with a black watch cap pulled low on his forehead steps out of the shadows and approaches the car. Johan begins to lower the window when the man salutes him as if he is a commander in a military operation. Johan smiles as the front gate opens, allowing us to gain entrance.

"A friend of yours?" I ask.

"A friend of Oskar's. I told you I'd hired some protection."

"Yes, I know, and thank you. I guess I just hadn't thought they would all look like street thugs."

"Would you have preferred a few fellas a bit more elfin? Ek and his crew are a dangerous lot."

"Point taken. I just wouldn't want to meet that guy in a dark alley."

"That guy's name is Rock."

"Well, isn't he aptly named. I just hope Rocky understands that we are on the same side." Johan chuckles as I call this mountain of a man by a diminutive version of his name.

By the time we are out of the car, both Mother and Father are at the door waiting to greet us. "Johan, Saga, please come in. You must be exhausted from your long drive."

"Johan may be, but I slept most of the way back."

Mother wraps an arm around my shoulder and gives me a squeeze as she whispers conspiratorially into my ear, "Tell me where you were. Father told me, but I'm afraid I forgot."

"It's okay," I whisper back as I kiss her on the cheek. "We're just getting back from visiting with the Sámi elders up in the Sápmilands. Grandmother Lejá and Bierdna asked me to send you their best regards."

A warm smile and a faraway look cross my dear sweet mother's face. She remembers. "It has been so long since I last saw them. These are good and honorable people. We must do what we can to help them."

Father takes our coats and hangs them in the closet. "Maryan already has dinner ready. Let's eat and then we can talk about your adventure in the North Country."

"Sounds great. I'm starving," I say as we enter the dining room. The table is set with a simple repast of beef stroganoff and a cucumber salad. I wish we had thought to call Maryan earlier as she knows I don't eat much red meat.

Johan looks me in the eye as I pass him my bowl. He ladles the steaming meat, noodles, and gravy into my bowl. "Bless it and eat it, Saga," he says with a smile as he passes the bowl back to me.

I haven't eaten since before dawn, and I will not make a fuss. I am grateful to have something warm to eat.

Father starts the salad around the table, and once everyone has filled their plates, he says a few words of gratitude and offers a blessing over the food.

"Amen," we say in unison.

I take a bite of the warm noodles. "Mmmm." It has been years since I had any of Maryan's stroganoff, and I'd forgotten how delicious it is. "Perfectly seasoned, as always."

"You are a good sport, Saga," Father says as it dawns on him I don't usually eat meat. "You'll be happy to know we're having rose hip soup and vanilla ice cream for dessert."

"You can count me in for some of that," Johan says with a laugh, and it is remarkable how much he still sounds like a twelve-year-old.

Once dinner is over, we retreat to the living room. The Christmas tree is still up but will be coming down on Tuesday as we always leave it up past the Feast of the Epiphany.

"So, what gifts of wisdom have the two of you brought back from your travels to the North?" Father asks.

Johan looks to me as if he wants me to decide how much I want to divulge to our parents. Before I can say anything, our mother looks at him and says, "Out with it, Johan."

I nod to him, giving him my consent to tell our parents the whole story, not some abbreviated version meant to lessen their fears and concerns.

"Saga, what's going on? We know something is up or that strong-armed bruiser wouldn't be pacing around the perimeter of the estate," Mother adds before Johan has even begun.

So, with that, Johan delves into the story as he knows it. Both Mother and Father sit in silence as the story of the Sámi, the mining, and Johan's run-in with Klaus Ek unfolds. At last, Mother speaks. "I know which treaty you are speaking of. It was always kept in the safe in the study. But it is no longer there. Perhaps it has been moved to the archives, but if I had it moved, well, I'm afraid I don't remember."

"I had a dream or a premonition or whatever you want to call it, but I think Klaus Ek has the original. I think he took it from the safe."

"Don't you think that might be just a little preposterous?" Father asks as I can hear just a slight element of hope in his voice.

"I wish it was so," I tell my father. "But Klaus grew up in this house, visiting his mother every day after school while she finished the household chores. He is smart and conniving. I think he learned long ago to crack the code on the safe. He has been waiting patiently for the right time to take what he needed."

"And what would that be?"

"This time what he wanted was the treaty signed by Baroness Kristina Lundstrom and the Sámi elders in 1635, allowing them to herd their reindeer unencumbered over their ancestral land."

"I remember the signing of that treaty," Mother says. "I think I was there. I think I signed it. Is that possible?" she asks as she shakes her head, trying to make sense of what she knows in this reality with what she remembers from another lifetime.

Johan opens his mouth to speak, and then thinks better of it and keeps quiet.

"I want to check the safe to see if that document might have been overlooked," Father says.

"It's not there," Mother says definitively.

Johan stands and pours us both a measure of the iced cold aquavit as we wait for Father to return.

"Mother's right. The safe is empty. When was the last time you opened it, Sigrid?"

"The day before yesterday. I tried to tell you, Edward. Klaus Ek came by the house looking for Saga. He's shifty and couldn't look me in the eye. I knew he was lying about his reason for coming by. He asked if he might borrow a book from my library. When I asked him the title, he stammered, just like he did when he was a child. I asked him to wait for me as I was needed on a conference call. Then I had Maryan keep tabs on him in the receiving room while I emptied the safe. When I returned, he spent about fifteen minutes alone in the library while I sent Maryan off on an errand to the Royal Bank of Sweden. Everything that was in the safe is now in the safety deposit box in the vault. But the deed was not there. I think he took it another time. I don't know what he was looking for yesterday, but I can assure you he did not get what he came after," Mother says as she settles in on the sofa. "Johan, fix me one of those," she says, indicating she too would like a glass of aquavit. "Just a thimbleful, dear."

"Well, I'll be," Father says, as he sits down beside his wife. "Sigrid, you never cease to amaze me, my dear."

"These memory failings of mine are a bit like an electrical circuit. Sometimes all the circuits are firing just fine, and other times I'm completely in the dark. Fortunately, yesterday was a good day, or was it the day before? See what I mean?"

Johan hands our mother her drink as Father raises his right index finger and lifts his chin, "Get me one too, will you, son?"

"How do we prove the existence of the treaty and the nature of the agreements our foremothers made with the Sámi people without the treaty?" I ask, as I am not sure how to proceed.

"Two copies were signed," Mother says with confidence.

"One of the originals is likely to have been filed at the National Archives of Sweden. It was established in 1618, about seventeen years before the treaty was signed," Father says as if this is common knowledge.

"You really do know a little bit about everything, don't you?" Johan says in a tone filled with admiration.

"How about a lot about everything?" I am always amazed at our father's treasure trove of knowledge.

"A lot of useless knowledge, I'm afraid. Still, the National Archives may not even be open tomorrow as it is the Feast of the Epiphany, *Trettondagen Jul.* Besides, even if it is there, the document's authenticity would need to be verified and translated from Old Swedish, and that may not be possible before seven o'clock tomorrow night in time for the board meeting," Father says.

Silence fills the room as we all contemplate this reality.

"I may have some connections from the university who can help us. I'll check into it first thing in the morning," Father offers. He is not willing to give up that easily.

"Just be careful. We are dealing with dangerous people who have a lot at stake," I say to my father.

"My how the tables have turned. I think it is you and Johan who are stepping into the most dangerous territory. Please heed your own good advice." Father paces in front of the fireplace. "I suppose I should have worn gloves when I opened the safe, now my fingerprints and Mother's will be all over the dial obscuring any evidence that Ek broke into our safe."

"I guess you don't know everything about everything," I tease my Father. "The curse of an honest man, but I can assure you that Ek's fingerprints will be nowhere near that dial. You may have forgotten to wear gloves, but there is no way in hell that Ek forgot."

"I suppose you are right, Saga," Father concedes the point.

"It's getting late, and tomorrow will be challenging, to say the least," Johan says. It is only then that I truly see how exhausted he is.

Always the picture of health, tonight his skin has taken on an unusual ashen cast and dark shadows appear beneath his eyes. The stress of this dire predicament we find ourselves embroiled in is taking a toll on my beloved brother and weighs heavily on him, to say nothing of the fact, he has been up before dawn and driving through the snowstorm while I slept.

Recapping the agreed-upon strategy, I say, "The plan is that Johan will meet in the morning with our in-house legal counsel to determine how we enforce an agreement that was signed nearly four hundred years ago, Father will attempt to locate the treaty at the National Archives, and I will meet with Anders and the team of legal experts to discuss the international violations, determine who we need to inform, how to bring this to light and stop Kommendor Klaus Ek and his minions before it is too late. And if we can save the Sámi, the reindeer, and Lundstrom Enterprises too, well, that will be a good day's work."

"And I will pray for your success," Mother adds.

We make our way to the foyer, and Father retrieves my coat. "Oh, I nearly forgot. I got you a new laptop to replace the one that was stolen. I've had it loaded with some basic software and transferred the photos you sent to Maryan from your trip to the mine," Father says, and he hands me a new computer bag.

"Would you look at this," I say, as I admire the beautiful designer bag that holds my new computer.

"I can't take credit for that. Ulla picked out the bag." Father smiles, clearly pleased that I like it.

"Did you get the computer from the IT department at Lundstrom Enterprises?" Johan asks anxiously.

Father laughs, "I may be old, but I'm no fool. Those old techies have been in Ek's pocket for years. No, I walked into the store and waited in line just like everyone else. This model is very intuitive, and if this old goat can manage it, I know you won't have any difficulty." Father smiles as I lean in to kiss him on the cheek.

"Thank you, Father," I say as tears start to well up in my eyes when I think about his thoughtfulness and how well cared for I am by my family.

"Do you want me to drive you home?" Johan asks as he tries to stifle a yawn.

"I don't think so. I'm more than capable of driving myself. Besides, I will need a car tomorrow. Can Father's driver bring you into the office?"

"Of course," my father says. "Or he can use my car. Don't worry about that. We'll work it out. However, I don't like the idea of you driving home alone tonight, all things considered. Why don't you have one of Johan's goons drive you home? I'm sure there are more than one of them at his beck and call who can stay behind and keep watch over the Damgården, tonight."

Johan must have some sort of pager in his pocket, for before Father has even finished speaking there is a knock on the front door and a burly man dressed in all black has pulled the car under the portico and is waiting to take me home.

Father smiles, "Well done, Johan."

Both Father and Mother wish us luck as they embrace us at the door before I leave for home, and Johan heads up to bed.

For all her clarity earlier this evening, once again, Mother has a faraway look in her eyes. She speaks softly to herself, or perhaps to others we cannot see. Father gently calls her back from wherever she has been, "Sigrid." She shakes her head and then nods as if in response to questions put to her by voices we cannot hear.

Mother no longer whispers in my ear. She speaks aloud, as if she is addressing the Riksdag, the national legislative assembly, "Fiona, Sofia, my beloved Saga, you have traveled far and endured. You have learned your lessons well in the schools of life. Past incarnations and challenges have been preparing you for this moment. You are up to this. Now is the time to be brave and speak the truth. Call on those who have loved you in this life, and those in the realm of spirit. All of us are here to help you. You, my darling, do not stand alone."

I can't help but wonder if she is channeling this message from someone and somewhere else. Her voice sounds disembodied and does not sound as if it even belongs to her.

A look of confusion and despair crosses Father's and Johan's faces, for they do not *see* what I have seen, and they are not privy to what Mother and I *know*. Mother gently squeezes my hand three times slowly, once for each word—I Love You. She and I have shared this unspoken signal over other lifetimes. I return the three squeezes. Tears fill both of our eyes as we part.

CHAPTER 15

I hadn't told my family that I had no intention of going home, and now I am being driven there by someone who believes he is my chauffeur and personal bodyguard. I had made plans to go to Anders's place tonight. We have things to discuss before tomorrow's meeting, and besides, I am in great need of a little tenderness. It has been a long time since I have been in a real relationship with a man, and if the world is rapidly heading for demise, well, I could use a little love. Lately, I have spent so much time wandering about in my past lives that I'm afraid I may completely miss the beauty of this one. There have been times when I could not see it, but now I am aware of how important it is to me to be fully present to all this life has to offer.

The car pulls out of the portico and heads down the long driveway towards the road. "Could you wait just a moment?" I ask as I send a text message to Anders.

Still want me to come by?

Instantly my phone dings with a response.

Of course

It's getting late, and I was afraid you'd been detained

or worse, changed your mind

Hmm, with all else going on, this is clearly not the worst-case scenario, but I decide not to comment on that.

I'm just leaving my parents now,
accompanied by a chauffeur/bodyguard,
but I'll need your address

Again, my phone dings.

Chauffeur/bodyguard???

I text him back.

So much to tell you

And with that, Anders sends me his address.

See you in about 20 minutes

"There has been a change of plans. I need you to take me to Gåsgränd and Stora Nygatan in Gamla Stan," I give the driver the crossroads in Anders's neighborhood. "Do you know how to get there?" I ask.

"Well, this vehicle is equipped with the latest GPS, so that is not the problem, but I report to Herr Johan."

"Herr Johan, is it?" I say, it has been decades since anyone used formal titles here in Sweden, except perhaps in a courtroom. But times are changing with the neoconservatives in power, and people are reverting to old customs in their efforts to restore *Sweden for the real Swedes.* Just who is this man that my brother has entrusted my care to? I consider calling my brother and straightening this out once and for all but decide against it. I don't need the drama tonight, and Johan needs his sleep. Instead, I send Anders another text.

Change of plans
Can you meet me at my apartment?

The phone dings as he responds:

I'm on my way

"We will have to clarify some of this in the morning with Herr Johan. But let me be perfectly clear, you may work for my brother as he was the person who hired you, but neither my brother nor anyone else is my keeper. I make my own decisions about where I go and with whom. Now take me home."

"Just following orders, ma'am. Right away."

I bristle as he calls me ma'am. I can't say exactly why, but perhaps it is a throwback from another lifetime when I was always under the thumb of some man or an other and made to feel less than as I grew older and past my prime. Fuck him and fuck them all. Men fear powerful women, and that is who and what I am. I take a deep breath; I have more important things to think about now.

When we pull up to my building, another one of Johan's thugs is waiting outside the front door, looking like an attack dog just ready to tear someone's leg off. He nods to me, acknowledging my presence but does not speak. Is this some kind of squad of mercenaries, or thugs for hire? What if someone offers them more money than Johan is paying them? Will they change allegiances? A shiver runs down my spine as I contemplate my personal safety when Mother's words ring clearly in my head, *'Be Brave.'*

Anders is already waiting inside the lobby with my doorman, Dagvin. "Stay right there," Dagvin shakes a finger at Anders and speaks to him in a stern tone that I have never heard from this kindly man before. He takes me by the arm and ushers me into an alcove near the bank of elevators. "Ms. Saga, are you okay? What in the world is going on here?" He asks, barely able to keep the panic from his voice. He has been keeping up the tough-guy façade too long, and fear threatens to overtake him.

"It will be okay, Dagvin." I take his hand in mine and try to reassure him that I am not afraid. "Can you tell me what has happened?"

"Someone broke into your apartment last night. I don't know how they got past me. I was at my post all evening, except when I helped old Frau Gertrude in 17B bring in her groceries. I'm so sorry."

I remember the break-in at the Arctic Lodge. Was that yesterday or perhaps the day before? What else are these people looking for? "This is not your fault in any way; please do not burden yourself with this kind of thinking."

"Then the guy in the black coat and black glasses with that ski cap pulled down over his forehead shows up here, taking over and talking about 'securing the premises.'"

"He's a bodyguard hired by my brother. This is only temporary," I try to reassure Dagvin, but I'm afraid I'm not doing a very good job.

"Bodyguard?" he says, as his eyes become big as saucers. This is beyond the routine daily duties he typically encounters as a doorman. "Bodyguard? Are you in some kind of trouble, Ms. Saga?"

"This will all be over soon, Dagvin. Just think of the man in all black as a security officer, you know, like they have at the bank."

"What about that handsome young man who arrived just a few minutes ago? He says he is supposed to meet you here for some kind of business meeting. It's nine at night. Who has a business meeting in their apartment at nine on a Sunday night? I don't mean to get all up in your business, but what I can say is that you've lived in this building for almost ten years, and never has there been a day like today."

"Let me talk to my friend, Anders, and then if you would accompany us up to my apartment. I would appreciate it. I want to take a look at my apartment to see if anything is missing or see if I need to file a police report."

"What about the front door?" Dagvin asks. Clearly, he is afraid to abandon his post.

"We'll let the guy in black know that you will be stepping away for a few minutes. I'm sure he can watch the door."

When we step out of the alcove, Anders gives me a look that asks—what's going on? I raise my index finger to him, indicating I need another minute as I step through the front doors where two men in black, the security team, converse in hushed tones. At that moment, I decide it is wiser to leave Dagvin under the protection of the officer at the door and have the bodyguard/chauffeur, accompany Anders and me up to my apartment. I speak to both men and request their assistance, and simultaneously they agree. "Yes, ma'am."

Grrr.

Anders bends in to kiss me on the cheek then reaches over to help me with my suitcase.

"You are a sight for sore eyes," I say as I link my arm with his free arm, and he pulls me in close to his side.

"Looks like you've had an interesting week." He smiles and holds me with his gaze for just another moment.

"That would be one way to describe it."

We pass Dagvin, who is now sitting and staring at a bank of security monitors projecting black and white images of the entrances and exits, elevator interiors, as well as the shots from each of the hallways. He rises from his chair, intent on following us to the bank of elevators.

"I've had a change of plan, Dagvin. I think it would be better if you stay down here to keep an eye on the monitors for anything unusual. Would you do that, please?"

He looks visibly relieved, "Of course, Ms. Saga. You can count on me."

The elevator door closes behind us but does not move. The man dressed in black presses the elevator button marked *close door,* and a red light goes on, indicating the elevator is stopped and will not be going anywhere until the button is released. He extends his hand to shake mine, "I'm afraid we got off on the wrong foot. My name is Oskar, and this is Elias," he gestures to the man who flanks him on the right.

I take his hand to shake it, and a current of certainty runs through me, and I know—there is more to this story than he is sharing. "Tell me Oskar, do you and your compatriot have surnames?" My voice is icier than I intended but aptly reflects my apprehension.

"I think we'll stick with first names for the moment. I can tell you that my team and I have been brought in by your brother, Johan. I'm the guy who swept your car this morning for surveillance devices up at the Arctic Lodge, and then we followed you and your brother all the way back to Stockholm."

Big deal. As if this is all the reassurance I require.

"We are operating as Saint Michael's Security Agency."

"Clever, St. Michael the Archangel, the patron saint of paratroopers, police officers, and military personnel."

"How did you know that?" Oskar asks as he gives me a quizzical look.

"I read. I suppose you've heard that *a well-read woman is dangerous,* and I read a lot. What did you mean by *operating as?*"

Anders reaches over and squeezes my elbow. He has not seen this feisty side of me, and if I wasn't so angry and afraid, I might have found his loving gesture patronizing. "Look, I'm going to say this once, Oskar, or whoever you are, I don't like to be lied to, so you better start telling me the truth."

Anders tightens his grip and turns me towards him, so we are face to face, "I was put in touch with this man yesterday as I began investigating the international safety and security implications of Klaus Ek's nefarious business dealings," Anders says as he looks me in the eye. "It seems that Johan and I were coming at the problem from two different directions and ended up at the same place."

"Okay, you want the truth. Elias and I are part of the Swedish National Security Service and operate under the auspices of the Ministry of Justice."

"Oh," I take a deep breath as I consider the ramifications of pissing off gun-toting officers of a state-sanctioned national police organization. "I'm sorry, sir," I apologize. "Something just felt off, and given the lies I've been told by Klaus Ek, I don't know who to trust, and I feared I was being played and manipulated."

"It is quite alright; I haven't been totally honest with you. But in my defense, some people are much more comfortable being kept in the dark. I see now you are not one of them. Let me elaborate on our function. The Swedish National Security Service is responsible for counterespionage, counterterrorism, as well as protection of dignitaries and the constitution. We investigate crimes against national security, and it appears you and your brother have stumbled into a major one. We have had our eyes on Klaus Ek and his paramilitary brethren for quite some time," Oskar says as he releases the red button. The elevator begins to move upwards until the door opens onto the third-floor corridor leading to my apartment.

As I look down the hallway, I can see another security officer is stationed right outside my door.

"Someone has broken into your home and has rummaged through your things. We don't know what the person or people were after, or if anything is missing. We will need your help to determine that," Oskar says as the three of us make our way down the hall.

Wearing white cotton gloves, the other security agent stationed by the door turns the handle to allow us in.

"Rummaged through? You have to be fucking kidding me! This place has been ransacked!" I take a deep breath as I walk into my apartment. My bookcase has been emptied, and my favorite books are strewn about the room with pages bent and covers torn. My mattress has been turned over and split with a knife as if someone was looking for something inside, and my undergarments are sliced up and ruined. Even the vase holding the beautiful roses that Anders sent earlier this week has been upended, and the flowers lie wilted and dying on the pale woolen rug. A cold chill runs down my back. This feels personally threatening in some kind of obscure and sexual way.

I stand there in silence, just taking it all in, when Anders's voice, low and gentle and slow says, "Oh Saga, I'm just glad you were not here."

I try to muster up more bravery than I feel. "It's only stuff, and stuff can be replaced." Then I move toward my bedside stand. The hand-painted antique lamp shade lies shattered on the oak floor. I cautiously step over the shards of glass. The drawer to my bedside table stands open, and it is empty. I quickly scan the floor littered with broken glass, my lingerie, and treasured books. Where are my journals? They are not here. Trying to keep from crying, I say, "Whoever was here has taken my journals, my personal diaries, my dream logs."

The men look perplexed, and then one of the three asks, "Whatever for?"

"Father Brendan intends to use them against me," I whisper, as the tears begin to fall.

Anders puts his arm around me and holds me close, "Who?" he asks gently.

"Klaus Ek," I respond. "One and the same."

"She can't stay here tonight. It's not safe. This looks personal. They've taken her diaries and shredded her undergarments for God's sake. The security here has already been breached." Anders acts as if he has the authority to speak on my behalf, and in this moment, I am grateful. "Let me take her back to my apartment. Send your officers to my home, but we have to leave right now. We have work to do to prepare for tomorrow's meeting with members of the International Atomic Energy Agency and the Euro Foreign Affairs and Security Council."

The security officers turn their backs to Anders and me and whisper amongst themselves. A minute later, the man who calls himself Oskar says, "Get what you need, Saga. We will take you somewhere with Mr. Andersson so you can work and be safe tonight."

I find my overnight bag unlatched and discarded in the middle of my living room. Then I begin to pick through some of my clothing that lies in a heap on the closet floor. My mind is racing. Still, I take a deep breath as I try to decide what I will need to take with me. My navy suit for tomorrow's meeting and the gray one for the board meeting tomorrow night, two silk blouses, a nightgown, panties, stockings, and a bra. I shake out my clothing to be certain there isn't any residual broken glass hiding in the folds. I fold the garments as if they are the sacred remnants from another time, a time when I felt safe and secure. I grab my toiletries and add my cosmetic bag to my suitcase.

Walking out into the shambles of what was once my living room, the men whisper as they wait. I don't know what comes over me.

Perhaps after all that has happened, I am just on high alert. "This is my apartment, and this is my life. If you have something to say, I want you to say it to me directly and not speak of anything that concerns me behind my back. Do I make myself clear?"

The men are shamed into silence and nod their heads.

"I want to see some identification before I go anywhere with you," I say as I plant my feet in a wide stance and place my hands on my hips. I feel a bit like a fool. If they are not who they say they are, they could hurt me or take me captive without blinking an eye. They know this, too, as all three of them start to smile as they reach for their identification.

"Not you, Anders," I say as I shake my head.

"Glad to know you trust me. I was starting to worry," he says as he puts his wallet back in his pants pocket.

The other men pass me their Security Council IDs. Their faces match the photos on their identification. "They could be forgeries," I say.

"Saga, do you trust me?" Anders asks gently.

"I think so," I respond.

"I checked their identification, and while you were on your way over here. I called Johan to verify who they are. Oskar has already provided Johan the identification papers for him and his colleagues. They have already been run through a Mobile Identity Document Scanner before you even left the Arctic Lodge this morning. These men are who they say they are. They are highly respected security agents with the Swedish National Security Service."

"Oh, okay. Sorry." I say, feeling more than a little bit foolish for this last display of bravado.

"You have every right to be afraid and suspicious. You are embroiled in something eminently dangerous. It would be foolish not to exercise caution without ascertaining who we are and why we are here. However, it might have been wiser to ask us for some verification before you got in the car with us or led us to your residence and invited us into your home," Oskar says with a smile.

"Yeah, I was just thinking that, too," I say as I return their smiles. "Okay, let's get out of here."

We take the elevator back down to the lobby, where Dagvin sits minding the monitors. He stands as we approach, "I'm so sorry, Ms. Saga. Is there anything I can do?" he asks with great sincerity.

"No need to apologize, Dagvin. You have done nothing wrong." I take his hand in mine to reassure him. "Perhaps you could contact Ethel and Luis. They clean for many of us in the building and see if they could come by tomorrow and set things to rights."

"Absolutely."

"Just one minute, this is still officially a crime scene. Our investigators will be in later tonight to gather any additional evidence that might be necessary," Oskar says. Then he directs his comments to Dagvin. "They will let you know when they have finished, and it has been cleared for re-entry. I'm guessing you can safely schedule the cleaning for tomorrow afternoon."

"Yes, sir," Dagvin says.

"Please have them bag everything that is torn, ripped, or sullied. I may want to look through it before it's discarded."

"Yes, Ms. Saga."

"Dagvin, have you made copies of the security tapes that we spoke about?" Oskar says.

"Yes, sir, but there isn't much to see. It appears someone messed with the lens on the third-floor camera as all the images are out of focus. If the camera had been totally disabled, an alarm would have been set off. Whoever did this knew exactly what they were doing. Here is the log of everyone who signed in and out of the building yesterday and this morning, and there is nothing unusual here."

"Unless one of your residents was involved," Oskar proposes.

"I know these people. I can't believe that is possible," Dagvin objects.

"You'd be surprised what people will do for money," Oskar says. Horrified is more like it as I know he speaks the truth.

"I'll need a copy of all the films, including the films from the front door, the lobby, all the floors, all exits including the utility and maintenance areas."

"I can have them all for you in about an hour," he says, attempting to be as courteous and cooperative as possible.

"Elias will wait for them and keep an eye on things just in case our intruders decide to return." Oskar gives the orders, and Elias complies without discussion.

As we make our way to the waiting vehicles, I find I am thinking about Elias and his willingness to follow orders. And then there are Ek and his minions. Are they just following orders? Do they fear Ek and the repercussions of failing to do so? Or are they motivated to disregard what is right and choose what is wrong because they are greedy? What was it that Oskar just said? 'You'd be surprised what people will do for money.' Somewhere in the recesses of my brain, a quote from the American social and cultural critic Henry Louis Mencken resurfaces:

Morality is doing what's right, no matter what you're told.
Obedience is doing what you're told, no matter what's right.

Where does this thought come from? It must be something I read, and as I've already said once today, *a well-read woman is dangerous.* But, dangerous to whom? I fear I may be told to be obedient. There are times when obedience is expected, when really what is needed is morality. I must do what's right, no matter what is expected or what I am told.

CHAPTER 16

Anders opens the car door for me, and I climb in while he puts my suitcase and new computer bag in the trunk.

He drives, and the agents follow behind us. "Well, I must say I saw a side of you I had not seen before. What happened to the genteel sophisticate I was out with New Year's Eve?"

"Oh, her? She's a bore," I say, and Anders roars with laughter. "What can I say? I've been primal and feisty all my life. It's just not always called for. Let's say it's my secret weapon. If I use it all the time, then it wouldn't be a secret, would it?"

"I must say I'm a little intimidated," he says as he reaches for my hand.

"I can see how terrified you are," I say as I swat his hand away. Again, he laughs.

"From what I hear from Sigge Markus, it was this feisty version of you who showed up at the Lars Löfgren trial and brought Ulf Lang, that pompous ass, to his knees."

"Tell me, counselor, am I on trial? If so, I object. You're badgering the witness. I'm pleading self-defense, as well as excited utterance and any other cock 'n bull legalese that will get me off this hook."

Anders smiles, and I am glad he can see the humor in what we have just been through. A bit of laughter breaks the tension and is a welcome relief. "I'm glad to see you have it in you because I fear we are in for a fight against some pretty rough international junkyard dogs," Anders says as he reaches for my hand again. This time I let him hold it, and I'm glad he's on my side.

We cross the bridge onto the island of Gamla Stan and onto the cobbled streets lined with multicolored buildings from the seventeenth and eighteenth centuries. We turn the corner of Gåsgränd and Stora Nygatan. Anders pulls into the gated underground parking, and another black SUV pulls up directly behind us. "It's Oskar. He's been on my tail the whole way over here."

Anders puts his car in park, and in an instant, he is out of the car talking to Oskar as they execute a plan that they've concocted without any input from me.

Oskar makes certain the elevator from the parking deck into the apartment building has been secured. He raises his hand to Anders giving him an *all-clear* signal. Anders gets my things from the trunk before he comes around to the passenger side and opens my door.

"Pretty precious cargo," he says with a smile, and I can't decide if I want to punch him or kiss him. He escorts me to the waiting elevator, which takes us up to the only apartment on the fifth floor.

Oskar is standing outside the elevator as the doors open, "All clear," he says as he steps back in the elevator. "Call me if you need anything or see anything. I'll be downstairs."

I suppose this is supposed to make me feel better, but everything just feels awkward. This is the first time I've been to Anders's apartment. He has seen my undergarments all cut up and strewn about the floor, but he's never seen them on me. We have never been intimate or spent the night together, and now here I am with my suitcase packed like I'm going to a pajama party. Although things have been progressing between us, it wasn't supposed to be like this. "I could do with a little more romance and a little less intrigue."

"Doesn't it feel a little like one of those old James Bond movies from the late 1900s?"

"Oh please," I laugh, "If you think I am one of those empty-headed sex kittens, you are going to be sorely disappointed."

"No, you are a *lioness* if ever there was one. Just be gentle with me," he says with a laugh.

"Don't push your luck. Now be a gentleman and fix me a cup of tea while I run myself a bath."

"Whatever you say," he smiles. "The bathroom is down the hall. I think everything you need can be found in the cupboard."

"Thank you, I've been up since before dawn, and a hot bath will be delightful. Do you have a couple of hangers I might use so I don't look like a wrinkled mess in the morning?"

"Just leave your clothes on the bed in the guestroom, and I'll hang them up for you," he calls from down the hall.

While I'm still soaking in the tub, Anders knocks. "I have a nice terry robe for you. It's just outside the door when you're ready."

"The truth is I could stay here all night, but I'm afraid you'll find me under the water if I don't get out now." So, I force myself out of the tub and wrap myself in a soft plush towel before reaching my hand outside the door I find a soft white spa robe.

When I emerge from the bathroom, the small table in the dining room is set for two, and the room is bathed in golden candlelight. "I thought you might be hungry," he says.

There are two plates with truffle oil salmon and mushrooms and a beautiful green salad. "When did you have time to cook?" I ask.

"Well, I had everything already prepared before I got the call to meet you at your place." He pulls my chair out for me, and I take my seat.

"I'm afraid I'm not exactly dressed for dinner," I say as I look down at myself drowning in Anders's oversized robe.

"You look lovely. That robe never really suited me. I know you said you wanted tea, and I've made a pot, but are you sure you wouldn't rather have a glass of wine?"

"Sounds tempting, but I thought you said we had to prepare for the meeting tomorrow morning with members of the International Atomic Energy Agency and the Euro Foreign Affairs and Security Council."

"I know I said that, but that was just a ruse to get you out of there. I wanted to bring you home with me." Anders breaks into a large grin as he begins to fill my crystal wine glass with a chilled Chenin Blanc.

"Oh really..."

"I've been thinking about tomorrow's meeting. It will likely be an investigatory hearing, and no doubt, you will be under oath. I think *they* will have a lot of questions for you about what you know and what you saw. You just need to answer honestly. I think it will be best if you don't appear too well-rehearsed."

What he says makes sense to me.

"Oh, and one more unsolicited comment from your lawyer."

"Yes, and what might that be?"

"Perhaps you might try to tame the lioness, at least during the hearing."

"Oh her? You expect much of me." I say as I reach for my wine glass.

"So, let's just relax and have a little dinner. Skål," he says as he lifts his glass and clinks mine.

"Telling the truth will not be difficult, for I may be many things, but a liar is not one of them. As for relaxing, well, that may be easier said than done." I worry that what I know comes from so many different places. Some of it is from this world and some from other lifetimes. I just don't want to get confused and caught up in it all while being interrogated under oath.

He looks confused, and I fear I may have cracked open a door I would have just as soon have kept closed. "You look worried. Do you want to talk about this?" Anders asks as the playfulness he exuded earlier leaves his tone and mannerism.

Part of me wants to open myself up and let him see me for who I really am, but not right now. I feel too vulnerable, so I decide to keep my worries to myself. "Perhaps we should save this conversation until after dinner and just enjoy this lovely meal you've made." I take a bite of the truffle oiled salmon. "Mm, this is so good. All this and he cooks, too," I say, trying to lighten the mood again.

By the time we finish our meal, Anders suggests we finish our wine in front of the fire. "Do you mind if I ask you a question?" he asks.

"I suppose that depends on the question."

"You seemed so upset when you realized that whoever broke into your apartment took your journals. Can you tell me about that?"

"Oh, dear Lord, I write almost every day and have for years. I write about a wide range of things—my thoughts and feelings, and much that I'd rather keep to myself."

"Why do you think *they* might be interested in your personal journals?"

The silence sits between us as I try to decide just how much I want to divulge. At last, I say, "There is a fine line between being psychic and psychotic." Anders looks bewildered, and I struggle to explain, "I'm afraid Ek will use some of my writings to portray me as psychotic and unstable. He is the chairman of the board, and I fear he will argue to have me removed from my position based on allegations of mental incompetence. If they find me mentally unstable, there will be little I can do to protect the reindeer, the Sámi people, and the planet from their malfeasance."

"Whoa, whoa. Slow down a little bit, Saga. Do you mean to tell me you believe that you are psychic, and there is evidence of this in your journal entries?"

"Anders, I am a Seer, and I have been across many different lifetimes and incarnations. Even my name, Saga, means the Seer of the Long Story." Perhaps it is the wine, or maybe I just need to unburden myself from all that I am carrying, or maybe at long last I just need to stand strong in my own reality of how the world works and my place in it. For whatever reason, it isn't long before I am telling Anders about the knowings and my earnest belief that I have been reincarnated not once, but multiple times.

"Oh, Sophia, perhaps you do not know, but I have looked for you across so many lifetimes."

Did he just call me Sophia? The room spins a little, and I fear I am about to transition to another time. A wave of nausea comes over me, and I start to sweat as I try to figure out what he means by this. I will myself to stay grounded in this reality.

"Do you remember what I said to you when we first met?" he asks me as he reaches for my hand.

"Anders, we only met a few weeks ago at my parents' home during their Winter Solstice party." I try to stick to what I know.

"I think I said, 'I can't believe you're here.' In fact, I know that's what I said. I have played those ill-chosen words over and over in my head and wished I had said something a little less baffling. I've wished I'd said something more eloquent and captivating, and at the very least, a lot less crazy."

"What did you mean by that?"

"You don't know, do you?" he says. I can hear the disappointment in his voice, but it is more than that. As we sit before the fire, and he holds my hands, I can feel his disappointment as if it is being transmitted through his hands and into my very being. I don't know how else to describe it, but it freaks me out. I pull my hands from his and fold mine in my lap.

"I've frightened you, and I hadn't meant to. I'm not sure how to begin. Perhaps it suffices to say that I, too, believe in reincarnation, and I believe we have known each other in other lifetimes."

"Really?" Now I reach for his hand as I try to pick up a clue or vibration from him that might help me determine who he is and where over the course of humankind our lives may have crossed.

We sit in the firelight silently holding hands as I look upon his face to see if I can figure this out. There is that same déjà vu feeling I've had before, but the images of where and when still elude me. "Can you help me out?" I ask, as I gently squeeze his hand three times. This gesture represents the words I Love You. In some ways, this feels more than a little premature given the length of time Anders and I have known each other, and yet I know it to be true. I love this man from somewhere in the depth of my soul and very being. He squeezes my hand back three times. Each squeeze is slow and deliberate. Does he know what this means?

"Perhaps love is just love, and it takes different shapes and forms in different relationships in different lifetimes."

"I believe that to be true." I think about my brother, Johan. I am convinced he was once my beloved partner, Dev, when we lived other lives. We love each other now, but differently from how we loved each other then. Dev abandoned me long ago in another life, and now Johan stands with me, steadfast and true. It isn't long before I'm lost in another daydream from another lifetime.

"Sophia," gently and softly, Anders calls me back from the deep dark recesses of my mind. He calls me by another name, a name I was once called. "Sophia. Ophelia. Fee," and lastly, "Saga."

And then I know.

"You were once my father, a scribe who was upright and honest, and the Cardinal had you burned at the stake for refusing to alter the sacred scriptures."

"Yes, and you were my daughter, Sophia. When you were just a young girl, you witnessed my execution at the hands of the powerful."

The tears run down my face.

"I was also your husband back in a land we called Armenia. The Young Turks and the Ottoman troops marched on our village, and all the men, including me, were taken out, shot, and buried in a mass grave. I was unable to protect you then. My death left you as a widow and a single mother to endure unspeakable atrocities. I am so sorry, my beloved Ophelia."

"Oh, my God, how I grieved for you. And now here we are again, given another chance at love and happiness."

Overwhelmed with the situation we find ourselves in, Anders wraps me in his arms and holds me.

"How is it that I could not see you before now?" I ask, trembling. "When did you know it was me?"

"The first time I saw you standing beside your mother in the foyer of Damgården. I would know you anywhere, for I have been searching for you across many lifetimes. I would have told you earlier, but I didn't want to frighten you. You see, I didn't know you had the gift this time. I didn't know you were a Seer."

I hold his hands and look into his eyes to see if I can see. In another lifetime, my beloved's eyes were as dark as night, and now they are the palest blue, and still I know he speaks the truth. These are the eyes of my long-lost love. "We have unfinished business, and somehow the Universe, the Creator, or God, take your pick, has blessed me with another chance and another life with you."

Before I can say anything else, Anders takes my hand and leads me to his bedroom. The bed has already been turned down, and the sheets smell lightly of roses in summer. Tonight, enveloped in love and the sweetness of our reunion, all memories of past traumas are eased. Here is the man I have been seeking and the answer to my heart's longing.

I have no idea how much time has elapsed, but beyond the bedroom, the last of the embers still glow in the fireplace. Feeling safe and greatly loved, I fall into a deep and dreamless sleep.

I wake to the smell of coffee and bacon. It takes me just a moment to remember where I am. Ah yes, sweet memories of last night linger as I twist my long hair up in a knot and wrap the flannel sheets around my nakedness as the only thing I wear is the golden necklace of the Yggdrasil. Fingering the medallion, I say a prayer of gratitude for the intertwining of lives and second and third chances to right the wrongs and live in the glory of all this life has to offer. So much has come full circle.

As I lie there with my head cushioned up against the pillow, Anders comes into the bedroom carrying a cup of coffee. He places the coffee cup on the bedside table then leans in to kiss me, and I think for a moment that maybe we will make love again this morning. He sighs deeply and groans reluctantly as he frees himself from my embrace. "As enticing as you are lying naked in my bed, today is an important day for you. I'm afraid we will have to wait."

I smile as he reaches for his robe from where it lies on the floor and hands it to me. I vaguely remember being freed from it last night. We sit for a moment on the edge of the bed, as he passes me a cup of coffee with cream and sugar.

"Just the way I drink it. How did you know?"

"It is interesting how some small things stick in our memories, and other seemingly more important things elude us."

"Don't be so quick to dismiss this, for how I like my coffee is not just any small matter," I say with a smile, then take a long draw from the cup. "What time is it?" I ask, as I have no idea where my phone is.

"Just a little before seven. We should probably leave here in an hour just in case the traffic is heavy this morning. Will an hour give you enough time?"

"Yes, do you want to shower first, or should I?"

"I've already showered, so go ahead, and I'll finish getting breakfast together."

Once I've showered, washed and dried my hair, I am delighted to find that not only did Anders hang my clothes, but they have also been steam pressed and are wrinkle-free. What a kind and thoughtful man.

Walking into the kitchen, I see that Anders has also dressed. He wears a dark gray suit and a white shirt. "Don't you look dapper," I say with a smile.

"Not that you'll see my natty ensemble for very long as it will be all covered up with my robe once the proceedings begin."

"Oh, yes, silly me. I keep forgetting you're my attorney."

"Yes, I fear I may have crossed a line somewhere late last evening, but today I'm all business as we attempt to get a dangerous predicament safely resolved. Today I am your attorney, and you are my client, and I will protect you and your interests as best as I am able."

"I trust you completely," I say as I take my seat at the kitchen counter where Anders has set out a light breakfast of toasted bread, bacon, and cucumber and a glass of green juice.

"So much has changed in the ten years I've been practicing law. Not long ago, the advocates and the judiciary all went to court dressed in civilian clothes. The robes are a throwback to another time and perhaps another place. Ever since the Swedish Democrats have taken control of the Parliament, our country has become more and more conservative with a heavy emphasis on enforcing the law and maintaining order rather than on justice."

"Hmm, I wonder what you would look like in one of those long white wigs the British advocates and judiciary wear."

"Let's hope we never have to find out."

And with that, there is a knock on the door. Looking through the peephole, Anders announces, "It's Oskar. I invited him up for a bite to eat as he has been up all night on duty." He opens the door to let Oskar in. "Good morning. Cup of coffee?"

"Yes, thank you. Just black," he says, as he steps into Anders's apartment.

"Quiet night?" I ask.

I nod. "Just the way I like it."

"Can I fix you something to eat?" Anders asks.

"If you have any more of that bacon and toast, I'll just take it with me. The car is warmed up and ready to go. I think we should be on our way."

And with that, Anders holds my coat for me, and then I grab my new computer bag and my purse. "Okay, let's do this," I say, and we all head down to the waiting car.

CHAPTER 17

Anders and I sit in the backseat, and he holds my hand in silence as Oskar drives us over the Vasabron Bridge. I hadn't realized how close Anders lives to the Government Offices of Sweden, where we will meet with representatives from the International Atomic Energy Agency and the Euro Foreign Affairs and Security Council.

Oskar pulls into the circular drive, and we get out of the car. The sky is still dark, but the Government Center is already abuzz with activity. The drive over was short, but the security check is comprehensive and consumes nearly all the time we had allotted as we walk through metal detectors and have our bags and documents checked. Anders's papers are in order, as he has been here often in his legal capacity.

"I need to get my robe on," he says as he gives me a wink. "I'll see you inside." As he departs, I am directed to a humorless man in uniform who puts me through a lengthy interrogation as to who I am and why I am here. When at last I am released, it is nearly nine. Then I am shown to a windowless meeting room and told to wait.

There is a large round table, light pine and contemporary. Legal pads and pens have been placed on the table in front of each of the seats. I choose a chair closest to the door. I count the chairs; there are twenty. I can't help hoping that I haven't selected a seat reserved for some high-ranking bureaucrat or dignitary. I think of the Biblical parable of the lowest seat. Still, it is difficult to determine which chair is the seat of humility when the table is circular. I cross and uncross my legs, shifting in my chair, trying to get comfortable, but the chair is not the problem. My unease is internal.

At last, the door opens, and a uniformed officer of the Swedish Police Authority lets Anders enter, and I breathe a sigh of relief. Anders asks the officer, "Can I assume this room has been thoroughly checked for surveillance equipment?"

"Yes sir, a member of the Special Investigations Unit just left. The room has been secured, and only those people who have passed through all checkpoints will be admitted."

It is only at this moment that I realize how frightened I am. The last thing I can afford to do today is to slip away from this reality. I search my brain for a grounding mantra, but nothing comes to mind. Anders takes the chair beside me and places a hand on my shoulder as I whisper, "I just want to get this over with."

"Why don't you just close your eyes for a moment and breathe. You know how, both slowly and deeply."

I do as he suggests while he methodically unloads the contents of his briefcase, placing each item carefully on the table in front of him. Focusing on my breathing, my anxiety begins to lessen, and I start to feel a little more in control until I hear the door behind me open and a parade of people all clad in black robes walk in single file until one person is standing behind each of the chairs. Anders touches my shoulder as he stands, and I know he wants me to do the same.

An elderly gentleman with white hair and benevolent blue eyes takes the seat directly across from me and smiles in my direction. He appears to be in charge as he says to me and all the others in the room, "Please, would everyone kindly take their seat. We have much that needs to be discussed today."

I know that looks can be deceiving, but I sense I have at least one ally in the room, other than Anders. As I look around the table, others meet my gaze with a scowl, and I fear their disapproval before we have even begun.

Anders stands, "Good Morning, Your Honor." The elderly gentleman nods in acknowledgment. "My name is Anders Andersson, counsel to my client Saga Svensson, Chief Executive Officer of Lundstrom Enterprises." Anders extends his right hand towards me as if there might be any question about who I am. Again, the older man nods.

"Please sit down, Mr. Andersson. There will not be a formal hearing today, but rather what I hope can be a comprehensive inquiry where *we*," he spreads his arms wide to indicate all of the robed men and women in the room, "can determine what Ms. Svensson has seen and what she knows. What has been alleged, if in fact true, is of utmost importance and requires our thorough investigation so we can collectively decide how best to deal with this situation." Now there appears to be a general agreement as people around the table nod their heads. I suspect the format of this inquiry has already been discussed at length in meetings neither Anders nor I have been privy to. "Given that Swedish national law is subject to European law as well as international law, we will be asking Ms. Svensson to swear under oath that the testimony that she will give is the truth."

This time it is Anders and I who nod our heads indicating our agreement.

"Before we begin, I would like to ask the members of this panel to introduce themselves and indicate the organizations that they are representing." The elderly gentleman is clearly in charge, and so he begins, "I am Gunther Holm, Chief Legal Counsel for the European Security Agency. As previously decided, I will assume the responsibility to chair this morning's proceedings. You should know I am a by-the-book fellow, and I assume this role as chair, not to be the judge or decide the outcome of these proceedings, but rather as a presiding officer enforcing procedure and maintaining the dignity of the inquiry." Then the person to his right introduces himself by name and title, then indicates he represents the International Atomic Energy Organization, and the next woman follows suit. She is from Euro Foreign Affairs. Moving around the table, each person offers their name, title, and the name of the organization they represent. This illustrious delegation encompasses the gamut of Swedish, European, and International atomic and security organizations.

The men outnumber the women about three to one. There are fifteen men, including Anders and only five women, including me. It is still a man's world; nobody can tell me differently. I come from a long line of strong women, and I vow not to let this old boys' club intimidate me.

Once the introductions are complete, Herr Gunther Holm, the chair of this panel instructs his colleagues, "Let me be clear, although this is not a trial and simply an inquiry, we will be operating under a basic set of rules that all members of this panel must follow in compliance with ethical standards that have been agreed upon by international courts of law. A basic rule is that members of this panel must decide the validity of this case only on the evidence presented today in this room. You must not communicate with anyone, including friends and family members, about this case, the people and places involved, or your service on this panel. You must not disclose your thoughts about this case until all the testimony has been heard, only then will we decide how to proceed. This will be done collectively and without outside interference.

"I want to stress that this rule means you must not use electronic devices or cell phones to communicate about this case, including tweeting, texting, blogging, e-mailing, posting information on a website or chat room, or any other means at all. Do not send or accept any messages to or from anyone about this case or your panel service. In addition, your cell phone, and all other electronic devices must be turned completely off while you are in this room.

"You must not do any research or look up words, names, maps, or anything else that may have anything to do with this case. This includes reading newspapers, watching television, or using a computer, cell phone, the internet, any electronic device, or any other means at all, to get information related to this case or the people and places involved in this case. These agreements apply whether you are here in Government Center, at home, or anywhere else.

"All of us are depending on you to follow these rules so there will be a fair and lawful resolution to this case. Unlike questions that you may be allowed to ask in court, which will be answered in court in the presence of the judge and the parties, if you investigate, research, or make inquiries on your own outside of the courtroom, there would be no way to assure they are proper and relevant to the case. The parties likewise have no opportunity to dispute the accuracy of what you find or to provide rebuttal evidence to it. That is contrary to our judicial system. Any panel member who violates these restrictions jeopardizes the fairness of these proceedings. If you violate these rules, you may be held in contempt and face sanctions, such as serving time in jail, paying a fine, or both. If you become aware of any violation of these instructions or any other instruction I give in this case, you must inform me."

The members of the panel raise their right hands and vow to abide by the instructions they have just been given.

Before I can testify, I, too, am sworn in.

Anders starts by asking me to identify myself by name and position in the company. He starts with the easy questions, but that doesn't last for long. When he asks how long I have been in my current position and how it has come to pass that I hold the position of chief executive officer in a multinational corporation, some of those around the table begin feverishly taking notes, while others signal the chair that they too would like to speak.

The litany of questions that follows seems endless as we spend the first hour discussing how my family gained access to the land and how my maternal ancestors decided to distribute the family assets and accumulated wealth based on matrilineal inheritance.

I can't help but wonder had everything been passed from father to son if anyone would have batted an eye, or just let it go.

I answer their questions the best I can, but it is easy to see some of the conservative older men are getting incensed at the very notion of wealth, position, and power being aggregated amongst the women of my family.

My irritation with this line of questioning has been growing all morning, even the few women who are in the room seem angry they had to work for their power and position, and mine was simply handed to me. Jealousy knows no gender.

The woman sitting two seats away from me writes the word *nepotism* in large letters across the top of her notepad. My eyes leave the notepad and come to rest on her face. There is something familiar about her, and a rush of fear carried from past betrayals threatens to overpower me. But who is she? How do I know her?

It is this woman who finally crosses a line as she glowers at me. "How do you justify your wealth and position when you've never had to work for anything? Don't you think years and years of this matrilineal nepotism puts Lundstrom Enterprises and all of its employees at risk for financial ruin?"

Whoa, what the hell was that? This woman is coming at me like a moth to a flame. Is she drawn to the light, or is this something personal? It feels personal. I take a deep breath and begin slowly calling on every bit of self-control I can muster from somewhere deep within my being. "I will be the first to admit, I hit the natal lottery. Perhaps, I was born under a lucky star. I have a wonderful family, and I am grateful for the multitude of blessings I have because of the fortunate circumstances of my birth. Had I not been born into the Lundstrom family, it is indeed doubtful that I would be the CEO of Lundstrom Enterprises. But I don't have to justify my wealth or position to you or anyone else. My family and our business have prospered under a policy of matrilineal inheritance for the past four centuries. Lundstrom Enterprises is a multinational organization that relies on the decision-making capability of many people to be good stewards of the land and keep the business both honest and profitable. I can assure you, decisions are not made unilaterally, and I will not be running our family business into bankruptcy. Thank you for your concern. Lastly, no one is enslaving our workforce. Every person we employ works for us because they choose to, and in return, we compensate them fairly for the work they do. Internal evaluations indicate that our retention rate is high, and so is employee job satisfaction. People work for us because we are a good and fair employer. How dare you imply otherwise." I stop for a moment to breathe and regain a modicum of composure before continuing.

Anders leans in and whispers, "Do you think you might try and tame the *lioness*?"

"Oh, her. Sorry, I'll try," I whisper back to my beloved.

Then turning back to the panel, I take a moment and try to wrap this up, "Forgive me, but I thought we were here to discuss the illegal mining of uranium on property owned by Lundstrom Enterprises and the illegal sale of what may be weapons-grade uranium across international borders by the chairman of our board, and thus, the violation of the international atomic energy agreements endangers all of us should this uranium end up in the wrong hands. Now, you may not agree with how my family has decided to run our business, but that is not what is up for discussion here. Please excuse the expression, but don't we have much bigger fish to fry?"

Anders speaks and directs his question to the chairman, "Shall we move on?"

"Indeed, Herr Andersson. I am in complete agreement. Let us leave this line of questioning behind and return to the reason we are here. Ms. Svensson, would you please tell us what you know and what you believe to be the truth in this matter. And if the delegates to the panel would kindly hold your questions until she has finished, then maybe we can make an informed decision and do what we came here to do."

Anders gives me a great deal of latitude to discuss all that has happened in the last week. I talk about my new position and the board of directors meeting that is scheduled for this evening at seven and how the first item on the agenda is the Sámi land dispute. My anxiety begins to dissipate as I start to find my pace and describe the trip to the Arctic Circle with my brother, Johan. "The purpose of the visit was to meet with the Sámi elders to see if we could get a better understanding of what could be lost if we were to mine for *gold* in the migratory path of the reindeer."

Just as I am about to talk about our trip out to see the mine, the same woman who questioned me earlier interrupts me. "Do you really expect us to believe that you had no idea the mine was already in operation and that they were not mining gold but were mining weapons-grade uranium?"

The intonation of this woman's voice takes me back to another time. Her skin is very fair and flawless. It is almost luminous, but there is something in her dark, shifty eyes that makes me think I know her. I didn't catch her name when introductions were made, but I believe in another lifetime she may have been my nemesis when her name was Tova. My stomach clenches as I remember how she manipulated me and ultimately betrayed me. If she is who I think she is, then I have good reason to be wary of her motives. What does she want from me now? To whom has she sold her allegiance this time? I cannot help but be suspicious of her. Perhaps this is the reason for my knowings.

Anders speaks up on my behalf. "I object to this line of questioning. Do not question my client's integrity. Ms. Svensson is under oath and is here voluntarily of her own free will."

"It's just all seems a little preposterous and more than a little hard to believe," she says as she tosses her long, dark hair and then rolls her eyes as if this is the theater and she is performing for the others in the room. "Perhaps she's known of this all along and is only here now seeking revenge because they cut her out of the deal—"

"Ms. Pryvid," the chairman interrupts her before she can go on, "I caution you to avoid speaking in this manner and using language not conducive to civil discourse." His words and his tone leave little doubt he is rapidly losing patience. "I ask the members of this panel to please refrain from offering any commentary whatsoever. If you are unable to do so, I will ask the Sergeant-at-Arms to remove you from these proceedings."

With that, Anders decides to take charge of the inquiry, asking me questions about my visit to the mine. His questions relate to the location, date, and time of our visit, who was with me, how we gained access, and the size and scope of the mine.

There is some dissension in the room, and one does not need to be psychic to know it. One of the men raises his hand to be recognized. He directs his question to me, "You do understand, young lady, every one of us in this room is here because it is our individual and collective responsibility to monitor anything and everything related to the mining, sale, and distribution of uranium and atomic energy. We have built our entire careers on assuring the non-proliferation of nuclear weapons and keeping the peace. It is more than a little bit offensive for you to imply we have been asleep at the switch, and something like this has happened on our watch. Now I may not be any more enamored with the politics of the right-wing Swedish Democrats than you are, but to imply one of their party leaders is involved in something so evil and nefarious without our knowledge is nothing short of egregious and highly offensive to our integrity on so many levels." His colleagues murmur their collective assent.

I feel so disheartened until Anders stands and addresses his comment to Chairman Gunther Holm, "I'd like to have this entire set of eight by ten photographs, which were taken at the site of the mine, admitted into evidence." He passes a sealed document envelope around the table to the chairman.

Herr Holm opens the envelope and removes the photographs one by one, turning each one over face down on the table in front of him after he has looked at it. The rosy color drains from his face. "Did you bring copies of these photographs for the other members of the panel, Herr Andersson?"

"Yes, sir."

"Please distribute the envelopes to the members of this panel."

Anders passes half the sealed envelopes to his left, and I pass the other half to my right until everyone has a complete set of the photos, including the pictures of cargo containers being loaded for transport at the shipping facility. But it is the enlargement of the shipping labels that need no explanation. These people are knowledgeable about the issues at hand. Audible gasps are heard around the room for these people now know what I only suspected. This is indeed uranium, and it is being shipped out to the Port of Kaliningrad in Russia and then will be transported to Rosatom, the Russian State Atomic Energy Corporation, in Almaty, Kazakhstan, which is in gross violation of the Nuclear Non-Proliferation Treaty.

Once the photographs are distributed, the tenor and mood of the meeting changes. There is something about seeing the scale of the operation that strikes fear in their hearts.

One by one, we go through the photographs, and I explain where they were taken and what we are looking at.

Many of the people are feverishly taking notes; the collective anxiety in the room is rapidly rising. Others begin gathering their things together as if they have seen all they need to see and have somewhere else they need to be. Immediately.

A tall blond man from Euro Foreign Affairs raises his hand to be recognized, "I move that we adjourn and table any further discussion until another meeting can be scheduled."

Someone else seconds it.

"Discussion?" the chair asks.

The dark-haired woman who gave me a hard time earlier in the morning raises her hand to be recognized. "Before we break into an all-out panic, I want to know if anyone has determined if what is being mined is indeed uranium, and secondly, if anyone has verified the authenticity of the photographs."

Without waiting to be recognized, another man says, "Good God, woman! Do you really think we can afford the luxury of doubt when the downside of failing to act puts the entire planet at risk for destruction?"

"I have the floor," she raises her voice angrily, "and I have not yielded it. I ask Ms. Svensson again, how do you know this is uranium and not any other raw material that is being dug out of the earth and being transported legally?"

"I do not know for certain," I say as calmly as I am able. "The reason I suspect this is not iron ore, copper or gold, as I had been led to believe is because the type of mine that has been dug is consistent with photographs I have seen of how uranium is extracted from the earth and secondly, I met with two of the Sámi men who work at the mine. They, along with other miners, are already exhibiting symptoms of radiation poisoning."

"Excuse me, but are you also a doctor?" she says with a snarl as her dark eyes flash with anger.

"No, ma'am."

The man who made the motion to table this meeting until after lunch stands, "Herr Holm, there is a motion on the floor and said motion has been seconded. I would like to call the vote."

The chairman stands, "Will everyone please return to your seats? With all due respect, sir, given the impact of Ms. Svensson's testimony and the supporting photographic evidence, I understand everyone's need to immediately attend to the potentially disastrous ramifications should we not intercede. However, when we entered this morning, we all took an oath not to communicate the findings of this investigation with anyone until we as a panel had a unified and agreed-upon plan. This is of the utmost importance. We do not want to inadvertently create widespread pandemonium. And I fear that is exactly what would happen if word of this were leaked."

The room is filled with an uneasy feeling. Nearly everyone looks as if they are on tenterhooks as they hold this information about the very real threat of nuclear proliferation while struggling with the ethical dilemma they now find themselves in given the solemn oath they made this morning. And Herr Gunther Holm has no intention of releasing them from this moral obligation.

"Will the Sergeant-at-Arms please stand guard. No one is to leave this room without my express permission. Anyone who attempts to leave will be taken directly into custody."

I can see why this guy was put in charge; he's not fooling around.

Everyone settles back into their seats, and the room goes quiet, and even from across the room, I hear the Sergeant-at-Arms bolt the door.

Once the lock has been thrown, Herr Holm continues, "I would like to ask our esteemed colleague from Euro Foreign Affairs to withdraw his motion to adjourn." Then he turns to address the tall blond man directly as he explains his rationale for the request, "If you would be so kind as to do so, then we could go into closed session to discuss the evidence, Ms. Svensson's testimony, and collectively develop a comprehensive plan delineating our best course of action before we let the worldwide community know what is happening."

Another man calls out, "I withdraw my second."

The man from Euro Foreign Affairs says, "Given the motion has not yet been formally stated by the chair, I believe I can withdraw without violating procedure. Therefore, I move to withdraw the said motion to adjourn."

The panel members chat quietly to the people sitting next to them as they try to recall the specifics of Robert's Rules of Order. Ms. Pryvid, the woman who has been harassing me all morning, smirks, exuding confidence as if somehow this course of action plays right into her hands. Again, I wonder what her agenda is and how she came to be seated on this panel. Minutes hang like hours as members of the panel sit around the table, attempting to size one another up. What had looked like a cohesive group of legal scholars has disintegrated into a suspicious gathering, where people are questioning one another's motives and allegiances. I don't know how I know this, but I do.

When at long last, an older woman, with a long gray braid and gnarled, arthritic hands, leans heavily upon her cane as she stands to speak. "I move we dismiss Ms. Svensson and her wise counsel with our profound gratitude, after which I move that the entire panel be sequestered in a closed session and that someone sees to ordering us some lunch."

Someone calls out a second.

The older woman returns to her seat, as I hear her muttering to those seated around her, "We might as well get on with this. I don't think we will be going anywhere anytime soon."

The chairman stands and repeats the motion as required by Robert's Rules of Order. "It has been moved and seconded that we dismiss Ms. Saga Svensson and her legal counsel, Herr Anders Andersson. Once dismissed, this entire panel will be sequestered while we go into closed session to discuss what we have heard this morning and attempt to come up with a plan as to how to proceed. And of course, lunch will be forthcoming. Discussion?"

Two hands go up simultaneously, one from the cantankerous woman, I believe is Tova Nielsen from my past, and the other from a man who appears anxious to get to some resolution. Herr Holms looks first to the agitated man and nods in his direction.

"I call the question."

It is seconded almost immediately.

Ms. Pryvid gets to her feet, shouting, "Point of order, point of order!"

Gunther Holm is clearly irritated with this woman, and I feel his pain, "The question has been called and seconded. All in favor."

Nearly all the hands go up, while in unison, they call, "Aye."

"Opposed."

Two people raise their hands, shouting, "Nay." Their frustration and anger are evident in their tone.

"The Ayes have it, and the motion carries."

Ms. Pryvid stands and speaks directly to me without being recognized, "I have many more questions for Ms. Saga Svensson. So much has been left unanswered. But you will answer for this, Missy!" She spits the words at me.

"Excuse me, but are you threatening me?" I ask.

"Ms. Pryvid, I think I was perfectly clear about the need for civil discourse and the importance of maintaining a sense of decorum,"

Herr Holm says as he stands. "This is three times today that I have had to speak with you about the aggressive nature of your verbal attacks on Ms. Svensson." Then he nods to the Sergeant-at-Arms, who stands guard at the door, "Please remove Ms. Pryvid and have her taken into custody."

She yells and screams at me, as she is being restrained. "You have crossed the wrong people again, and there will be consequences for your actions. Oh, dear little Mizfee, how is it that you just don't seem to learn?"

Given the strength of her accent, the word sounds like *mizfee*, unrecognizable to most. But I know what she said. She just referred to me as Miss Fee. I fold my hands in prayer and ask for God's protection. Across other lifetimes, I have been known as Fee. I now know for certain this screaming woman who threatens me was Tova when I was Fiona. She was also Wafa when I embodied Ophelia in the days of the Armenian diaspora. Anders reaches over and covers my folded hands with his own, adding his prayers to mine.

Before she is led from the room, Herr Holm gives one more instruction to the Sergeant-at-Arms. "She needs to be placed in isolation, so none of the information from this meeting is leaked."

The other man who voted against the motion opens his mouth to object, but closes it again, thinking the better of inflaming the situation any further.

"I'm sorry, Ms. Svensson. Are you all right?" Herr Holm asks, his concern for my well-being is filled with compassion.

I nod my head before asking, "What did you say her name is?"

"Her name is Radmila Pryvid. She serves on the International Atomic Energy Agency as a representative of the conservative Right Alliance Party which is now in power in Belarus."

"I see," I reply, but I really don't have an idea how this might be relevant.

"Do you know her?" he asks.

I pause for a moment before answering. "I believe she has mistaken me for someone else." I am under oath, so I respond truthfully, even if my response does not answer the question asked. This seems to satisfy him.

"Ms. Svensson, I must say, given everything that has happened today, I have concerns for your safety."

Anders speaks on my behalf. "We have already hired personal protection for Ms. Svensson and her family until there is a satisfactory resolution of the crisis at hand."

"I'm glad to hear that. Please let me know if there is anything I can do to be of assistance. I think you both know how absolutely important it is that this information you have shared with us is held in the strictest secrecy. It is in the interest of international safety and security."

I think about tonight's board meeting, which is now just hours away. Anders must be having the same concerns as we exchange glances.

"Is it possible, Herr Holm, that we might have a word with you in private?" I ask.

The panel begins to stir, and it is obvious to all that they are not in favor of this idea.

Anders speaks up before anyone can formally object, "A sidebar, if you will."

This bit of legalese the panel understands.

Herr Holm nods. "Why don't the rest of you have your lunch." He must have hit a button under the table near his seat as almost simultaneously, there is a knock on the door, and a man enters pushing a cart filled with sandwiches, coffee, and cold drinks. "Now, if you would meet me in chambers, we can discuss your concerns."

Both Anders and I stand and follow the chairman into the study, and then he closes the door behind us.

"I have a board meeting scheduled tonight at seven."

"Yes, you mentioned that earlier today in your testimony."

"The first item on tonight's agenda is the Sámi land dispute. I had hoped to expose and discuss with the other members of the board the building of the mine, the lies, and deception and specifically our Chairman Klaus Ek's role in this nefarious scheme."

"If I may offer a bit of unsolicited advice, Ms. Svensson."

"Please call me Saga."

"As you wish, Saga. I think you should have plenty of evidence of unethical business practices without ever exposing the fact they are mining uranium and shipping it into countries in flagrant violation of international law. These are extremely dangerous people you would be crossing. I fear if you were to do so, Klaus Ek would not be the only person you would need to be afraid of."

"What you say makes sense."

"Then will you agree to abide by the oath to not speak of the uranium, the radiation sickness, or the shipping and transport until we can settle this crisis diplomatically?"

"Yes, sir. You have my word."

"Who else already knows of this?"

"Just Anders, my brother, my parents, members of the Swedish Security Services, and some of the Sámi people living up near the mine, and then there are those Klaus Ek may have in his inner circle." This list seems pretty long, pretty damn long. Ensuring silence and secrecy seems nearly impossible.

"Well, there is not much we can do about those people. However, please speak confidentially to your family, friends, and close associates and ask them to keep silent and let them know we will be working towards a diplomatic solution."

"You have my word," I assure him as I agree to his request. But I can't help but wonder how long it may take to come to a diplomatic solution, particularly if the uranium is ready to be shipped.

"We should go," Anders says to Herr Holm. "You have important business to attend to, and so does Saga."

"Thank you both again," Gunther Holm says, extending his hand to shake first mine and then Anders. He leads us back into the main chamber, where the panel has been reseated around the table having lunch.

Herr Holm walks us to the door and indicates the Sergeant-at-Arms can allow us to leave.

Anders puts his hand around my back and says, "Let's go get something to eat."

CHAPTER 18

Oskar is parked in the special lot for security officers. He must see us as soon as we exit the building, for he pulls up in the circular driveway almost immediately. Before we can even mention going to get some food, he says, "I've taken the liberty of ordering lunch. It has already been delivered to your home, Herr Andersson."

"Sounds good to me," I say. "I wouldn't mind eating and then maybe having a short nap before the board meeting."

"Perfect," Anders says, "and thank you, Oskar."

Oskar drops us off outside the door, where another of the Swedish Security agents waits to escort us upstairs to Anders's apartment.

Someone has lit the fire in the fireplace, and the dining table is laden with a colorful variety of food for our lunch. The room feels cozy and warm as the last of the daylight fades from the winter sky. "Would you like to freshen up before we eat?" Anders asks.

"Indeed, I would. I like to get out of this suit and into something warm and comfortable, but I'm afraid in my haste last night I didn't bring anything with me."

"I'm afraid all I can offer is an old cotton sweatshirt and a pair of sweatpants. The good news is they are just back from the laundry."

"Oh, that sounds delightful, if you're sure you don't mind."

"I don't mind at all, but no doubt you will be swimming in them." Anders is well over six feet, and although not in the least bit heavy, he is muscular and built like a Viking of old.

"I'll lay them out for you on the bed," he says as I head off to the washroom.

Once I've changed into something comfy, I find Anders is waiting for me at the table. "You must be starving," he says. "I know I am."

"A little," I admit. "It's been a stressful morning, and no doubt tonight will not prove to be any less so."

He pours us both a cup of hot tea, and the fragrance of cinnamon and cardamom fills the room. I wrap my hands around the mug while waiting for it to be cool enough to drink. In the meantime, Anders fills our plates with a variety of salads, a generous slice of gravlax, and dark bread.

Anders eats with gusto while I pick at my food until he asks, "So who was she?"

I know who he means, as I've played the scenes from this morning's meeting over and over in my head. Still, I ask, "Radmila Pryvid, the representative of the conservative Right Alliance Party of Belarus?"

"Yeah, her."

"Well, let's just say you know as much about her as I do, at least in this lifetime."

"Oh, *in this lifetime*, those appear to be the operative words." Anders turns his hands up towards the ceiling, fully expecting me to fill in the gaps in an old convoluted story.

Fearful of divulging too much and reliving the devastating horror of this woman's actions, I close my eyes and ask God to be with me. I take a deep breath, attempting to ground myself in the here and now. "Most recently, I have known her as Tova. She was one of my classmates when I was Fiona and a student at the University of Chicago. I didn't trust her as she traded in gossip and used information to blackmail and betray. Fortunately, in that life, I was savvy enough to elude her. In a previous life after the Armenia diaspora, I was not so lucky. She was involved in what today would be considered sex trafficking."

I look at Anders, and tears fill his eyes. "I'm so sorry, my beloved."

"She was the madam for a Bedouin sheik, and in control of his harem and concubine. In my grief and my desperation, I did not meet his expectations and became expendable. She betrayed me as she stood back and watched while the other women did her bidding. I was beaten, and my face was tattooed with the symbols of my captors. I was left to beg on the street in a country far from my home where I did not even speak the language, and ultimately I starved to death."

Now, both Anders and I are crying. It is such a release to finally be able to put words to this unspeakable tragedy. The images and feelings from this lifetime play on and on in my psyche, and then I know.

"Now, I know. Somehow there is a part of me that must have always known."

Anders looks confused but waits patiently in silence as I try to find the words.

"The Cardinal, the Sheik, Father Brendan, and Klaus Ek are all different incarnations of the same dark soul." Speaking the words aloud grounds the knowing in the here and now.

Anders knows the Cardinal from another lifetime. "I may not have met Klaus Ek, but the Cardinal, of whom you speak, had me burned alive as a heretic when I refused to acquiesce to his demands. If Ek is who you say he is, and I have no reason to doubt your knowings, then he must be stopped by whatever means necessary. The man is the embodiment of evil, and I fear he will have no qualms in destroying everything and everyone who gets in his way."

I put my fork down, then wipe my mouth with my napkin, "I feel sick to my stomach."

"I'm sorry, Love. Perhaps you should lie down and rest for a little while."

I look at the clock on the wall. It's already three forty five. "The meeting is at seven. We should probably leave here by six fifteen at the latest. I need to call Johan and see how his meeting went and fill him in on what happened this morning, so he doesn't accidentally step in it tonight."

"Why don't you make your phone calls from the bedroom, and then try to get some rest. I have a few things I need to attend to. What time do you want me to wake you?"

"How about by five thirty? All I have to do is change my clothes and freshen up my makeup. That won't take very long."

"Try and get some sleep, Saga." He kisses me gently on the lips as I leave him in the hall and enter his bedroom alone. Part of me wishes he was coming to bed, too.

The bedside lamp glows with a soft golden light as I pull the covers back and climb in, pulling the eiderdown up around my body before adjusting the pillows to support my back against the headboard. Looking at my phone, I see that Johan has called twice in the past twenty minutes but has left no messages. He must be out of his meeting. I call him back, and he picks up on the first ring.

"Johan?"

"Hi, where are you?"

"I'm at Anders's. How did your meeting go?" I ask.

"Not as well as I'd hoped. Nothing is ever easy when dealing with lawyers and bureaucrats."

"Tell me what happened."

"Well, Father was amazing, as always. We know he is a really good person, and apparently, others know that, too. As we suspected, the National Archives were locked up tight this morning, given today is the Feast of the Epiphany, *Trettondagen Jul*. But either he knows people in high places or else he just used his charm and charisma to gain entry. Or perhaps it was a little bit of both. But by the time the meeting was called to order at two this afternoon, Father was seated at the table with a certified copy of the document, and he'd already had it translated by a world-renowned professor of ancient languages in the doctoral program at the University of Stockholm.

"Give me a second and let me pull out my notes." I hear the rustling of papers before Johan continues. "This is where the problems began. The translation of the document was clear in intent, at least to Father, the professor, and me, but our in-house legal team had a field day with it, debating the translation and interpretation of every single word."

"Can you read me the translation from the certified document?"

Johan clears his throat before beginning, "The land given to the Baroness Kristina Lundstrom by the King Gustavus Adolphus in 1632, is to be held in safekeeping for the Sámi people with a promise to respect the land and the water and the people who live here. At anytime that the earth is disrespected, then the Lundstrom Family and said descendants will be asked to return it, or the Sámis will harness the strength and the power of all creation to set things to rights. No one owns the earth, but jointly we agree to use it and be good stewards of the earth."

"Oh, I see. So, they are saying that a contract entered into and signed in 1632 doesn't follow the standards for legally binding contracts in 2035. Is that what the issue is?"

"These yahoos wanted to take the whole thing apart word by word. They insisted it would need to be re-authenticated by a panel of experts and would need to be subjected to a panel of translators before any decision could be made in a court of law."

"Did anyone want to hazard a guess on just how long that might take?"

"It could be years."

"I see."

"And Saga, clearly Ek has some of the legal team in his pocket. Once the meeting was over, Thea Bergman, the head of our legal department, pulled me aside and confided in me that if you try to unilaterally go against the board on this, they are already looking into ways to have you removed from your office as chief executive. I'm sorry, Saga."

"Okay, none of this should come as a surprise to me, but that doesn't make it any less painful."

"I'm sure," Johan says. "How did your meeting go?"

"Let's just say both Anders and I have been sworn to secrecy, to be certain that news of Ek's activities does not create international pandemonium. We are to keep quiet while the powers that be attempt to resolve the breaches diplomatically. We are legally bound by our oath to say nothing tonight at the board meeting about the mining of uranium, the miners with radiation poisoning, and the transport of uranium across international borders."

"Dear God, we've been thwarted on all fronts."

"I think we should stick with what we know, and that is plenty. Let's assume he is indeed mining gold, as he would like us and the Sámi people to believe. Although we know this is not the case. We do know Klaus Ek has spent a fortune building a mine on property that does not belong to him. He is harvesting minerals from the land that does not belong to him, shipping it out of the country without any documentation indicating what has been sold, to whom, and at what price, and he has gone ahead and done this without securing any of the appropriate permissions. My goal for the meeting tonight is to have the board remove Ek from his position as chairman of the board, ask that he be indicted for fraud and embezzlement, and have the mine closed down immediately for further investigation of Ek's predatory business practices and determine where the money from this operation came from and where it has gone."

"I will back you on this, but please be careful. We don't know who else is in Ek's pocket. We are dealing with very dangerous people, and they are gunning for us. I'll see you in the boardroom at seven."

Falling back on the pillows, I fall asleep almost instantly but awake in Anders's arms. "Saga, are you okay, honey? You were crying in your sleep."

"I guess I was just dreaming, but I can't tell you what it was about."

"It's just about time for you to get ready to go."

"I think I'd like to have a bath if that's okay."

"Of course. Are you hungry?"

"No, not at all. I'm still a little queasy."

"How about some tea?"

"That sounds good," I say as I drag myself from the bed and head for the washroom to get ready.

When at last, I am ready to go, I'm more than a little surprised to see that Anders is dressed in a different suit. "I should have asked if you wanted me to accompany you, but I'm feeling uneasy about this whole thing. If it's all the same to you, I'd like to be there when you get out. I'll stay with Oskar and out of your way. I promise."

Anders shoots me an uneasy smile as he pleads for permission to come along. It's kind of childlike, yet charming on a full-grown man.

"I can't risk losing you when I've only just found you again."

"Okay," I say, and return his smile.

Just finishing my tea, I hear a knock on the door. It's Oskar, and it's time to go.

CHAPTER 19

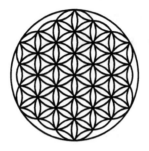

Driving the dark winter streets towards Lundstrom Enterprises, the streetlights glisten on the snow piled high on either side of the road. I sit in silence, and both Anders and Oskar seem to understand and respect my need for quietude. I am filled with angst and an overwhelming need to gather my loved ones in close. I am so glad Anders is here with me. I send a text message to my mother and father and ask them to pray for me. I send a similar message to Annika, and then I bow my head and call upon all the angels and saints, my ancestors, and all my loved ones in this world and the next to watch over and protect me. Lastly, I pray to God in all divine forms: The Creator, the Almighty, the Father, his holy son our Lord Jesus, who shows us the way and the face of love, and the Holy Spirit that dwells in all of life. I humbly ask them to be with me as I face the forces of evil. In this incarnation, I know evil wears the face of Klaus Ek.

Oskar and Anders leave me at my private entrance, and I use the optical scanner to gain entrance to the building. Everything is pretty quiet on the second floor, but I can hear a conversation in the hallway as I cross the atrium towards the boardroom. Ulla steps out of my office to greet me. "Welcome back, Saga."

"Ulla, I'm surprised to see you here so late. Is everything okay?"

"I've always acted as the recording secretary when your mother was here. I just assumed you would need me to continue."

"Of course. There is so much about how this place functions that I don't know yet."

"I'm guessing you're coming up to speed very rapidly," she says under her breath as she looks towards the men gathered outside the conference room. "Will you be bringing your personal computer to the meeting?"

"I had planned to," I say, wondering why she is asking.

"Your mother used to. That way, if she wanted to send me a private message during the meeting, she could, and the other way around, too."

"I see, and you think this might be advantageous?"

"Something is afoot. There has been a great deal of secrecy and whispering going on all day. We may need to be able to communicate privately, to ensure your safety."

Oh God, she feels it, too.

I leave my coat and gloves in my office and carry my new computer bag into the boardroom. Chairman Klaus Ek stands in the doorway where he is surrounded by an aura of muddy brown light. I now see what others have seen. He shakes hands with each of the board members as they enter the room. This is his party, and I am in his domain. I force myself to smile at him as he extends his hand to shake mine. His hand is sweaty, contradicting the smiling confidence he exudes. My stomach clenches. Johan follows me in and places a hand at the small of my back as he guides me toward the far end of the table.

"This is your seat. The CEO sits at one end and the chairman at the other. I will sit to your left, and Ulla will sit to your right." Johan says. I take my seat as another young woman scurries about offering coffee, tea, and cold drinks.

"Would you like a cup of tea or a cold drink, Ms. Svensson?"

I look at her name tag. "Just water, Astrid. Thank you."

"Astrid is a friend of Oskar's," Johan says nonchalantly as if this just everyday conversation.

"I see."

She sets a glass of water in front of me as I open my computer on the table. By now, all ten members of the board are seated, and Klaus Ek sits at the head of the table directly across from me as his assistant distributes paper copies of tonight's agenda. The agenda has been altered. The early part of the evening is to be filled with committee reports, and the Sámi land dispute has been moved to the end of the agenda. Perhaps Ek plans to limit the amount of time available to discuss this, or more likely, he is hopeful we won't get to it at all.

"Good evening, and welcome to the first board meeting of 2035," Klaus Ek addresses the group. "I would like to welcome you all back after the holidays. And in particular, I'd like to extend a heartfelt welcome to our new chief executive officer, Ms. Saga Svensson. I'm sure many of you know Saga as she has been wandering the halls of Lundstrom Enterprises since before she was out of diapers."

That asshole is trying to minimize and demean me in the presence of the board. Still, I smile as they offer me half-hearted and obligatory applause. I'll give him a point for that.

Ek looks from his end of the table to mine. "Saga, you don't need your laptop tonight. Ms. Ulla will take the minutes." He tries to school me and embarrass me again.

"Oh, Klaus, I am well aware of that. It is just that I have some things on my computer that might be of interest to the board. But you need not worry about that now. I'll show you all later." This time it is Ek's turn to blanch, as I hold his gaze. When I was at the Arctic Lodge, my laptop was stolen, right out of my hotel room, along with the photographs of the mine and the shipping facility. Given the look on his face, I'm quite sure Ek is unaware that a back-up set of photographs had already been sent to Maryan, my parents' housekeeper.

"Well then, let us begin with a call to order." He recovers nicely. "It is now seven oh five on Monday, January 7, 2035. Ulla, call the roll."

She calls each member by name as I try to connect their names and their faces with what Johan has told me about each of them. I recall some are clearly in Ek's camp.

"All present," Ulla reports.

One of the men on the right says, "I move that we approve the agenda. We're expecting more snow, and I can't be stuck here all night." I chastise myself for I have forgotten his name already.

"Forgive me, but I have met so many people in the last week. Would you each be so kind and introduce yourselves before you speak so I can begin to learn your names."

"No problem, I'm Elton Wahl."

A middle-aged woman with light eyes raises her hand to be recognized. "My name is Linea." She does not give her surname. I look into her face and engage an old trick to help me remember her name— Linea Light Eyes "Let's hold off on that motion for a moment. This is not the agenda we were sent last week. I think we should begin with a discussion of the Sámi land dispute before we get into all the other committee reports. We have been waiting for Saga or rather, a change in leadership and putting off making a decision about this dispute for months. We can always table the other committee reports until another time, if need be."

I'm not sure whose side she is on. Did they table this because they knew my mother would never agree to it, and now, they want to push it through? Or does she expect me to object and blow the cover off of this covert operation? The look on Ek's face makes me believe she has spoken out of turn, and he is not pleased.

A message from Ulla appears in the lower right corner of my screen. She has your back.

"We have a motion on the floor," Ek tries to rein her in.

"I think Linea makes a good point. I withdraw the motion," the man on my right says. Elton Wahl, that's his name. Wahl the worrier.

"I move we discuss the Sámi land dispute as the first item on the agenda," Linea says.

The members of the board stir uncomfortably in their seats as they look to Ek for some direction, as their plan appears to be derailed already. "I second the motion," I say as everyone in the room turns to look in my direction. "What? Am I not a voting member on this board? Am I not allowed to second a motion and participate freely in the meeting?"

"No, it is allowed," Ulla speaks up, as the acting parliamentarian. "It is just that your mother rarely did. The only people here who cannot vote are Johan Svensson, as he is here as the Director of Public Relations and myself the Acting Recording Secretary.

"Thank you, Ulla, for clarifying," I smile in her direction before continuing. "Okay, then I call the question," I say with a tone of defiance.

This may be Ek's meeting, and there may be some board members who are his carefully selected sycophants, but I will not go easy or be pushed around without a fight. My mind shifts to the conversation Johan and I had a couple of days ago about Sun Tzu.

'If you know your enemy and know yourself you need not fear the result of a hundred battles...'

Ek may or may not know himself, but he certainly does not know me.

All heads turn to Ek, and he gives a nod before he calls for the vote, "All in favor."

In unison, the members vote: "Aye."

"Fine, it appears to be unanimous," Ek says, but it is clear he doesn't like having his carefully crafted plan disrupted. "Can we hear from the committee on the Sámi land dispute?"

One of the men sitting close to Ek shuffles some papers before he begins to speak. As I look in his direction, I have a sense that I know him. Who is he? Where and when have we crossed paths? These answers elude me, but he is dangerous. This I know for certain. "My name is Fara." His voice is low and deep. He has a thick neck and looks like a weightlifter or a lumberjack with muscles on muscles. He, too, omits his surname.

He pauses as if unable to think of what to say beyond this. Perhaps he has a muscle cramp in his brain. Wow, what is wrong with me? This poor guy hasn't said a thing, and already I am judging him to be an idiot. Still, it isn't lost on me that his name means *danger*.

"I have asked Fara to report on the Sámi land dispute, which is a subcommittee of the Committee for New Business Development," Ek speaks up to help this poor guy out. "Fara, can you briefly summarize what the dispute is all about?"

"Gold has been found on our land up near the Arctic Circle. This land is owned by the Lundstrom Enterprises Trust. We would like to mine for this gold, but the Sámi reindeer walkers insist the mine would interrupt the migration of the reindeer." It is obvious to me by the halting way he speaks and stumbles over the words that his statement has been scripted and rehearsed. "They are objecting to our moving ahead and building the mine on the grounds that a contract was signed nearly four hundred years ago, giving them the right to trespass on our land."

I'm put off by his choice of words, 'our land.'

Other members of the board begin to ask questions. They ask about the location, how long it will take to dig the mine, how much money this mine is projected to yield. The answers to these questions are already known. I have read the transcripts from all the past board meetings. This inquiry has also been scripted and is designed to waste time and divert my attention from the fact the mine is already operational.

I raise my hand to be recognized, but other hands are also raised, and people continue to comment and discuss issues not the least bit germane to the topic at hand. Only after everyone else has been recognized is Linea called upon. Ek is obviously irritated with her for proposing a change in the agenda. "For the love of God, Klaus. I have had my hand up for the last thirty minutes, and you have allowed multiple members to speak multiple times before calling on me."

"Forgive me, Linea. It was simply an oversight on my part. I meant no offense."

She takes a deep breath. "I yield my time to our new CEO, Saga Svensson, as she has been waiting to be recognized even longer than I have."

Ek has been outplayed. Clearly, he doesn't know this woman either. I begin, "I have just returned from the Sápmilands up near the Arctic

Circle and met with some of their elders. I wanted to get a firsthand understanding of the nature of the dispute and what is at risk for being lost if Lundstrom Enterprises was to pursue this opportunity to mine for gold in the migratory path of the reindeer. Have any other members of this board actually met with the Sámi elders to understand their objections to the mine?"

Hands go up around the table.

"That is very interesting because Herr Bierdna Heibmu indicated he has called and written many times, and his requests to sit down and talk with someone from Lundstrom Enterprises have gone unanswered. I would like to see the reports from those of you who met with the Sámi elders as I can find no evidence in the files that any of these meetings ever took place."

Another man who fails to identify himself raises his hand to speak, and this time I recognize him, "Some of those meetings were just preliminary, you know, nothing formal."

"I see. In the medical community where I have been working for the last decade, if you don't document it, then legally, you didn't do it."

The room goes silent until I continue. "Has anyone reviewed the document allowing the Sámi people and their reindeer to legally migrate across the land now owned by Lundstrom Enterprises?"

Another man looks to me and raises his hand to speak, while Ek frantically tries to get his attention. "We have looked for that document and been told it doesn't exist. We've concluded it is part of some convoluted scheme to allow *those people* to continue to trespass on our land."

I look straight into Ek's eyes and see him grimace. "Do you want to tell him, or should I?"

Ek chooses to speak. "Only just today has the document resurfaced. Apparently, it had been filed at the National Archives. Our legal team has been charged with reviewing the document for authenticity, and of course, it will need to be translated from Old Swedish before any decision can be made about its validity."

"I would like to show the members of this board some images that were taken over the last few days of the land in dispute." Johan stands near the door and electronically lowers first the screen and then the lights as I project a photo of the mine on a screen located directly behind Klaus Ek. The photo includes a crane and a full-size dump truck at the bottom of the mine to show the magnitude of the operation. "This mine has already been built and is fully operational on land that is owned and held in trust by Lundstrom Enterprises." I switch the picture from my laptop, and an image of the shipping facility fills the screen. "Where is the ore, dug from the land owned by Lundstrom Enterprise, going? Who is buying it? And where is the money? This mining is unsanctioned, illegal, and is the equivalent of embezzlement."

"Holy shit," someone says, just before the lights go back on, and my computer screen goes dark.

Now Ek begins another tactic, and I know I am running out of time. "I don't know where those photographs came from, but I can assure you there is no mine of that scale operating anywhere in the north of Sweden. I hate to go down this path, but when you make these wild accusations and besmirch the reputations of everyone on this board, I am afraid that I have no choice. Ms. Svensson, dear Saga, is it true you have been consulting with a paranormal guide and believe that you are capable of time-travel?"

"How did you come by this information? How is this relevant and any of your business?"

"You may believe yourself to be psychic, but perhaps you are merely psychotic. A reasonable and alternative explanation is that our dear Ms. Svensson suffers from paranoid delusions brought on by visual or auditory hallucinations. Perhaps Ms. Svensson may be having difficulty discerning the difference between what is real and what is simply imaginary."

Ek pulls a stack of my journals from somewhere beneath the table and places them on the table in front of him for me to see.

"Those were stolen from my bedside stand when my apartment was ransacked the night before last."

He smiles, giving me a condescending smile, as I become more and more incensed.

"You have been blessed beyond measure and have the good fortune to have been born into one of the great landed families of the Swedish aristocracy, and still you choose to spend your time with nomads and squatters. Have you no shame? We have it on good authority while you claim to be off doing company business and conferring with the Sámi elders, in reality, you were partaking in psychedelic drugs with the indigenous people. There was a time when people were burned alive as witches for participating in those ceremonies.

"You do know those ceremonies and the use of fly agaric or Amanita muscaria mushrooms have been outlawed again by the State. Now that the Swedish Democrats are back in power, this violates our drug laws and is once again a very serious offense and is punishable with incarceration.

"Perhaps a leave of absence from your position as CEO is advisable, at least until you get your substance use and mental illness attended to. Dear Saga, I fear in your current state that you are dangerous to yourself and possibly to others, and clearly are not capable of taking on a leadership role in an organization of this complexity. Therefore, I move that Saga Svensson be removed from office and placed in a psychiatric facility until your mental competency can be verified—"

And as someone calls out to second the motion, all of the lights go out, leaving the windowless room in complete darkness. People start to panic as they do not know who is in control, or what is happening. Some of the board members try to push and shove their way towards the door.

Someone grabs my arm, and I instinctively pull it away, fearing I am going to be locked up. "It's me, Astrid," a woman's voice whispers in my ear as she holds me close, and I do not resist.

As we approach the door, Johan whispers to me, "Go with her Saga, it will be okay," and then he unlocks the door and I am dragged out into the hallway. The door locks behind us, and we can hear the angry voices of those locked inside as Astrid leads me down the hallway. The entire building is black as night.

"I'll get you out of here. We're leaving through your private entrance." She presses my face close to the optical sensor, and the door to the passageway opens before us. "Oskar and Anders are downstairs waiting."

"What about Johan and Ulla?"

"They'll be okay. They have a plan."

Once in the car, Anders enfolds me in his arms, and Oskar speeds away.

"Oh my God, Ek was going to have me hauled away to a psychiatric facility and locked up."

"How did you get us out of there?" I ask Astrid. "There was no light, and it was impossible to see."

"I wore night-vision goggles. They were in the pocket of my apron the whole time."

I take a deep breath as I try to come to terms with what has just happened.

"You were amazing in there," Anders says.

"How do you know?" I turn to look at Anders.

"Do you really think we would let you dance with that devil and leave you unprotected?" You had enough to worry about today, so Johan, Oskar, Astrid, Ulla and I concocted the plan to get you out of there if things started to fall apart," Anders says.

"Ulla was in on this, too?"

"She always uses her computer as the recording secretary, so it didn't take much persuasion at all to add the surveillance software. Astrid merely posed as a member of the catering staff, and Ulla spent the afternoon acquainting her with the entrances and exits in the boardroom, your office, and your private entrance," Oskar fills me in on how my escape was orchestrated.

"Ulla controlled all the lights from her computer, and Johan unlocked the door so you could escape and then locked the others in," Astrid adds.

I am dumbstruck as I try to recreate it all in my head. Everything happened so quickly and flawlessly. "I remember a prayer my father used to say, 'in all things give thanks,' and I am so thankful for each and every one of you for delivering me from evil."

"I'm afraid we are not out of the woods just yet." Then Astrid reveals the rest of the plan. "We're heading up to Sápmiland tonight. Bierdna, Grandmother Lejá, and the others will be waiting for us.

Johan and Ulla will pick up your parents then meet us at the rest stop on the northbound highway."

"How do you know Bierdna and Grandmother Lejá?" I ask Astrid.

"I am Sámi, and Bierdna is my grandfather," she says with a smile. "May the Ancestors smile upon you, for you were very brave tonight, and our people will sing your praises as the *Great Noaidi* for generations to come."

"Amen," Oskar says from the front seat. "For you see, I am Sámi too."

"It is amazing for all that my gift allows me to see, and still I miss what is right in front of my own face."

"Isn't it though?" Astrid says, and we all laugh. "You don't know me, do you?"

The only light is from the dashboard and from the headlights reflecting back from the snow-covered highway. I take Astrid's hand in mine to see if I can feel the connection that I cannot yet see.

"I have come to repay a karmic debt, for you were once my older sister. You stood by me. You loved and supported me and my beloved daughter when we had nowhere else to turn."

I reach for Astrid and enfold her in my arms as we both dissolve to tears, "Oh Bridgie. Praise be to God. Thank you for coming to my rescue."

"No, Fiona, it is I who must thank you. We will always be sisters."

CHAPTER 20

The snow is falling as we pull onto the highway. It's already nine o'clock. There is something quite unbelievable about the nature of time. Sometimes it speeds by so quickly that a multitude of hours pass completely unnoticed, and then there are the times when unbeknownst to us whole lifetimes are lived in the span of one single hour. Was I really only walking into the boardroom two hours ago, and now I am speeding down the highway like a criminal in a spy novel just hoping to avoid detection? It is all so difficult to wrap my head around.

The roads are snow-covered and slippery as Oskar pulls the big, black SUV in behind the snowplow. He follows closer than I am comfortable with, but there is so much about this evening that makes me uncomfortable. I bite my tongue and refrain from asking him to please drive a little slower. I close my eyes and slide in close beside Anders. He, too, is quiet as we travel north, putting mile after mile between us and the urban metropolis of Stockholm.

The sound of the metal plow, throwing sparks on the asphalt highway while scraping off the ice and snow, adds to my unease.

I am grateful for my escape and my freedom. Still, I can't help but feel this is not over, and that makes me feel exceedingly vulnerable. Ek is a dangerous man. Although I have just escaped due to the clear thinking and kindness of others, the truth is Klaus Ek has outsmarted me every step of the way. He has foiled my plans. Now it looks as if he may have the votes to have me ousted as CEO and take over Lundstrom Enterprises. He has the wherewithal to sell the weapons-grade uranium to any two-bit despot who can meet his price. After nearly four hundred years of a continuously profitable operation, I will be the shortest reigning CEO. In less than two weeks, I will have lost a company that generations of women before me have worked so hard to grow and preserve. But that is not just my personal failing; the bigger issue is: if this uranium gets into the wrong hands, the subsequent nuclear weapons proliferation threatens the destruction of our planet. The raw material and scientific technology to make a nuclear bomb will be available to every power-hungry despot who gets his nose tweaked or has a bad hair day. I have made promises to the Sámi people, and to the reindeer. I cannot let this go.

If we do not stop Ek, there could be mass extinction as we cannot survive a nuclear winter.

Despite Astrid's kind words, I feel so utterly helpless and despondent.

It is only then that an idea comes to me. It is true I do not have the personal power to stop Klaus Ek, for in this physical realm, I am in way over my head. But I haven't yet harnessed the power of the spirit world, the power of my angels, the power of my ancestors who have gone on before me, and neither have the Sámi people. What would happen if we all called upon our loved ones in the spirit world to protect this sacred land from destruction?

We travel behind the snowplow for hours and hours, when Oskar engages his turn signal to pull off into a rest stop. He flashes his bright lights, and two black SUVs pull in behind us. "Who is following us?" I ask.

"Johan and your parents are in the first vehicle. Your friends, Annika and Ulla, are in the second one. We will caravan up Sápmiland, and God willing, if we can maintain our speed, we will be there before the sun rises."

"Excuse me, but where exactly are we going to be for sunrise?"

"Oh, Saga, this was all your idea. We are going to the mine," Anders says.

"I don't know what you are talking about," I confess.

Anders explains. "Oskar and I heard you praying aloud on the way to the board meeting and calling on the spirit world for help. You remember your Sunday school lessons from the Gospel of Matthew, don't you?"

"Help me out," I say, quite uncertain just what he is talking about.

"Jesus said, *'Where two or more are gathered in my name, I am there among them.'*"

"Yes, of course," I say. "Were you reading my mind?"

"I don't know if it was telepathy or maybe just empathic energy. You're not the only one here with spiritual gifts," he says, as he pulls me close. "You have tried appealing to Ek's humanity, and to his sense of right and wrong. But sociopaths have no conscience. You have appealed to the board of directors, presented evidence of gross wrong-doing, and even engaged the legal system to hear the case, and to right the wrong. But I fear by the time they rule, it could be too late. It is time to call upon the Divine and the powers of the spirit world." Anders's words hang in the air, and for a moment, no one speaks.

Anders reaches into the back of the vehicle to retrieve that exquisite long, white reindeer cape I wore when I first met the Sámi people, traditional gákti, and fur-lined snow boots. Thankfully someone had the forethought to bring this warm clothing for me.

The men and Astrid turn their heads towards the windows to provide me some privacy as I change my clothes in the darkness.

"Now I suggest we travel on in silence and in prayer. So much hangs in the balance. We have a long cold night ahead of us," Oskar says as he turns his face towards the snow-covered road and grips the steering wheel tightly.

Oskar pulls up to the gateway to the mine, and the gate is wide open. Silvu and Márten come out of the guardhouse. "Ah, so good to see you again, Saga. Is your brother here?"

"Johan and our parents are in the next vehicle."

"Good, I had hoped we would see them again," Márten says. "Kommadant Ek and several of his henchman arrived about an hour ago by helicopter. They landed deep inside the mine, but none of the miners showed up today."

"Grandmother Lejá has called a strike, and all of the workers are already on the ridge," Silvu adds.

"Bierdna, Grandmother Lejá, and the others have been here all night praying. Our friends and relations from other *siidas* across the North have been arriving throughout the night. They are camped out up there on the ridge. They are expecting you. The food is plentiful, the campfire is hot, and so is the coffee. Can we catch a ride up there with you?" Márten asks.

"Of course," Oskar says. "There are two nice women in the second car. I'm sure they will have room for you." Oskar gets out of the car and goes with the two men to ask Ulla and Annika if they would be willing to bring our friends to the gathering on the ridge. Of course, this is not an issue.

"I don't understand how all of this has come to be," I say aloud to Astrid and Anders while Oskar introduces Silvu and Márten to Ulla and Annika.

"When you ask for help with a pure heart and the best of holy intentions, the universe hears and conspires to answer your prayers. This gathering is simply the answer to your prayers, Saga. You asked for us to help you, and we are here. You are not the only one amongst us who hears the voice of God. You are a powerful *Noaidi*, perhaps more powerful than you realize," Astrid says as Anders holds my hand and nods his head in affirmation.

And so it is that we meet at just before sunrise on the highest ridgeline of Scandes Mountains, from here we can see all the lower mountain ranges and even the valley and tundra below. It is a day to honor Máttaráhkká, Mother Earth, to whom we gather and pray. Sámi from far and wide have traveled to join us in solidarity.

There are people clothed in their finest traditional dress standing side by side across the ridge for as far as I can see. We stand in solidarity, and then just as the first rays of the sun cross the horizon, Grandmother Lejá honors the new day as her old arthritic hand grips a padded drum hammer and taps out a slow and steady beat on the ceremonial drum of the *Noaidi*. The drum echoes throughout the canyon and comes pulsing back to us, both strong and confident. The others stand shoulder to shoulder and listen in the quiet of the new day until the young tenor with his beautiful voice begins to *joik* in a manner that begins softly, then one voice followed by another joins in until the music reaches around the ridge and everyone is singing. These people have an oral tradition, and the elders have long ago taught their children who have taught their children's children. The volume increases as more and more people join in the song until it is loud and echoes and reverberates off the mountains. The sound is more magnificent than anything I have ever heard in any of the grand cathedrals of Europe.

From down on the lower ranges, we hear a slow roar begin to sound. It grows louder, calling our attention to the slopes below. And still we sing as the drummer beats the drum.

Avalanches of cascading snow tumble down the mountainside, covering the fields of shipping containers and blocking transport. There is a collective gasp as we look on from the ridge far above.

It is then that the sound of our collective voices drops an octave, becoming both low and deep as we are joined by those unseen. They, too, are angry at the betrayal of our Mother Earth and on behalf of all the creatures who share our home. The deep resonance starts like a rumble and increases in volume until it crescendos into a deep, loud roar. It is as if this were some kind of call and response. The Sámi people call, and Mother Earth responds. The earth begins to rumble beneath our feet, but we stand our ground and keep singing while *she* cracks wide open and swallows the mine, the pit, all of the equipment, and all the uranium ore.

When the rumbling ceases, and our Mother has gone quiet, all that is left is the wide barren tundra forming a land bridge for the reindeer and the reindeer walkers to use when it is again time for them to leave this region and return to their summer grazing lands.

Mother Earth has spoken, and she has the last word.

FULL CIRCLE

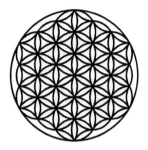

Standing there in the traditional dress of the Sámi people I am awestruck by the power and the majesty of what has happened, images begin to take shape within my mind's eye of all the women I have been, not just now but also in other incarnations. But I am not alone in this vision, I stand with the others, wise women and men who have loved me and supported me all along my journey in all of their different incarnations. They are smiling, knowing, but they do not speak. I know they are with me and they are within me. They always have been and always will be. I can feel their energetic reverberations stirring deep within my soul and I know what they are saying...

Our spirits are infinite, eternal, and whole and destined to return to the Circle of Life until we have learned what we are here to learn, and have done what we have been sent here to do. Within the Great Circle, there is no us and them. There is only us. Each of us and all of creation is a unique manifestation of our Creator, and therefore worthy of great love and reverence.

JEANNE SELANDER MILLER

The Full Circle Trilogy was created out of the author's imagination, her yogic journey, and her undying curiosity to ask the big questions: What if?

The idea for the Full Circle Trilogy started with a question, and then another, as so many discoveries do—What would reincarnation and karma look like in a world where people were raised with a completely different mindset and understanding of how life works? And what if we could remember all the lessons we learned in other lifetimes?

An internationally acclaimed author, Jeanne has also written a trilogy of memoirs which have been awarded the Best Spiritual Book at the London Book Festival and Honorable Mentions at the Paris International Book Festival and the New York Book Festival. In her first novel, *Privileged*, Jeanne reveals truths about life in a college prep school and shines a bright light on the grim underbelly accompanying such privilege.